Justin looked, and then could not look away.

He'd turned to see whether the daughter carried the stain of her mother's sin.

Head high, she stared at a point above the king's crown. But then, just for a moment, she glanced around the room. Her eyes, violet, brimming with pain, met his.

They stopped his breath.

Wide-eyed, still looking at him, she did not complete her step. Then she gathered herself, lifted her skirt and approached the throne.

Justin shook off her spell. The woman's glance had been enough to warn him. Her mother had bewitched a king. He would be on guard.

* * *

The Harlot's Daughter
Harlequin Historical #870—October 2007

THE HARLOT'S DAUGHTER

BLYTHE GIFFORD

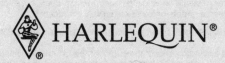

HARLEQUIN®

TORONTO • NEW YORK • LONDON
AMSTERDAM • PARIS • SYDNEY • HAMBURG
STOCKHOLM • ATHENS • TOKYO • MILAN • MADRID
PRAGUE • WARSAW • BUDAPEST • AUCKLAND

ISBN-13: 978-0-373-29470-1
ISBN-10:   0-373-29470-0

THE HARLOT'S DAUGHTER

Copyright © 2007 by Wendy B. Gifford

This edition published by arrangement with Harlequin Books S.A.

www.eHarlequin.com

Printed in U.S.A.

Available from Harlequin® Historical and
BLYTHE GIFFORD

The Knave and the Maiden #688
The Harlot's Daughter #870

DON'T MISS THESE OTHER
NOVELS AVAILABLE NOW

#867 A WESTERN WINTER WONDERLAND—
CHERYL ST.JOHN, JENNA KERNAN, PAM CROOKS
Love and family—the recipe for the perfect Christmas.
Three new novellas from three of your favorite authors!

#868 LORD LIBERTINE—GAIL RANSTROM
Andrew Hunter, cynical, disillusioned and dangerous, has
secrets to keep—and Isabella is determined to find them out!

#869 THE WARLORD'S MISTRESS—JULIET LANDON
Dania draws influential Roman officers to her House of Women
to learn their secrets, but one masterful warrior could all too
easily seduce her into his arms.

For my mother, a trailblazer.
And with great thanks to Pat White,
who kept me going.

Author Note

My fascination with the English royal bastards began in junior high school when I read a novel about the mistress of one of the sons of Edward III. Her romance had a happy ending. She married her prince, their children were legitimized and their descendants sat on the throne of England.

The story was a testament to the role that love has played in shaping history.

The story of Edward III's notorious mistress, Alice Perrers, did not end so happily. Universally hated, she was stripped of her position and her wealth when the king died. Her children rate barely a footnote in history.

Yet her daughter intrigued me. What was it like to grow up nearly a princess and then be banished from the court? How would she view love, and the world, as a result? This story is my answer to these questions.

And it reflects my view of the role love plays in shaping the history of our lives.

I hope you enjoy it.

Chapter One

Windsor Castle,
Yuletide, 1386

The shameless doxy dragged the rings right off his fingers before the King's body was cold.

They used to whisper that and then look sideways at her, thinking that a ten-year-old was too young to understand they slandered her mother.

Joan had understood even then. It was all too clear the night the old King died and her mother, his mistress of thirteen years, gathered their two daughters and fled into the darkness.

Now, ten years after her father's death, Joan stood poised to be announced at the court of a new King. Her mother hoped Joan might find a place there, even a husband.

Foolish dreams of an ageing woman.

Waiting to be announced, she peeked into the Great Hall, surprised she did not look more outdated wearing her mother's made-over dress. It was the men's garb, colourful and garish, that looked unfamiliar. Decked in blues and reds, gold chains and furs, they looked gaudy as flapping tournament flags.

Except for one.

Standing to the left of the throne turned away from her, he wore a simple, deep blue tunic. She could not see his face fully, but the set of his jaw and the hollow edge of his cheek said one thing: unyielding.

For a moment, she envied that strength. This was a man whose daily bread did not depend on pleasing people.

Hers did. And so did her mother's and sister's.

She pulled her gaze away and smoothed her velvet skirt. Please the King she must, or there would be no food in the larder by Eastertide.

As the herald entered the Hall to announce her, she heard the rustling skirts of the ladies lining the room. They whispered still.

Here she comes. The harlot's daughter. No more shame than her mother had.

She lifted her head. It was time.

Amid the whispers, Lady Joan, twenty summers, illegitimate daughter of the late King and his notorious mistress and the most unmarriageable woman in England, stepped forward to be presented to King Richard II.

Lord Justin Lamont avoided Richard's court whenever possible. He had braved the crowded throne room only because he had urgent news for the Duke of Gloucester.

Last month, Parliament had compelled the reckless young King to accept the oversight of a Council headed by his uncle, Gloucester. Since then, Justin had been enmeshed in the business of government. He was only beginning to uncover the mess young Richard and his intimates had made of the Treasury.

Thrust upon the throne as a boy when his grandfather died,

Richard had inherited the old King's good looks without his strength, judgement or sense. Instead of spending taxes to fight the French, he'd drained the royal purse with grants for his favourites.

When he demanded more tax money, Parliament had finally balked, installing the Council to gainsay the King's outrageous spending.

Now, the King had put forth another of his endless lists of favours for his friends, expecting the new Council's unquestioning approval.

He would not get it.

'Your Grace,' Justin said to Gloucester, 'the King has a new list of gifts he wants to announce on Christmas Day. The Council cannot possibly approve this.'

Distracted, the Duke motioned to the door. 'Here she comes. The doxy's daughter.'

Justin gritted his teeth, refusing to turn. The mother's meddling had near ruined the realm before Parliament had stepped in to save a senile King from his own foolishness. This new King needed no more misguidance. He was getting that aplenty from his current favourites. 'What do they call her?'

'Lady Joan of Weston,' Gloucester answered. 'Joan the Elder.'

Calling her a Weston was a pleasant fiction, though the old King's mistress had passed herself off as Sir William's wife while she bore the King's children. 'The Elder?'

Gloucester smirked. 'There were two daughters. Like bitch pups. Call "Joan" and one will come running.'

Wincing at the cruelty, Justin reluctantly turned, with the rest of the court, to see whether the daughter carried the stain of her mother's sin.

He looked, and then could not look away.

Her mother's carnality stamped a body that swayed as if it

had no bones and her raven hair carried no hint of the old King's sun-tinged glory. 'She looks nothing like him,' he murmured.

Gloucester whispered back, 'Maybe the whore simply whelped the children and called them the King's.'

Justin shook his head. 'She moves like royalty.'

Head high, she stared at a point above the King's crown, walking as if the crowd adored instead of loathed her.

But then, just for a moment, she glanced around the room. Her eyes, violet, brimming with pain, met his.

They stopped his breath.

Wide-eyed, still looking at him, she did not complete her step. Tangled in her gaze, he forgot to breathe.

Then she gathered herself, lifted her skirt and approached the throne.

He shook off her spell and looked around. No one had noticed that her eyes had held his for an eternity.

She dipped before the King, head held high. Justin thought of the lad on the throne as a boy, though, at twenty, he had been King for half his life. Yet he still played at kingly ceremony, instead of grappling with the hard work of governing.

'Lower your gaze,' the King said to the woman before him.

A flash of fury stiffened her spine. Then, she bent her neck ever so slightly.

'Kneel.'

She dropped gracefully to her knees as if she had practised.

Justin took a breath. Then another. Still the King did not say 'rise'. A smothered cough in the crowd breached the silence.

Her hands hung quietly at her sides, but her fingers twitched against the folds of her deep red skirt.

He squashed a spark of sympathy. The woman's glance had been enough to warn him. Her mother had bewitched a King. He would be on guard.

He had been deceived by a woman's eyes once—long ago.

* * *

Joan had known the King would test her. *Kneel.* So she did. Her mother had taught her well. *Read his needs and satisfy them. That is our only salvation.* This one needed deference, that was obvious. She would give him that and whatever else he asked if he would grant them a living from the royal purse.

At least there was one thing he would not ask. The blood of the old King flowed through both their veins. She would not have to please a King as her mother had.

She heard no whispers now. Silent, the court watched as the King left her on aching knees long enough that she could have said an extra Paternoster for her mother's sins.

Eyes lowered, she looked toward the edge of the wide-planked floor. The men's long-toed shoes curled like a finger crooked in invitation. She stifled a smile. Men and their vanities. Apparently, they thought the longer the toes, the longer the tool.

Yet when her eyes had met those of the hard-edged man at the fringes of the crowd, she had nearly stumbled. His severe dress and implacable gaze sliced through the peacocks around the throne sharply as a blade. For that instant, she forgot everything else. Even the King.

A thoughtless mistake. She had no time for emotion. Only for necessity.

Finally, the King's high-pitched voice called a reprieve. 'Lady Joan, daughter of Sir William of Weston, rise and bow.'

With no one's hand to lean on, she wobbled as she stood. Forcing her shaking knees to support her, she curtsied, then dared lift her eyes.

Tall, thin, and delicately blond, King Richard perched on the throne overlooking the hall. A golden crown graced his curls. An ermine-trimmed cloak shielded him from the draughts. She wondered whether his cheeks were clean shaven from choice or because the beard had not yet taken hold.

His slope-shouldered wife sat beside him. Her plaited brown hair hung down her back, a strange affectation for a married queen. Of course, Joan's mother had whispered, after six years of childless marriage, she wondered how much of a wife the Queen was.

'We hope you enjoy this festive time with us, Lady Joan,' she said. Her eyes held a gentleness that was missing from the King's.

Joan, silent, looked to the King for permission.

He waved his hand. 'You may speak.'

'Thank you, your Grace.'

He sat straighter and lifted his head. 'Address us as Your Majesty.'

'Forgive me, Your Majesty.' She bowed again. A new title, then. 'Your Grace' had served the old King, but that was no longer adequate. This King needed more than deference. He needed exaltation.

The Queen's soft voice soothed like that of a calm mother after a child's tantrum. 'I hope you will not miss Christmas at Weston Castle too much, Lady Joan.'

She suppressed a laugh. A Weston in name only, she had never even visited the family estate. It was her mother and sister she would be thinking of during the Cristes-mæsse, but no word of them would be spoken aloud. 'Your invitation honours me, Your Majesty.'

Queen Anne said, 'Perhaps you might pen a short poem for our entertainment.'

'Poem, Your Majesty?'

'Not in French, only in English. If you feel capable.'

She swallowed the subtle insult. The Queen's words denigrated not only her mother, but Joan's ten years spent away from Windsor's glories. Still, as a daughter of the King, she had been taught both English and French. 'Your Majesty, if my humble verse might amuse, I would be honoured.'

The King spoke. 'Of course you would, Lady… What was your name?'

'Joan, Your Majesty.'

He frowned. 'I do not like that name. Have you another?'

'Another name, Your Majesty?' Odd, she thought, then she remembered. The King's mother had been called Joan. And his mother had been a bitter enemy of hers. Of course she could not be called by the name of his beloved mother. 'Yes, Your Majesty, I do.' It would not be the Mary or Elizabeth or Catherine he expected. 'My mother also calls me Solay.'

'Soleil?' he said, with the French inflection. 'The sun?'

'Yes.'

'Why would she give you such a name?'

She hesitated, fearing to speak the truth and unable to think of a way to dissemble. 'She said I was the daughter of the sun.'

Whispers ricocheted around the floor. *I was the Lady of the Sun once,* her mother had said. The Sun who was King Edward.

The King dismissed her with a wave. 'Your name matters little. You will not be here long.'

Fear twisted her stomach. She must cajole him out of anger and gain time to win his favour.

'Your use of the name honours me,' she said quickly, 'as much as the honour of knowing I share the exalted day of your birth under the sign of Capricorn.' She knew no such thing, but no one cared when she had come into the world. Even her mother was not sure of the day.

He sat straighter and peered at her. 'You study the stars, Lady Solay?'

She knew little more of the stars than a candle maker, if the truth be told, but if the stars intrigued him, flattery and a few choice phrases should suffice. 'Although I am but a student, I hear they say great things of Your Majesty.'

He looked at her sharply. 'What do they say?' he said, leaning forward.

What did he want to hear? She must tread carefully. Too much knowledge would be dangerous. 'I have never read yours, of course, Your Majesty.' To do so without his consent could have meant death. She thought quickly. The King's birthday was on the twelfth day of Christmas. That should give her enough time. 'However, with your permission, I could present a reading in honour of your birthday.'

'It would take so long?'

She smiled and nodded. 'To prepare a reading worthy of a King, oh, yes, Your Majesty.'

The King smiled, settling back into the throne. 'A reading for my birthday, then.' He turned to the tall, dark-haired man on his right. 'Hibernia, see that she has what she needs.'

She released a breath. Now if she could only concoct a reading that would direct him to grant her mother an income for life. 'I will do my humble best and be honoured to serve Your Majesty in any way.'

A small smile touched his lips. 'I imprisoned the last astrologer for predicting ill omens. I shall be interested in what you say.'

She swallowed. This King was not as naïve as he looked.

Done with her, he rose, took the Queen's hand and spoke to the Hall. 'Come. Let there be carolling before vespers.'

Solay curtsied, muttering, 'Thanks to Your Majesty', like a Hail Mary and backed away.

A hand, warm, touched her shoulder.

She turned to see the same brown eyes that had made her stumble. Up close, they seemed to probe all she needed to hide.

The man was all hardness and power. A perpetual frown furrowed his brow. 'Lady Joan, or shall I say Lady Solay?'

She slapped on a smile to hide the trembling of her lips. 'A turn in the carolling ring? Of course.'

He did not return her smile. 'No. A private word.'

His eyes, large, heavy lidded, turned down at the corners, as if weighed with sorrow.

Or distrust.

'If you wish,' she said, uneasy. As he guided her into the passageway outside the Great Hall, she turned her attention to him, ready to discover who he was, what he wanted and how she might please him.

God had blessed her with a pleasing visage. Most men were content to bask in the glow of her interest, never asking what she might think or feel.

And if they had asked, she would not have known what to say. She had forgotten.

Yet this man, silent, stared down at her as though he knew her thoughts and despised them. Behind him, the caroller's call echoed off the rafters of the Great Hall and the singers responded in kind. She smiled, trying to lift his scowl. 'It's a merry group.'

No gentle curve sculpted the lips that formed an angry slash in his face. 'They sound as if they had forgotten we might have been singing beside the French today.'

She shivered. Only God's grace had kept the French fleet off their shores this summer. 'Perhaps people want to forget the war for a while.'

'They shouldn't.' His tone brooked no dissent. 'Now tell me, Lady Solay, why have you come to court?'

She touched a finger to her lips, taking time to think. She must not speak without knowing whose ear listened. 'Sir, you know who I am, but I do not even know your name. Pray, tell me.'

'Lord Justin Lamont.'

His simple answer told her nothing she needed to know. Was he the King's man or not? 'Are you also a visitor at Court?'

'I serve the Duke of Gloucester.'

She clasped her fingers in front of her so they would not shake. Gloucester had near the power of a king these days. Richard could make few moves without his uncle's approval, a galling situation for a proud and profligate Plantagenet.

She widened her eyes, tilted her head and smiled. 'How do you serve the Duke?'

'I was trained at the Inns of Court.'

She struggled to keep her smile from crumbling. 'A man of the law?' A craven vulture who never kept his word, who would speak for you one day and against you the next, who could take away your possessions, your freedom, your very life.

'You dislike the law, Lady Solay?' A twist of a smile relaxed the harsh edges of his face. For the first time, she noticed a cleft in his chin, the only softness she'd seen in him.

'Wouldn't you, if it had done to you what it did to my mother?' Shame, shame. Do not let the anger show. It was over and done. She must move on. She must survive.

'It was your mother who did damage to the law.'

His bluntness shocked her. True, her mother had shared the judges' bench on occasion, but only to insure that the King's will was done. Most judges could not be trusted to render a verdict without an eye on their pockets.

Solay kept her brow smooth, her eyes wide and her voice low. 'My mother served the Queen and then the King faithfully. She was ill served in the end for her faithful care.'

'She used the law to steal untold wealth. It was the realm that was ill served.'

Most only whispered their hatred. This man spoke it aloud. She gritted her teeth. 'You must have been ill informed. All her possessions were freely given by the King or purchased with her own funds.'

'Ah! So you are here to get them back.'

She cleared her throat, unsettled that he suspected her plan so soon. 'The King honoured me with an invitation. I was pleased to accept.'

'Why would he invite you?'

Because my mother begged everyone who would still listen to ask him. 'Who can know the mind of a King?'

'Your mother did.'

'A King does as he wills.'

A spark of understanding lit his eyes. 'Parliament turned down her last petition for redress so she has sent you to beg money directly from the King.'

'We do not beg for what is rightfully ours.' She lowered her eyes to hide her anger. Parliament had impeached one of the King's key advisers last autumn, then given the five Lords of the Council unwelcome oversight of the King. It was an uneasy time to appear at court. She had no friends and could afford no enemies. 'Please, do not let me detain you. My affairs need not be your concern. You must have many friends to see.'

'I'm not sure that anyone has many friends these days, Lady Solay. You asked about my work. Among my duties is to see that the King wastes no more money on flatterers. If you try to entice him into raiding the Exchequer on your behalf, your affairs will become my concern.'

The import of his words sank in. She risked angering a man who had power over the very purse strings she needed to loosen.

'I only ask that you deal fairly.' A vain hope. She had given up on justice years ago.

She stepped back, wanting to leave, but he touched her sleeve and moved closer, until she had to tip her head back to see his eyes. He was tall and lean and in the flickering torch fire, his brown hair, carelessly falling from a centre parting, glimmered with a hint of gold.

And above his head hung a kissing bough.

He looked up and then back at her, his eyes dark. She couldn't, didn't want to look away. His scent, cedar and ink, tantalised her.

Let them look. Make them want, her mother had warned her, *but never, never want yourself.* Yet this breathless ache—surely this was want.

He leaned closer, his lips hovering over hers. All she could think of was his burning eyes and the harsh rise and fall of his chest. She closed her eyes and her lips parted.

'Do you think to sway me as your mother swayed a King, Lady Solay?'

She pushed him away, relieved the corridor was still empty, and forced her lips into a coy smile. 'You make me forget myself.'

'Or perhaps I help you remember who you really are.'

Her smile pinched. 'Or who *you* think I am.'

'I know who you are. You are an awkward remnant of a great King's waning years and glory lost because of a deceitful woman.'

Gall choked her. 'You blame my mother for the King's decline, not caring how hard she worked to keep order when he could not tell sun from moon.'

When he did not know, or care to know, the daughter he had spawned.

'I, Lady Solay, *can* tell day from night. Your mother's tricks will not work on me.'

Then I must try some others, she thought, frantic.

What others did she know?

He *had* made her forget herself. She had been too blunt. Next time, she must use only honeyed words. 'I would never try to trick you, Lord Justin. You are too wise to be fooled.'

Muttering a farewell, she turned her back and walked away from this man who lured her into anger she could ill afford.

* * *

Shaken, Justin watched her hips sway as she walked, nay, floated away. He had nearly kissed her. He had barely been able to keep his arms at his side.

He had been taken in once by a woman's lies. Never again.

Still, it had taken every ounce of stubborn strength he could muster not to pull her into his arms and plunder her mouth.

Well, nothing magical in responding to eyes the colour of purple clouds at sunset and breasts round and soft. He would not be a man if he did not feel something.

'There you are.' Gloucester was at his elbow. 'What possessed you, Lamont, to whisper secrets to the harlot's daughter?'

Gloucester's harsh words grated, although Justin had thought near the same. 'Such a little difference, between one side of the blanket and the other,' he said, turning to look at the Duke. 'You share a father. You might call her sister.'

Gloucester scowled. 'You are ever too outspoken.'

'I'm just not afraid to tell the truth.' But about this, he was. The truth was that he had no idea what possessed him to nearly take her in his arms and he did not want to dwell on the question. 'The woman sought to tempt me as her mother did the old King.'

'You looked as if you were about to succumb.'

'I simply warned her that she would not be permitted to play with King Richard's purse.'

Gloucester snorted with disgust. 'My nephew is a sorry excuse for a ruler. The French steal my father's land and all the boy does is read poetry and wave a little white flag to wipe his nose. As if a sleeve were not good enough.' Gloucester sighed. 'Now, what was it you wanted to tell me?'

Justin brought his mind back to the King's list. 'He wants to give the Duke of Hibernia more property.'

'And what of my request?'

Justin shook his head.

Gloucester exploded. 'First he gives the man a Duke's title that none but a King's son has ever held. Then he gives him a coat of arms adorned with crowns. Now he gives him land and leaves me at the mercy of the Exchequer? Never!'

'I'll tell him, your Grace. Right after vespers.' To Justin had fallen the task of delivering bad news. He was not a man to hide the truth. Even from the King.

But he suspected that Lady Solay was. Nothing about her rang true, including her convenient birth day. As he and Gloucester returned to the hall, Justin wondered whether one of the old King's servants might remember something of her.

If she believed she was going to tap the King's dwindling purse with honeyed kisses, she would be sorely disappointed.

He would make sure of that.

Chapter Two

In the hour after sunset, Justin strode towards the King's chamber, dreading this meeting. The King expected an answer on his list of grants. He wasn't going to like the one he would hear.

But Justin would deliver it, and quickly. He had another mission to accomplish before the lighting of the Yule Log.

Entering the solar, Justin saw Richard on his knees, hands clasped. He paused, thinking the King at prayer, but when Richard dropped his pose and waved him in, Justin saw an artist, squinting over his parchment, sketching.

As Justin forced a shallow bow, the artist left the room, handing his drawings to the King.

'Aren't these magnificent, Lamont?' The man had drawn Richard kneeling before a group of angels. 'The gold of heaven will surround me here and my sainted great-grandfather will stand behind me.'

Only young Richard would call the man a saint. 'Your great-grandfather died impaled on a poker for incompetence in government.' And sixty years ago, most had cheered at his death.

The King narrowed his eyes. 'He was deposed by ruffians who had no respect for their King. Do you?'

Justin clenched his fingers, his sergeant-at-law ring digging into his fist. 'I respect the King who respects his realm and the advice of his barons.'

Years ago, Justin had respected this King. Then, the young boy bravely faced rebellious peasants and promised them justice. That promise, like so many others, had been broken many times over.

Frowning, the King put down the sketches. 'It's abominable, having to go to the Council every time I need the Great Seal. Give me the list.'

'The Council has said no.'

The King, stunned, merely stared at him. Only the crackle of the fire broke the silence.

'Even to Hibernia?' he asked, finally.

'Especially to Hibernia. The man tarries at court with his mistress while his wife waits at home in embarrassment.'

'You go too far!' The King shook his fist. His voice rose to a squeak. 'That's not the Council's concern. These are my personal gifts, not governmental ones.'

Obviously, the King did not understand the new order. 'They affect the Treasury, so they come under the Council's purview.' There might be a legitimate grant or two on the list, but in the end, he suspected, he would be serving summons to the lot of them. 'Until we complete a full review of the household expenses, there will be no new grants.'

'Is this the legal advice you gave the Council?' The King spat 'Council' as if he hated the very word.

'Parliament made the law, Your Majesty.'

'And by that law a Council can rule a King?'

'For the next year, yes.'

The King narrowed his eyes. 'You tell your Council that

by Twelfth Night I want the seal affixed to this list. The entire list.' A wicked smile touched his lips. 'And add a grant of five pounds for the Weston woman.'

Justin clenched his jaw. The amount would barely keep a squire for a year, but the woman had done nothing to earn it. The King was simply trying to flaunt his power. 'I will convey your message,' he said. 'I do not expect them to change their minds, particularly for the woman.'

Barely suppressed fury contorted the King's face. 'Remember, Lamont, according to your precious law, by this time next year, I will be King again.'

The King's very softness of speech caused him to shiver. This was a man who never forgot wrongs.

Well, that was something they had in common.

As Justin left the room, laughter laced the halls as the court gathered for the lighting of the Yule Log. He did not slow his steps. The Lady Solay had to be stopped. Quickly.

Scolding herself for speaking harshly to Lamont, Solay took her small bag of belongings to the room she was assigned to share with one of the Queen's ladies-in-waiting, wondering whether the choice was an omen of the King's favour or a sign that he wanted her watched.

She unpacked quickly as Lady Agnes, small, round, and fair, hovered in the doorway. 'Lady Solay, hurry. We mustn't miss the celebration.'

Shivering in her outgrown, threadbare cloak, Solay crossed the ward with Lady Agnes, who had not stopped talking since they left the room.

'The Christmas tableaux for his Majesty tomorrow will be so beautiful. I am to play a white deer, his Majesty's favourite creature.' Agnes had come to England from Bohemia with Queen Anne and still trilled her *r*s. 'And for the dinner, the cook is fixing noodles smothered in cheese and cinnamon and saffron. It's my very favourite.'

Solay's mouth watered at the thought. Her tongue had not touched such extravagant sweetness in years. As they entered the hall, Solay looked around the room, relieved when she did not see Lord Justin.

All her life, she had ignored the prejudice of strangers, yet, unlike all the others, his condemnation had unearthed her long-banked anger, exposed it to the air where it threatened to burst into flame, stirring her to fight battles long lost.

Worse, he had touched something even more dangerous. Close to this man, she felt *want*. The unruly emotion threatened the control she needed if she were to control those around her. And her ability to influence others was her family's only hope.

Lady Agnes left to attend the Queen, who was touching the brand to the kindling beneath the Yule Log. Solay looked for another woman companion, but each one she approached drifted out of reach.

The men were not so reticent. One by one they came to study her face and let their eyes wander her body. Feeling not a speck of desire, she turned the glow of her smile on each one, circling each as the sun did the earth.

She learned, as she smiled, that the King had bestowed a new title, Duke of Hibernia, on his favourite courtier.

The men did not smile as they told her.

'Congratulations, Lady Solay.' Justin's words came from behind her. 'The King has put your name on his list already.'

Only when she heard his voice did she realise she'd been listening for it. Yet surely the excitement she felt was for the news he brought and not for him. 'His Majesty is gracious.' She wondered how gracious an amount he'd given.

'The Council is not. It will not be allowed. The Council cares not that you pick a birth date to please the King.'

Her cheeks went cold. 'What do you know of my birth?' Few had known or cared when she came on to this earth. The deception had been harmless. Or would be unless the King found out.

'One of the laundresses served your mother twenty years ago. She remembers the night of your birth very clearly. It was the summer solstice and all the castle was awake to hear your mother's moans.'

She bit her lower lip to hold back a smile of delight. Her birthday. She finally knew her birthday.

But she must cling to the tale she'd told. 'She must have mis-remembered. It was many years ago.'

'She was quite sure she was right. And so am I.'

Fear swallowed her reason. If the King were to believe her reading, he must have no doubts about her veracity. 'Would you take the word of a laundress over that of a King's daughter?'

'The laundress has no reason to lie. The King's daughter apparently does.'

She raised her eyes to Justin's, forgetting to shield her desperation. 'You haven't told the King?'

'No.'

Relief left her hands shaking. 'He need not know.' Surely a few light words and a kiss would cajole this man to silence. She touched his arm and leaned into him, pleading with her eyes. Her lips parted of their own accord. 'It was harmless, really. I thought only to flatter him.'

The angry set of his lips did not change as he stepped away. 'When next you think to flatter the King, remember that, for the next year, the power belongs to the Council.'

Fear smothered her joy. Now that he knew the truth, he held a weapon and could strike whenever he pleased. This man, so able to resist a woman's persuasion, must want something else.

She had a moment's regret. She had thought he might be different. 'I see. What is it you want for your silence?'

He raised his brows. 'Don't confuse my character with yours, Lady Solay. I do not play favourites.'

'So you will hold your tongue and then call the favour I owe you when it's needed.'

Seemingly surprised, he studied her face. 'Do you trust no one?'

'Myself, Lord Justin. I trust myself.'

'Surely someone has given you something without expecting anything in return?'

Her thoughts drifted to memory. All those courtiers who had fawned over her mother while the King lived disappeared the night he died. All their kindnesses, even to a little girl, had only one purpose—access to his power. 'Not that I remember.'

'Then I am sorry for you.'

She saw a trace of sadness in his eyes, and steeled herself against it. 'I don't want your pity. You'll want something some day, Lord Justin. They all do.'

'You are the one who wants something, Lady Solay. Not I.' He turned his back and left her standing alone in a crowded room.

She shrugged as the next man approached. What Lord Justin said did not matter. His actions would tell the tale.

Justin strode down the stairs and out into the upper ward, glad to be free of her. The dark, her nearness, went to his head like mulled wine.

He should go to the King immediately with her deception, he thought, rubbing his thumb across the engraved words on his ring. *Omnia vincit veritas.* Truth conquers all. Just tell the king she had lied and she would be gone.

But all around him, the court was surging across the ward towards the chapel for midnight mass. It was hardly the time to interrupt one's monarch to say…what? That the Lady Solay had lied about her birthday? What lady had not? The King, never too careful of his own word, might either take it as a compliment or as an affront.

Justin's footsteps slowed. He could imagine the look on Richard's face. After the King digested the fact, the cunning would creep into his eyes. Then, just as she predicted, he would hold the knowledge as a weapon, waiting to use it until she was most vulnerable. And despite everything, Justin knew that the Lady Solay was vulnerable. When her violet eyes pleaded with him, they reminded him of another woman's. A woman so desperate she—

He blocked the painful memory as he walked by the Round Tower, looming in the centre of the castle's inner ward. There was no need to reveal Solay's secret tonight. The threat alone would give her pause. Besides, the Council would never approve her grant, so what did it matter?

But as he entered the chapel and bowed before the altar, the knowledge of her lie, and the desperation that caused it, lay in his gut like an undigested meal.

Right next to the admission that, for once in his life, he was holding back the truth.

Beside Lady Agnes, Solay walked out of the midnight mass with a stiff neck from craning to watch the King. She knelt when the King knelt, rose when the King rose, following his movements as closely as his shadow.

At least she did until Lord Justin blocked her view. He moved to his own rhythm, never glancing at the King, or at anyone else, except once, when he caught her eyes with an expression that seemed to say, 'Can't you even be yourself before God?'

Who was he to judge her? she thought, shivering beneath her thin cloak. He did not know her life.

But he already knew a secret that threatened her. And her clumsy attempt to kiss him had made matters worse.

Everyone wanted something. If she could learn what he wanted, perhaps she could help him get it in exchange for his silence.

Agnes must know something. 'Lady Agnes,' she began, 'what do you—?'

'I need the room to myself tonight,' Lady Agnes whispered back, not looking at her.

Craving the few hours of rest between the Christmas Eve and Christmas dawn Masses, Solay opened her mouth to protest, then stopped. This was why Agnes had offered to share a room with her. Agnes needed someone to cover for her when she had a rendezvous.

Lady Agnes had chosen wisely. Solay murmured her assent.

As the crowd fanned out across the inner ward toward the residential apartments, she wondered where she might pass the night. Lagging behind the others, she slipped around the Round Tower and over to the twin-towered gate her father had built before she was born. Perhaps it would shelter her tonight.

She slipped inside and started up the stairs, but, halfway up, she heard a noise in the darkness below. She climbed faster. Another set of footsteps echoed hers.

Who could it be? Even the guards had been given a Christmas respite.

The man was gaining on her.

Holding her skirts out of the way, she tried to run, but he was faster. As the scent of cedar touched her, her heart beat faster, the fear replaced with something even more dangerous.

'Lady Solay, you must be lost.'

She turned, holding back a laugh at the very idea. 'I cannot be lost, Lord Justin. I was born here.' The castle had been her playground when she was near a princess. At the memory, her chest ached with loss long suppressed.

'Born here, yet you can't seem to remember the day and you don't know the difference between the gate tower and the residential wing.' He took her arm. 'I'll take you to your room.'

'No!' She pulled her arm free, and turned gingerly on the narrow stair. He was still too close. 'Sleep is difficult for me,' she said. That, strangely, was true. She wondered why she had shared it with him.

'So you wander the castle like a spectre?'

She grabbed an excuse. 'I was going to study the stars to prepare for the King's reading.' He would not know that a horoscope came from charts and not from the sky.

He moved closer. 'Then I will accompany you.'

She released a breath, not caring whether he believed her. At least Agnes was safe.

Their steps found the same rhythm as they climbed to the top of the Tower. Cold air rushed into her lungs as they emerged from the dark stairway on to the battlements. After the darkness of the Tower, the night, lit by stars, seemed almost bright, although the half-moon shed only enough light to polish the strong curve of his jaw.

He waved his hand towards the sky, a gesture as much of dismissal as of presentation. 'So, milady, look out on the stars and make what sense of them you will.'

She looked up and her heart soared, as it always did. How many sleepless nights had she spent trying to discern their secrets? Now, like familiar friends, their patterns kept her company when sleep would not come.

She hugged herself, trying to warm her upper arms. He moved behind her, his broad back cutting the wind, suddenly making her feel sheltered, though his voice turned cold. 'Strange method of study. In the dark. Without notes or instruments.'

'I only need to watch them to learn their meaning.'

He snorted. 'Then all soldiers should be experts on the stars.' Behind her, he took her by the shoulders, his breath intimate as he whispered in her ear, 'Do you know any more of the stars than you do of your birth date?'

She swallowed. Was it his question or his nearness that caused her to tremble? 'I know more than most.'

Yet of the stars, like many things, she knew only the surface. By memorising the list of ascendants in her mother's Book of Hours, she had gleaned enough to impress most people, but only enough to tantalise herself.

Thankfully, he let her go and leaned against the wall next to her. 'You could not know what takes the University men years to learn.'

His dismissal rankled. 'I *had* years.' Years after they left court and her mother was busy with suits and counter-suits.

His dark eyes, lost in shadow, gave her no clue to his thoughts. 'And did the stars give you the answers you sought?'

His question surprised her. She had studied the heavens because she had nothing else to do. She had studied hoping they might explain her life and give her hope for the future. 'I am still searching for my answers, Lord Justin. Did you find yours in the law?'

He turned away from her question, so silent she could hear the lap of the river out of sight below the walls.

'I was looking for justice,' he said, finally.

'On earth?' She felt a moment's sympathy for him. How disappointing his life must be. 'You'd do better to look to the stars.' The stars surely had given her this time alone with him. She should be speaking of light, charming things that might turn him into an ally. 'Let me read yours. When were you born, Lord Justin?'

He frowned. 'Do you think your feeble learning can discover the truth about me?'

She touched his unyielding arm with a playful hand. 'My learning is good enough for the King.'

Her fingers burned on his sleeve. She swayed towards him.

He picked up her hand. All the heat between them flowed from his fingers and into her core. He held her a moment too long, then dropped her hand away from his arm.

'The King cares more for flattery than truth.' His voice was rough. 'I would not believe a word you say.'

She waved her hand in the air, as if she had not wanted to touch him at all. As if his dismissal had not hurt her. 'Yet you believe in justice on earth.'

'Of course. That's what the law is for.'

Was anyone so naïve? 'And when the judges are wrong? What then?'

'The condemned always claim they've been unjustly convicted.'

Fury warmed her blood. Parliament had given her mother no justice. 'Even if the judgement is right, is there never forgiveness? Is there never mercy?'

'Those are for God to dispense.'

'Oh, so justice lives on earth, mercy in Heaven, and you happily sit in judgement confident that you are never wrong.' She laughed without mirth.

'You believe your mother should be exonerated.'

Surprised he recognised a meaning she had missed, she was silent. Better not to even acknowledge such a hope. Better not to picture her mother back at court and revered for the good she had done. 'She was brought back to court before the year was out.' Restored to her position beside the King for his last, painful year.

'Not by Parliament.'

'No, by the King himself. The Commons never had the right to judge her. And neither do you.'

'It is you I judge. You've lied about your birth date. I suspect you are lying about why you are not abed. It seems truth means nothing to you.'

'Truth?' He talked of truth as if it were more valuable than bread. She held her tongue. She had already been too candid. If she angered him further, he would never keep her secret. 'Perhaps each of us knows a different truth.'

'There is only one truth, Lady Solay, but should you ever choose to speak it, I would scarce recognise it.' His voice brimmed with disgust.

'You do not recognise it now. My mother was a great helpmate to the King.'

He shook his head. 'Even you can't believe that.' A yawn overtook him. 'I'm going to bed. I leave you to your stars and your lies.'

'Some day when I tell you the truth, you will believe it,' she whispered to his fading footsteps.

Shivering and alone under a sky that seemed darker than before, she crossed her arms to keep from reaching for him as he descended the stairs.

Chapter Three

Solay snatched only an hour of sleep after Mass, then spent the feast day watching Justin and wondering whether he planned to expose her lie. Finally, exhausted, she escaped for a nap as soon as the King left the Christmas feast.

Her respite was brief. Before dark, Lady Agnes bustled into the room, carrying a white robe and two bare branches. 'Here's my costume for the disguising.' She held up the simple off-white shift and waved the branches over her head. 'Will I not look like a hart?'

A knock relieved Solay of responding. Agnes would resemble a horned angel more than a white stag.

At the door, a page, garbed in a vaguely familiar livery of three gold crowns on a blue background, handed Agnes a note and ran. She read it, then, smiling, closed the door.

'I need you to take my part in the disguising,' she whispered.

'I would be honoured,' Solay told her, trying to place the page's livery. How bold to ignore the King's entertainment for a private tryst. Did lusting make one so mad?

'Quick. We haven't much time.' Agnes helped Solay into the undyed gown, slipped a linen hood over her face, and tied the branches around her head.

'Tell me what I must do.' Beneath the hood, she squinted, trying to see out of the eye holes.

'Just watch the others in white. Do as they do and at the end, curl up at the feet of the one who plays the King.' Agnes stopped tugging on the robe and peered through the slits in the hood to meet Solay's gaze. 'They must think you are me.'

Behind the hood, Solay laughed. 'I'm disguised and I've just come to court. Who will recognise me?'

'Everyone saw you yesterday.'

Everyone watched in glee as the King humiliated her, Agnes meant. And then, of course, the men had come for a closer look.

But only Justin had really seen her.

Agnes squeezed Solay's fingers. 'Please. Do not remove your hood, no matter what. Too many know what part I was to take.' Agnes opened the door a crack, looked both ways, then pushed Solay into the hall. 'And thank you,' she whispered, her round blue eyes full of gratitude.

Solay crept down the stairs to the Great Hall, fingers touching the cool stone wall for balance. The branches wobbled uncertainly at the back of her head. Anonymous beneath her white hood, she felt strangely free as she entered the Hall.

Until she saw Justin.

Head down, he huddled with three other men. He was not costumed, of course. This man refused to disguise himself or his feelings.

As she walked towards the masked group gathering at the end of the Hall, his gaze drifted from the conversation to follow her. Knowing he was watching, she realised that Agnes's costume exposed her ankles and hung slack around her hips. She turned her back on him and touched her hood to make sure her hair was covered. A stray dark lock would betray her.

The King's herald called for silence and she pulled her attention back to the tableau. Like a mirror, the scene reflected the King who observed it. A pretend King sat on a mock throne. Heavenly beings in blue surrounded him. Beasts of the field came to lie at his feet.

As she moved to her place, the court seemed as much of a façade as the play, beautiful on the surface, but concealing each player's true nature. When she lay at the foot of the false throne and heard the applause, she wondered which player had donned Agnes's lover's garb.

'Up. Now,' someone behind her whispered.

Around her, players moved into the audience, pulling them into the scene. As she rose to follow, she glimpsed a deep blue robe through the slits in her hood. All around them, laughing men and women joined the pretty scene, posing like statues. Afraid to look up, she saw a hand, grasped it and pulled.

At his touch, her fingers seemed to dissolve. For that moment, there was no separation between them.

He ripped his hand away, refusing not with the good-natured, temporary reluctance of the rest, but with stubborn belligerence.

She made the mistake of looking up.

Beneath the heavy brows, she saw no doubt in his eyes. It was Justin. And he knew her.

She turned, reaching with both hands to draw in two courtiers next to him, trying to escape. As the real and the pretend court merged, the King applauded and some of the disguisers lifted their masks.

Ducking behind the pretend throne, Solay fled into the hall. The man in the King's garb left, too, mask still in place, turning in the opposite direction.

She had almost reached the stairs when Justin's voice licked her back.

'You do not raise your hood with the rest, Lady Solay.'

'You mistake me.' She climbed the first two stairs, back to him. Perhaps a carefully rolled *r* would fool him. 'I am a white hart, pious and pure.'

'You are neither pious nor pure and your accent sounds nothing like the Lady Agnes.'

She lowered her eyes, her lashes scraping the linen hood, still hoping to deny who she was.

Too late. He pulled off the hood, letting the fake antlers skitter down the stairs, and took her chin in his hand, forcing her to look into his eyes, dark with anger, and something more.

His breath touched her cheek. 'And her eyes are not the colour of royalty.'

Her lips parted and she struggled to catch a breath that did not smell of him.

He swayed nearer, his lips dangerously close to hers. One more breath, and they would touch.

He let her go and held out the hood. 'No, I see you are nothing like a hart.'

She snatched it back, her breath still coming fast. What good would she be to Lady Agnes now? 'Did you not think I played the part well?'

He dusted his palms, to brush off her touch. 'It seems all of life is a disguising to you, a deception for amusement.'

''Tis not true,' she said, though the idea gave her pause. She had mirrored the others in the play, just as she did every day, playing a part to please the watcher.

'Where is Lady Agnes this evening?' he asked, ignoring her answer.

'She was taken ill. She did not want to disappoint their Majesties.'

'So you lie for others as well as for yourself.'

'Why do you assume I lie?' Not only did the man demand truth, he had an uncanny knack of discerning it.

'Because I saw Lady Agnes just after the feast. She was laughing and excited about her part in the disguising. Where is she?'

'She was taken to her bed suddenly,' she said, hoping still to hide Agnes's sin.

'I'm certain she was, but not by illness and not alone.' His strong brows furrowed with disapproval.

'I told you, she didn't feel well.' Her tongue ran away with her, trying to make him believe. 'She must have eaten too much of the noodles and saffron.'

'You are the only one who thinks that Hibernia's trysts with Lady Agnes are a secret.'

Her cheeks went cold. 'I am newly come to court.' Where ignorance of such secrets was dangerous. No wonder the page's livery looked familiar. The Duke was the King's dearest companion. Poor, foolish Agnes. 'And if that is so, there's nothing to be gained by speaking of tonight.'

'You seem to have nothing but secrets, Lady Solay. Don't expect me to keep them for ever.'

'I denied you a kiss last night.' She had been told a woman's body could enslave a man, though she knew little of how. She leaned close to him, feeling her breasts soft against his hard chest, fighting her traitorous body as it weakened next to his. 'Perhaps you want it now?'

He raised his arms. She waited, wanting him to take her.

Instead, his hands curved into fists. Nothing else moved except the truth of his response, pounding below his waist.

Then, he pushed her away. 'You are just like your mother.' He spat the words like a curse.

She gripped his sleeve, fighting her anger. She had tried to tell him about her mother, but this implacable man had no compassion. And now, her foolish move had only strengthened his mistrust.

She swallowed her emotions and tried to think clearly. 'What do you want? What can I give you?'

The harsh planes of his face held no more feeling than a stone. 'Nothing. The Council will not be swayed by kisses, Lady Solay.' He uncurled her fingers from their grip on his sleeve. 'And neither will I.'

Shaking, Solay watched him leave, fear drowning both her want and her anger. She knew how to charm men. She had even cajoled the King, but this man, this man could resist everything she offered. This man could ruin it all.

She slipped the hood over her head and hurried back to her room, knocking cautiously before entering.

She opened the door to the scent of lovemaking. The smell tugged at her. What would that be like, to share such closeness?

She shut the door behind her. Dangerous. It would be dangerous.

Agnes sprawled under the covers, tears streaking her rounded cheeks.

Had Agnes's sad lesson come so soon? 'What's the matter?'

'His wife comes tomorrow.'

She had wondered where the Duchess was while all the King's favourites were gathered at Windsor. Perhaps she had stayed home to avoid humiliation. 'She travels on Christmas day?' The rumours must have driven her to protect herself. No wonder the urgency to bed him one more time. Surely, Agnes would see him no more after his wife arrived.

Agnes shrugged her answer, speechless in the face of disaster. She folded a little white piece of cloth and blew her nose.

Solay sat on the side of the bed and patted her arm. 'It's all right. Everything will work out,' she said, without sincerity.

Such naïveté could only lead to pain. What had the silly goose expected? That he would leave his wife for his mistress?

Agnes sat up in bed, sniffing back the tears. 'I know. You're right. I must be patient.' She squeezed Solay's hands. 'Thank you. You're a true friend.'

She blinked. She had known few women and never one who had called her friend. Women did not like her, as a rule.

Agnes blew her nose again and tried to smile. 'Now, tell me—how was the disguising? It was beautiful, no?'

'Oh, yes. The King clapped loudly.'

'No one recognised you?'

She turned away as she folded the wrinkled linen hood and slipped out of the shift. 'Nothing has changed.' Based on what Justin had said, the Duke and Agnes had no secrets left. 'Tell me, Agnes. What do you know of Lord Justin Lamont?'

Agnes's smile slipped into a frown. 'He's a terrible man. He's the one who led Parliament to impeach the King's Chancellor.'

Solay shuddered. Worse than a man of law, worse than a Council member. He was a man who would manoeuvre Parliament to destroy those closest to the King, just as her mother's enemies had done. 'So he truly is the King's foe.'

Agnes leaned forward. 'They want to attack my dear Duke as well,' she whispered, as if afraid someone might hear, 'but they do not dare. He is the King's right arm.'

Agnes had let slip her lover's identity. The poor girl truly believed he was safe, but in times such as these, no one was safe. Still, if Agnes trusted her, perhaps Solay could glean something useful. 'Lord Justin does the Council's legal work?'

Agnes snuggled back under the covers with a pout. 'I suppose. Who knows how any man spends his time when not with a woman? Documents, diplomacy, bookkeeping.' She shrugged, as if it were unimportant.

Solay stared, stunned. Her mother had taught her that the

work of the King was the work of the world. While feminine arts gave them diversion, money and power, law and war ruled the earth. How could Agnes not care about those things?

'But that's not what you really want to know,' Agnes continued, with a catlike smile. 'I saw him watch you with hunger during the Christmas feast. You want to know what kind of man he is.'

'He is the King's enemy.' *And mine.* 'That is all I need to know.'

'But not all you want to know. He's handsome, isn't he? Many women think so, but he has refused them all.' Agnes tilted her head. 'I heard he was to be wed, many years ago, and the girl died.'

'So he mourns still?' Somehow, he did not seem like a man who pined for a dead love.

'He has no interest in marriage.'

'His family allows it?' He was certainly nine and twenty. The family must want an heir.

'He is a second son. His brother has many children. But beware, Solay. He and the Lords Appellant would destroy the King.'

Should Justin demand more than kisses for his silence, how could she refuse? 'He does not tempt me. I am only trying to learn who's who.'

'Good. I saw you with the Earl of Redmon. He might make a good husband. His wife died on Michaelmas and he has three children who need tending. He might not be too particular. I mean…' A blush spread over her cheekbones. 'I'm sorry.'

'It's all right.' There would be no marriage for Solay. She had nothing to offer a husband but her body, unless the mere taste of royalty might titillate a man. 'I am not thinking of a husband.' Her hopes lay with a grant from the King, not with a group of lords with temporary power, and if she were to please the King, she must produce a horoscope and a poem.

'Tell me, Agnes, who is the King's favourite poet?'

Chapter Four

As the Lord of Misrule pranced around the table two days after Christmas, Justin felt no Yuletide spirit.

Across the room, Solay laughed gaily at something John Gower the poet said.

Justin was not laughing.

He sank his teeth into the roast boar. At least the King had bowed to convention and put a whole pig on the spit for the Yule feasts. Usually, the meat at table was spiced, sugared, and so shredded you could eat it with a spoon.

Robert, Duke of Hibernia, had left the King's side to wander the room and now stood laughing with Solay. That man alone was enough to make him scowl. He was so close to the King that he seemed to fancy that he, too, was royal.

And judging by her wide-eyed attention to him, Solay knew it as well.

He heard her husky laugh again.

Just like her mother, she would lie and cheat and use anyone to get what she wanted. He had avoided her for the past two days, but, mistrustful of her motives, had watched her from afar.

Be honest with yourself, Lamont. This has nothing to do with your distrust of her. You just can't keep your eyes off the woman.

How had he let himself be gulled into holding her lies? Now her falsehoods tainted him, too, and, instead of thanks, she accused him of some subversive purpose. He should expose her and have her expelled from court.

But then he would remember the pain in her eyes.

He was ever the fool for a woman in pain.

More than a fool, for the pain he thought he saw was probably as false as her offered kisses.

Gloucester joined him, swilling wine from his goblet. 'Your eyes are ever upon the Lady Solay.'

'Her eyes have turned on every man in the room.' Most had leered at her as long as she'd let them. 'I even saw her talking to you.'

Gloucester smiled. 'She has her mother's talent for pleasing powerful men, but if she seeks a husband, she'll be hard pressed to find one who will have her.' He lifted his goblet in a parting toast and laughed, moving on down the hall.

Husband. Startled, Justin looked for her in the crowd. She was smiling at the Earl of Redmon, a recent widower as a result of his third wife's fall down the stairs. Why had he never thought of marriage for her? A husband would do her more good than a grant, if he came with enough property and a willingness to take on Alys of Weston as a mother-in-law.

And the right husband would not require the Council's approval. Only the King's.

He looked to the dais. Despite the joy of the season, the King's scowl matched Justin's own. Since he had told the King that the Council refused his appointments, Richard had been in a foul mood.

Tonight, he sulked while the poor fool, the Lord of Misrule, tried to create merriment by ordering the most unlikely couples to embrace.

The Fool forced Hibernia into an embrace with Lady Agnes. Hibernia and Agnes seemed to be enjoying it mightily. The man's wife did not.

Solay had assumed a bland smile. He wondered what it hid.

The thought deepened his frown, so when the Fool waved his crown before Justin's eyes, blocking his vision of Solay, Justin only grunted.

The Fool would not be dissuaded. 'Now here's another man who needs to show more Yuletide cheer. Who would you like to kiss this evening?'

'No one. Leave me be.'

'Ah, but your eyes have been on the Lady Solay. Would you like to put your lips on her as well?'

Hearing her name, Solay turned to look.

His entire body surged to answer. He had refused her kisses before, but those she fawned over tonight might not. The wine had loosened his resistance. Surely, he, too, deserved a taste. 'Yes,' he answered. 'I would kiss the daughter of the sun.'

Her eyes widened and her lips parted, as if she inhaled to speak, but no words came.

The diners next to him went silent. Was it because he dared kiss the daughter of a King? Or because no one wanted to be reminded of who she was?

The jester's babbling broke the awkward silence. 'The Lord of Misrule makes all things possible.' He grabbed Justin's hand and pulled him around the table, to face Solay.

Trapped in the jester's grip, Justin watched her eyes darken with desire, and regretted his honesty. What would happen when he took her lips? He steeled himself against her. Nothing. She was a woman, nothing more.

The Lord of Misrule laughed merrily. 'Your wish is my command. Kiss the lady!'

She was too close now, close enough that her scent engulfed him. She smelled of rose petals hidden in a golden box, sweet, yet protected by metal that only fire would melt.

He wanted to take her in his arms, crush her to him and ravish her lips with his. He wanted to possess her, yet something warned him that she would possess him instead.

Her lips parted, but her eyes did not droop with desire. They were open, wide with fear.

He put his hands on her arms, deliberately holding himself away from her body, leaned over and put his lips on hers.

Her lips were soft as he'd expected, but they lay cool and unyielding beneath his. When she did not respond, something burst within him. She had teased him for days. For all those other men, she supplicated and simpered.

He would have what she offered.

He pulled her close, feeling her breasts, soft, pressing against him. Suddenly, he did not care who she was or where they were. He wanted her kiss, yes, but whatever else she hid, he wanted that, too.

The kiss she had dangled before him for days blossomed and the impossible scent of roses made him dizzier than the wine. When she opened to him, he took her lips and thrust his tongue into her mouth, wanting to taste all of her. Her stiffness became softness and he tightened his arms, fearing she would fall if he let go.

And only the beat of the jester's wand on his shoulder brought him to himself.

'The man's eaten nothing but oysters all night,' the jester said.

Drunken laughter around them brought heat to his cheeks.

He pulled away, torn between desire and scorn, and glimpsed on her face the truth he'd sought.

She wanted him.

Her eyes were dark with desire, her mouth ripe with lust. Then she touched her lips and blinked the softness from her eyes, and for once he was grateful—her disguise protected them both.

The jester turned to Solay. 'Since you have suffered this dullard's embrace, you deserve a wish of your own. What boon can I grant the lady?'

She grabbed her goblet and lifted it toward the King's table. 'I desire to toast our gracious Majesties, King Richard and Queen Anne. Long life, health and defeat of all their enemies.'

Tapered fingers hugging the chalice, she lifted it to drink, but instead of looking at the King, her eyes met Justin's.

He touched his goblet to his lips, wishing the wine could wash away her kiss.

Now that he had tasted her, he could no longer deny that her body tugged at his loins. Her eyes put him in mind of bedchambers and the pale skin of her inner wrist made him want to see the pale skin of her thighs.

All the better, then, if she took a husband, although none of the popinjays at court seemed right. As long as she kept out of the King's Treasury, she was no concern of his.

Gloucester returned to his side. 'How does she taste?'

Like no one else in the world. ''Twas but a Yuletide jest.'

'You obviously enjoyed it,' Gloucester said. 'And you put her in her place.'

The words kindled his shame. She had succumbed, yes, but he had forced her. No matter that she had tried to tempt him earlier. He had let his desire overrun his sense, spoken his want aloud, then forced it upon her.

And he had promised himself never to force a woman. He knew too well the bitter results.

For that, she deserved an apology.

* * *

Unable to sleep, Solay looked out of the window at the last star fading in the blue dawn light. An insistent rooster heralded the coming day, yet beside her in the bed, Agnes slept undisturbed, her gentle, drunken snore ruffling the air.

Solay, too, felt drunk, perhaps from the wine or the sweetness of the almond cake.

Or perhaps from his kiss. It still burned her mouth and seared her mind, speaking of promises not to be hoped for, particularly from a man who hated her.

Wide awake, she rolled over. What boon does the lady want? the Fool had asked. She wanted such simple things. To be safe. To be looked at without scorn. To sleep through the night without worrying whether they would have food to meet the morrow. To see her mother smile and hear her sister laugh.

And tonight, God help her, she wanted him.

She crept from bed and grabbed her cape as Agnes snored on. Crossing the ward, she climbed again to the roof of the tower. As a child, she had loved to watch the sun rise. Each time, she could begin life anew. For those few moments when first light touched the world, she had had no one to please, no one to *be* but herself.

Here, as the winter wind quieted in anticipation of the life-giving ball of light, she could believe that the stars ruled people's lives and that she was truly a daughter of the sun.

She recognised his steps, surprised that, after only a few days, she knew his gait. As he reached the ramparts, she composed her smile and turned, dizzy at the sight of him.

Impossible hopes danced in her heart. 'Did the Lord of Misrule send you after me again?'

He held himself stiffly, his hands clenched as if to keep from reaching for her. 'We must talk.' The words seemed forced. 'About the kiss.'

Kiss. The word lingered on lips that had moved soft and urgent over hers. The memory brought heat to her cheeks and to places deeper inside. 'What is there to say?'

'I should not have forced you.'

So. He regretted his passion now. Well, she would not reveal her weakness for him. He would only use it against her in the end. She shrugged. 'It is Yuletide. It meant nothing.'

'Really?'

His question trapped her. To admit he moved her would leave her with no defence. *Oh, Mother, how do I protect myself against the wanting?*

'Of course not.' She crafted a light and airy tone so he would not know she had dissolved at his kiss and no longer recognised the new form she found herself in. 'You took no more than I had offered.'

'Well, then…' He nodded, finishing the sentence and the incident. His rigid muscles relaxed, but he did not move closer. 'What brings you to the roof, Lady Solay? It is too late to see the stars.'

'I come to watch the sun.'

She was grateful that the breeze quickened and blew his scent away from her. One more step and she might reach for his shelter.

'The sun is near its lowest point, Lady Solay. It has withdrawn its light from the world.'

His words brought back her childhood fears. Sometimes, as her life had changed, she had watched for the sun to rise, uncertain that it really would. 'Yet it was at this, the darkest hour upon earth, that the brightest son was born.'

'Are you speaking of the Saviour or the King?'

She smiled. The analogy had not occurred to her, but it might make a flattering conceit for the King's reading. 'Both.'

'The sun comes up every morning.' He leaned on the battlements, facing her. 'Why do you find it worthy of watching?'

'Why? Just look.'

He turned.

In anticipation of sunrise, the sky erupted in colour—bruised purple at the horizon, then striped blue, and finally brilliant pink. 'The heavens are more reliable than your justice. The sun comes up every morning.' Her words came out in a whisper. 'Even in our darkest hours.'

'Have you had many of those?'

'Enough.' More than dark hours. Dark years after the death of the old King snuffed the life-giving sun from their sky.

'But you survived.' No compassion softened his words.

She blocked the memories. She had spoken too much of herself and her needs. 'Has the world never been harsh to you?'

'No more than to most.' Pain gilded his answer, but whatever weakness had sent him to the roof in near-apology was gone when he looked at her. 'Do not try to play on my sympathies. You will not change my mind about your grant.'

The memory of the kiss pulsed between them. Could an appeal to his sense of justice change his mind? 'King Richard has given his clerks more than we would need.'

'And the clerks didn't deserve it either.'

'Don't deserve?' Despite her resolution, harsh words leapt to her tongue. 'The King is the judge of that, not you.'

'Not according to Parliament.'

'Parliament!' She spat the word. 'Those greedy buzzards stripped us of everything, not only what the King had freely given, but lands my mother acquired with her own means.'

'Lands she took from others and did not need.'

'She needed them to support us after his death.'

'She had a husband to take care of her, more fool he. Better to ask for a husband to support you.'

'Now you mock me.' Husbands were for women with dowries and respected families. 'No one would have me.'

'If the King decreed, someone would.'

'Then perhaps I shall ask him.' The very idea left her giddy.

He grabbed her arms and forced her to look at him. Some special urgency burned behind his eyes. 'Don't let him force you. Only wed if it is someone you want.'

Her heart beat in her throat as she looked at him. That was why her mother had warned her against this feeling. If the King decreed, it would not matter whom she wanted.

She stepped back and he let his hands drop. 'If someone weds me, be assured that I will want him.'

Disgust, or sadness, tinged his look. 'And if you don't, you'll tell him you do.' The brilliant colours of daybreak faded as the sun emerged. The sky had no colour; the sun, no warmth. 'Here's your sun, Lady Solay,' he said, turning towards the stairs. 'May it bring you a husband in the New Year.'

As his footsteps faded, the image he had suggested tantalised her like the dawn at the edge of the day. Marriage. Someone to take care of her.

She pulled her cloak tighter and let the wind blow the fantasy away. Better to focus on pleasing the King with a pleasant poem and a pretty future.

But Justin's suggestion tugged at her. Perhaps he had deliberately shown her the path to circumvent the Council.

If the King had no power to grant her family a living, he might find an alliance for her with a family that would not allow hers to starve.

And if the King were gracious enough to find her a husband, she would take whomever he gave, even if the man's kisses did not make her burn.

Chapter Five

As the sun rose to its pale peak on the last day of the year, Solay set aside the astrology tables in despair. She read no Latin, so she could understand none of the text. In a week, the Yuletide guests would be gone, and she with them unless she could create a story from the stars to please a King.

Before she wove a fiction, she had tried to decipher the truth, but the symbols in the chart the old astrologer had drawn blurred before her eyes.

She trusted no one for help except Agnes. When she had asked what ill omens the old astrologer had seen, Agnes's already pale face turned white.

'He said the King must give up his friendship with the Duke of Hibernia or the realm would be in danger.'

No wonder the man had been jailed.

Idly, she flipped through the tables of planets, wondering when Lord Justin Lamont had been born. He had the stubbornness of the Bull, but his blunt speech reminded her of the Archer. Perhaps one of them was the ascendant and the other…

Foolishness. She put the tables aside and turned to her real work. Her future lay in the hands of the King, not in the kisses of Justin Lamont.

She studied the King's birth chart again. Some aspects didn't match the temperament of the King she knew. Aggressive Aries was shown as his ascendant, yet he seemed the least warlike of kings.

The eleventh house was that of friends; the twelfth of enemies. Surely just a slight shift could move the Duke from one to the other.

A different time of birth would do it.

She turned pages with new energy. She would populate the chart as she wished and suggest it had changed because she used a different time of birth.

Smiling, she began to draw.

By late afternoon, she derived a chart that suited her purpose, and, it seemed, the King much better. A square formed the centre of the chart, Capricorn, his sun sign. Four triangles surrounded it, forming the four cardinal points as triangles from each side. Then, the additional eight houses formed another square around the first.

The shift clustered more planets in the house of friends, but it also described his character more accurately. From this one, she could spin a happy future for the King and, she hoped, for her family.

She hesitated. If it were dangerous to change her own time of birth, what would she risk to change the King's?

Yet it was the only answer she had. At least she was sensible enough to tell him no bad news. No one was likely to know enough to dispute her conclusions and, if anyone did, she would laugh and say she was only a woman and not a real astrologer.

Justin's mind wandered as the Court wasted the afternoon listening to bad verse penned by courtiers playing poet. The words flowed around him unheard. He had spent the last week telling himself that he was relieved that the kiss had meant nothing to Solay, though it galled him that she could swoon in his arms like a lover and then laugh. He should have expected nothing less. Even the woman's body lied.

Across the room, she was fawning over Redmon again. Since he had told her to seek a husband, Justin judged every man she spoke to for the role. She would have few choices. The man must have money, not need it, for she would bring no dowry. He must be acceptable to the King, but not too important, for if he were, he would get a better bride.

She gave the Earl a dazzling smile as it came her turn to present. Then, she licked her full, lower lip, cleared her throat, glanced at Justin and started to read.

They call them men of law, an empty boast
They claim that law means justice
But justice comes quickest to him that pays the most.

His cheeks burned. Though no one looked his way as they laughed, he knew her words were directed towards him. Her poem told an amusing tale of a dishonest lawyer, brought to justice by a benevolent and pure King. The verse lacked polish, but it showed promise. The words were clever.

More than clever. Something about them seemed very familiar.

After the King applauded heartily and the afternoon's entertainment ended, Justin sought her out. Her small triumph had touched her lips with an easy smile.

'A pretty poem, Lady Solay,' he said. 'Did you suggest the subject to John Gower?'

Solay's smile stiffened. 'What makes you ask that?'

He did not dignify her lack of denial with an answer. 'I did not think him a man to be swayed by kisses.'

She did not blush, which made him think she had not tried physical persuasion of the King's favourite poet. Odd, he felt relieved.

'The idea was his, not mine. He told me he was trying something new and if the King did not like the poem, Gower would put it aside. Since the King liked it very much, I dare say he will finish it and then tell the King and they will both think it a good joke.'

'So now I must keep secrets for John Gower's sake, not yours?'

Behind the pleading look in her eyes he saw the shadow of resentment. It must gall her to beg his co-operation. 'You wouldn't spoil the surprise, would you, just because the verse doesn't flatter you?'

Shocked, he realised he had never even considered it. 'It is Gower you wronged, not me. You sling borrowed barbs about lawyers, but you know nothing about me at all.'

'I know you helped Parliament impeach the King's Chancellor on imaginary charges.'

'The charges were real.'

'Not real enough, I see.' She nodded towards the Earl of Suffolk, laughing with the King. 'The man is with us today.'

He gritted his teeth. 'The King released him. Not Parliament.' Richard had imprisoned the man for a few weeks, then, as soon as Parliament had gone home, set him free as if Parliament had never ruled. As if the law meant nothing.

She lowered her voice to whisper. 'You say you care about truth, but others say you care more about destroying those closest to the King.'

'And you let others decide what you think.'

She didn't answer, but turned to smile at Redmon across the room. The man smiled back, broadly, and she started to leave.

'I hope you are not thinking of him as a husband.'

She kept searching the room, not meeting his eyes to answer. 'When you suggested marriage you did not request approval of the choice. In fact, you told me only the King could decide.'

One of the young pups across the room winked at her, elbowing his companion, and she gave him a slow smile.

The boy's grin grated on him. 'That one is not looking on you as a wife,' he growled.

'How do you know?'

'Because I am a man.'

'Well, the Earl of Redmon is.' Behind the lilt in her voice he heard the edge of anger.

'Did the stars tell you so?'

'He was born under the sign of the goat. We should get along well enough.'

'Did the stars also tell you that he is old and rich with wealth and sons and three dead wives? All he needs is someone to grace his bed. That should not be difficult for you.'

She gasped, but instead of satisfaction, he felt remorse. 'You fault me for failing some standard of your own devising. What do you expect of me, Lord Justin?'

'Only what I expect of anyone. To be what you are.'

She dropped the smile and let him see her anger. 'No, you expect me to be what you think my mother is.' She turned to leave.

'So each of us judges the other wrongly, is that what you think?' He grabbed her hand, stopping her as if he had the right.

The shock was almost as great as touching her lips.

Both of them stared down at their clasped hands, her hand, cool in his, his large, blunt fingers, covering her pale skin.

And something alive moved through him, the feeling of kissing her all over again. Then, he had been in his cups. Easy to explain being set afire by a beautiful woman. But this… He had simply touched her hand and now stood transfixed, unable to—

'Lord Justin, please.'

He looked up. This time, her slow, sultry smile was for him.

He dropped her hand. As she walked across the room to Redmon, he could swear she put an extra sway in her hips.

He smothered his body's quick response. He was finished with this dangerous woman. Whether she married or not was none of his affair as long as she did not dip her hand into the King's purse.

Justin and Gloucester approached the King's solar shortly before noon on the last day of the Yuletide festivities. Their visit would be short and unpleasant, but at least Solay should be gone at the end of it.

'Lamont? Did you hear me?' Gloucester's voice interrupted his thoughts.

'Sorry,' he answered. 'What did you say?'

'I'm going to throw this list in his face.'

Justin gathered his thoughts. It would fall to him to keep things civil when the royal tempers slipped loose.

As they entered, King Richard extended his hand, imperially as if it held a sceptre. 'The list. Give it to me.'

Justin held out the list of grants to be enrolled on the Patent Rolls 'with the assent of the Council'. 'The Council has approved these four.'

The King glanced at the list. 'Where are the rest? Where is Hibernia? Where is the woman?'

'They have not been allowed,' Justin said.

'Not been allowed? It is the King who allows!'

'Allowed?' Now it was Gloucester who yelled. 'You've allowed France to seize our lands instead of defending them!' he snapped, sounding more like an uncle than a subject.

Richard reached for his dagger. 'You impugn the power of the throne? I'll have you hanged.'

They lunged towards each other, tempers flaring, while the guards hung back, uncertain whether to protect the King or Gloucester.

Justin stepped between them. 'Please, Your Majesty, Gloucester.' Each stepped away, glowering.

Richard gritted his teeth. 'I will see *all* these grants allowed, including…' he looked at Gloucester, hate glowing in his eyes '…the one for the harlot's daughter.'

'You'll see none of them,' Gloucester said. 'Least of all that one!' He stomped out of the room without asking for leave.

Richard stood rigid with shock. Or anger.

Justin repressed his resentment. The King cared nothing for Solay except as a pawn to infuriate his uncle and the Council. 'Your Majesty, the Council has finished its review. There will be no more grants.'

Richard turned to Justin, his entire face pinched with rage. 'Be careful, Lord Justin.' His voice quavered with anger. 'Your Council may have power now, but I was born a King. Nothing can change that, especially not you and your puny law.'

A shiver slithered down Justin's back. When this man returned to power, he would grab what he wanted without a care for justice or the law. And Justin had been very, very much in the way of what he wanted.

On the afternoon of the twelfth day of Christmas, Solay was ushered into the King's private solar to present her reading. The King dismissed everyone but the Queen and Hibernia, an indication that he was taking her reading very seriously.

Solay's fingers shook as she smoothed the parchment with her new drawing. Her family's fate lay on its surface.

'Your Majesty,' she began, 'was born under the sign of the

goat on the day three kings were in attendance on the babe in the manger. Surely this is auspicious. In addition—'

'This is all well known,' Hibernia scoffed. 'Can you tell us nothing new?'

She put aside the chart. Hibernia had tolerated her for Agnes's sake, but after what the last astrologer had said about him, he had no love of the art.

'Well, I believe there may be.' Her breath was shallow. Now. Now she must risk it. 'Is Your Majesty sure you were born near the third hour after sunrise?'

Silence shimmered. How could one doubt the King?

'Of course I'm sure. My mother told me.'

Next to him, Anne put a gentle hand on his arm and gave Solay a look that was hard to decipher. 'Why do you ask?'

Solay swallowed. 'My calculations suggest the hour was closer to *nones*.' That would have meant the middle of the afternoon.

'Impossible,' said the King.

Queen Anne stared at Solay, then turned to her husband and whispered. The King's eyes widened and they both stared at her.

She swallowed in the lengthening silence.

'Who told you this?' the King said.

'No one. I was simply trying to read the planets. Of course, I am no expert and could easily be wrong.'

'But you could not easily be right.'

She looked from one to another. 'Am I right?'

The Queen spoke with her customary calm. 'Richard's mother once told me she had put out a false time of birth so as not to give the astrologers too much power.'

Her body burned with a heat that did not come from the hearth. Power. The unfamiliar fire of power. The truth of her startling prediction had given her something she had never before possessed.

Power enough for him to fear.

The King leaned forward, pinning Solay with eyes that held an uneasy mixture of apprehension and curiosity. 'What new knowledge does that give you?'

She looked down at her chart, trying to think. Too much knowledge would be dangerous. 'There are differences in the two ascendants. Yours is now Gemini and your moon is in Aries.'

'But what does that mean?'

Flattery first. Then the request.

'Your people revere you, Your Majesty. You are a singular man among men, whose wisdom surpasses ordinary understanding.' She swallowed and continued. 'And you are exceedingly generous to faithful friends and those of your blood.'

'Such as you?' His smile was hard to decipher.

She should have known that a King had heard all the ways to say 'please'. 'And so many others.'

His mouth twisted in derision, but fear still haunted his eyes. 'What does it tell you,' he whispered, 'of my death?'

She took a deep breath. If she predicted long life incorrectly, they would only think her a poor astrologer. If she predicted death correctly, she could be accused of causing it.

'I see a long and happy reign for Your Majesty.' Actually, some darkness hovered over his eighth house, but this was no time to mention it. 'All your subjects will bless your name when you leave us for Heaven.'

He leaned forward, his teeth tugging at his lips. 'And when will that be, Lady Solay?'

She swallowed. 'Oh, I am but a student and cannot determine such a thing.'

'You were skilful enough to deduce the correct time of my birth. I'm surprised you could not be so precise with my life's end.'

She lowered her eyes, hoping she showed proper deference. She had stumbled into a dangerous position. It would take all her talent to balance the King's belief in her with his fear. 'Forgive me for my ignorance, Your Majesty.'

He leaned back in his chair, peering at her over steepled fingers. 'And are some of these things also true of you, since we share a birth day?'

Trapped by her lie, she decided the truth might serve her well. 'It is interesting that you ask, Your Majesty. Since I have come to court, I found that I, too, was misinformed about the time of my birth. I was not born on the same day as Your Majesty.'

He smiled, pleased, and did not ask when she was born.

Hibernia pinched the bridge of his nose and shook his head. 'You can hardly take this seriously, Your Majesty.'

He would be wise to say so. The old astrologer was right. Hibernia was bad for the King. She simply chose not to say so.

'Of course I don't,' the King said, chuckling, as if relieved to be given an excuse. He rose and nodded at Solay. 'You shall have a new, fur-trimmed cloak for your work.'

'Thank you, Your Majesty.' She sank to her knees in what she hoped was an appropriate level of deference for an extravagant gift.

'And Lady Solay. You shall not read the stars again.' The faintest sheen of sweat broke the skin between his nose and his lips. 'For me, or for anyone.'

She nodded, murmuring assent. Her work as a faux astrologer had accomplished its purpose. Her uncanny prediction had raised the least bit of fear in the King. Useful, if managed carefully.

Deadly, if not.

She must make it useful in finding a husband.

The King had turned back to Hibernia, whispering, leaving her again on her knees.

'Safe journey home,' the Queen said as she left the room.

This could not be the end. 'I had hoped—' she began.

The two of them turned to see her kneeling, as if surprised she was still there.

'I had hoped,' she continued, 'that Your Majesty might take an interest in my family.'

The King exchanged a glance with Hibernia. 'Ah, yes. "Generous to those of your blood," you said. What kind of interest?'

You'll get no money, Lamont had said. *Better to ask for a husband.*

She cleared her throat. 'In my marriage, Your Majesty.'

Hibernia smirked. 'Marriage? To whom?'

She let a cat's smile curve her lips. Would it be too bold to suggest the Earl? 'Any man would be honoured to be recognised by his Majesty.'

The King eyed her warily, indecision in his frown.

The Duke leaned towards the King, chuckling. 'She seemed to enjoy kissing Lamont. Marry the two of them.'

She felt as if a bird were trapped in her throat, desperately beating its wings. 'Oh, no, Your Majesty, that was just under the Lord of Misrule. Meaningless as the Duke's kiss of Agnes.' A kiss, she belatedly remembered, that was not meaningless at all.

But the King was not listening. 'Marriage to Lamont. A very interesting idea.'

Her damnable want warred with her family's need. She wanted no marriage to an enemy of the King, yet she dare not criticise the Duke's suggestion. 'How kind of the Duke of Hibernia to suggest it, but I'm sure Your Majesty was thinking of someone else.'

'You wanted a husband. If I choose to provide this one, are you ungrateful?'

Still kneeling, she looked down at the floor, hoping her deference would mitigate his anger at her small show of defiance. 'Of course not, Your Majesty. It would be just the expression of your generous ascendant planet to bring Lord Justin so close to the throne.'

She looked up through her lashes to see him frown at her subtle reminder that he was elevating an enemy.

A light flared in his blue eyes. 'And for my magnificent generosity, I ask only one thing of you.'

'Anything, of course, Your Majesty.'

'You will keep me informed of his actions for the Council.'

Suddenly, his purpose was clear. This marriage was to be for the King's benefit, not hers. She should never have thought otherwise. 'Do you not think they will be in constant contact with Your Majesty as well as Lord Justin?'

'That's what you are to discover.'

She bowed her head in defeat. 'Of course, Your Majesty.'

'Do your part and perhaps I will provide a grant for your family next year.'

Next year, when the Council's charter expired and she would still be married to a man who hated her. 'Your Majesty is ever generous.'

King Richard waved to a page standing outside the door. 'Summon Lord Justin.'

The King's summons bode ill, Justin thought, as he entered Richard's chamber with a brief bow to what looked like twin kings.

Solay stood before the King and Hibernia. She touched her lips when he entered and his blood surged as he remembered the taste of them.

The King's fury of two hours ago had been replaced with his dangerous, calculating look. 'It seems the Lady Solay would marry.'

Startled, he ignored the twist in his stomach. Was this not exactly what he had suggested? 'Most women do.' He should be grateful the King had backed down from a confrontation with the Council over the woman. Belatedly, the amount she needed seemed minor.

'You seemed to enjoy her kiss.'

No reason to deny the truth. 'What man would not?' He felt a flare of envy for the one who would be her husband and have the right.

'So, then, you will be pleased to have her as your wife.'

Lust surged through him from staff to fingertips, drowning logic. To be able to bed her, to take her, seemed the only *yes* in the world.

He saw a flash of fear in her eyes, but she blinked and it was wiped away. Lips slightly parted, she looked up through her lashes as if she were at once trying to seduce him and play the innocent.

He was sure, and the thought brought him pain, that she was not.

His mind regained control over his body. The woman had neither honour nor honesty in her. 'She is not what she seems,' he said, the words shaken up through a rusty throat. It was long past time for truth. 'She does not share a birth date with Your Majesty.'

She flinched and he fought the feeling that he had somehow betrayed her.

'So she told me,' the King said. 'She was misinformed about her birth.' He smiled. 'As was I. Lady Solay seems to have some talent as a reader of the stars.'

'Or so she has convinced you. Did she also confess that her flattering verse was borrowed?'

Her eyes widened in surprise. Justin smiled, grimly. Had she expected he would keep her secrets for ever?

The King frowned, shifting on his chair. 'So you already know what a clever woman she is.'

'I would prefer an honest wife to a clever one.' It was not only the King he must dissuade. It was himself.

'You have difficult requirements, Lamont,' the King continued. 'You've already turned down two honest heiresses most younger sons would have embraced with fervour.'

He met Solay's eyes again, full of fresh pain. Just as that first time when she entered the Great Hall, he could not break away from the force that flowed between them.

'Speak.' The King's voice seemed to come across a great distance. 'Will you have her?'

What would the King do if he said 'no'? Give her to Redmon? The man likely pushed his last wife down the stairs when she became quarrelsome over his dalliances.

Solay mouthed the word 'please'. Her pleading, desperate eyes held echoes of another woman, another time. He had not been able to save that one.

For a moment, nothing else mattered.

'Yes,' he said, his gaze never leaving Solay.

The word stood between them, a pillar of fire. She released a breath and a smile trembled on her lips.

Having broken the spell, he found a kernel of sense left in his brain. This time he would not sacrifice his happiness for a woman he could not trust. This time he would be sure there was an escape.

He faced the King. 'But I have a condition.'

The King frowned. 'Condition?'

'I must be convinced that she loves me.'

She gasped and he smiled at her. It was an unusual demand, and, in this case, an impossible one. Yet he had seen the disaster of a marriage forced. He would not brook it again.

The King dismissed him with a wave. 'I never thought you

a man who believed the love poems, Lamont. Love can come later as my dear wife and I discovered.'

Having planned his escape, he found he could breathe again. 'Nevertheless, the Church requires we both consent freely. If I have stated a condition that is not met, the marriage will not be valid.'

He and Richard glared at each other. Even the King could not deny the power of the Church.

Solay glanced at the King. 'Allow us a word, Your Majesty.'

They stepped out of earshot of the King. As she touched his arm, he struggled to keep his mind in control.

'I know you care nothing for my life, but have you no care for your own? You are angering the King beyond reason.'

'I told you not to let him force you. And I won't be forced either.'

'There is fire between us, Justin,' she whispered, but her fingers choked his arm. 'I am willing and I shall learn to love you.'

He steeled himself against the fear in her voice. 'If I believe a word of love you say, I'll be sadly deluded. I have bought you some time to find a man you really want to marry. Perhaps you can convince some other fool of your love.'

He stepped away from her to face the King again, relieved to be removed from her touch. 'I stand by my word.'

'Nevertheless,' the King said, smiling, 'I shall have the first banns read next Sunday.'

Sunday. The reality of what he had done pressed on his shoulders like a stone.

'So soon?' she asked. 'We cannot wed until Lent is over.'

Hibernia cut in. 'There's time enough for you to marry before Lent begins.'

'We won't be married at all unless I am convinced of her love,' Justin said.

The King shrugged. 'Very well. Lady Solay, you have until the end of Lent to convince him of your love.' His look turned menacing. 'And, Lamont, you have until the end of Lent to be convinced.'

Chapter Six

Solay ran after Justin as he left the King's solar, determined to begin her campaign to convince him she would be a loving and pliable mate.

She touched his arm to stop him before he reached the end of the hallway.

'I shall ask the King's permission to visit my mother and inform her of the impending marriage,' she began. 'Would you accompany me?'

'No.'

'Later, then. I would not interfere with your work—'

'Solay, stop. This is folly.'

'You were the one who suggested I marry.'

'I did not mean to me.'

'Then why did you agree?' Surely her whispered 'please' could not have convinced him. 'You care nothing for the King's approval.'

He met her eyes with that cold honesty she had come to know, yet a hint of caring shadowed his gaze. 'I did not want him to force you.'

'I was not forced. I want this marriage.' If she said the words more loudly, would they sound more convincing?

'You want a marriage, not a marriage to me.'

I don't have a choice! The thought screamed in her head. Without this marriage, she would return home empty-handed.

She tried to calm her mind. Fighting him would get her no closer to learning the Council's secrets.

She leaned against his chest. All those courtiers who had fawned over her mother for the King's sake, what words did they use? 'I think the King suggested we marry because he could see how much I already love you.'

He undraped her like an unwanted blanket. 'For someone with so much practice, you're a poor liar.'

No one else had ever thought so. 'Why can you not believe me? You feel the attraction between us.'

His eyes burned into hers. 'Lust, yes. I would lie if I denied that.'

She could feel his breath on her cheek, feel the tingle starting again deep inside her. He moved nearer and she closed her eyes, lifting her chin. Now. Now he would kiss her.

Suddenly the air was empty of him. She opened her eyes to see him standing out of reach, arms crossed. 'But lust is not love.'

She forced her eyelashes to flutter. 'But it can be a start, can it not?'

He shook his head. 'I am not a senile King looking for someone to warm my bed. I demand more than your body.'

What else did a woman have? 'The King lusted after many women who shared his bed. My mother shared much more.'

'Let me tell you why you said "yes".' He held a finger to her lips to stop her from interrupting. 'You agreed to please the King. And I assure you, whatever reasons he had for this marriage are for his benefit, not yours.'

She said a silent prayer that he never discovered the real reason. 'Perhaps they were for *your* benefit. Isn't it high time you took a wife?'

'I have no interest in a wife. And if I did, I would not want a viper in my bed. Do you think if we are married I will change my mind about the living you want from the Crown?'

Any ordinary man would. She held her tongue.

He did not wait for her to answer. 'If you think to share my life, then you will be wasting your time long past Lent. I agreed so you could have time to pursue one of those men who has stared at you moon-eyed. By the end of Lent, you could have a willing husband. One you want, or at least one who wants you.'

'If we are betrothed, I hardly think others will see me as a potential bride.'

'Marriage itself doesn't stop most men,' he muttered.

She shook his stubborn sleeve. The King had given her a husband. She would have no second chance. 'But I want this marriage!'

'Then you will be very disappointed come Eastertide. Nothing you say or do will convince me that you are capable of love for anyone, particularly me.'

As he walked away, she realised that instead of merely pleasing the King, she now had to convince a man who hated her that he should be tied to her for the rest of his life.

Given the task, the forty days of Lent seemed no longer than a flicker.

Within days, Solay left Windsor, riding in solitary splendour in a cart driven by one of the King's men, to inform her family of the impending marriage.

She rubbed her nose in the fur trim of her new cloak, rehearsing the smile she would wear when she told her mother she was to be wed. She knew not how to explain that she had failed to secure the grant her mother was expecting. Alys of Weston had been away from court too long. She would never understand that a Council might gainsay a King.

Despite her worries, peace melted her bones as the two-storey dower house with the six chimneys came into view. Pretending to be a castle, it was surrounded by a small moat. The whitewash had yellowed and the thatch needed patching, but it was all the home she'd had for the last ten years and more dear now than Windsor's corridors.

Jane ran out to meet her while her mother looked down from her upstairs window, smiling. Her fair-haired sister, clad in tunic and chausses, seemed to have grown in the weeks Solay had been away. Her boy's garb could no longer disguise her womanhood.

As they gathered in her mother's chambers, her mother's blue-veined hands stroked Solay's heavy cloak with reverence. 'The King has given you a magnificent gift. You must have pleased him.'

Solay handed her mother a box. 'And here is his gift for you along with a message of great importance.' The smile she had practised came easily.

Her mother opened the box and froze, not speaking, her hand still on the lid.

'What is it?' Jane asked.

Her mother lifted an amethyst-studded brooch, rubbing her thumb over the cabochon stones. 'It was yours, once, Solay,' she said, in a voice that held too much hope. 'A gift from your father.'

Solay reached for it, but her mother held the piece tightly in her fingers. 'Jane, please read the King's letter to us.'

As her sister read the clerk's prose announcing her betrothal, the lines in her mother's face deepened. When the simple statement was done, she rose and paced before the fireplace. 'What land does he bring?'

'He is a second son.'

'Even second sons can sometimes—'

Solay shook her head. 'He is a man of the law,' she answered, struggling to say the words without a sneer. Or perhaps the flutter in her throat was the memory of his lips on hers. 'He owns property in London.'

'How much? Where?'

How could she have been so ill prepared? 'I don't know.'

'What is his income?'

Solay flushed, ashamed she did not know. 'At least forty pounds a year.'

'A King's ransom, to be sure,' her mother said, archly. 'So he brings you no land and little money.'

'I bring little enough.'

Her mother drew herself straighter, trapping Solay with her gaze. 'The King called you daughter. That is more than enough.' For her mother, it would always be thus. At Solay's age, her mother had been a King's mistress for three years. Her mother sat back, sad understanding dawning in her eyes. 'Tell me, Solay, what does he want from this marriage?'

He doesn't want it at all.

Perhaps she should confess. Perhaps she should prepare her mother for the possibility that in this, too, she might fail. But as the two expectant faces gazed at her, she answered with half the truth. 'He wants someone who will love him.'

'What does that matter?' Her mother shrugged.

Jane tilted her head. 'And do you love him?'

She swallowed. 'I will convince him that I do before we are wed.'

'God has blessed you with a face and body that heat men's blood,' her mother said. 'You can convince him of anything.'

She nodded, unable to disappoint her mother with her failure to do exactly that.

'Now,' her mother said, 'what about our grant?'

Now she could not dissemble. 'The Council has blocked it.'

'Council? No Council overrules a King!'

So Solay explained about Parliament's law and Gloucester and the Council's year to bring the King to heel.

When she had finished, her mother stared at the brooch in her hand. 'So, this is the King's recompense for what he cannot give.' She dropped it back into the box and shut the lid, disappointment creasing her lips.

Her mother had endured so much. Solay had to give her some hope. 'The King has promised a grant in a year if…'

Her mother settled back into her chair and raised her eyebrows. 'If what?'

'Lamont works with the Council. The King wishes to be kept informed.'

Jane gasped. 'He wants you to spy on your own husband? How can you love him and do that?'

No one answered her.

Solay's mother nodded, as if all had become clear. 'The King has a right to know what the Council is doing. And you will tell him. In a year, he will give us our grant. And if you persuade your husband well, we might not have to wait that long.' She turned, briskly, to the present. 'Now, we must begin the wedding plans, meet the man's family—' Her mother stopped in mid-sentence as she saw the truth on Solay's face.

'The King has his own plans.'

'I see.' A mask of resignation settled on her face. 'And will I be invited to this wedding, whenever it may be?'

'I do not know,' she said, though she suspected. 'This has all come about quickly.' She rose, unable to witness her mother's pain. 'I am to return to the court in few days. Lady Agnes would have me as a companion.' And as a cover for her affair, but she did not add that. 'And Justin's work is at Westminster.'

'Excellent.' Her mother smiled. She swallowed disappointment and moved on to necessity. 'I expect you to parlay this into bigger things for us all. Your sister needs a husband, too.'

Her sister threw down the message. 'Stop it. Stop it, both of you.' She ran from the room.

Solay shared a moment's sigh with her mother.

Her mother shook her head. 'Jane fancies herself a student, but she was never as wise as you.'

Nor as cynical, Solay thought, wishing that Jane could stay in blissful innocence. She had shared the situation too frankly for a girl of fifteen to hear. 'I'll go to her.'

Solay found Jane in her chamber, with the few books her mother had not yet sold. Her sister's eyes had seen much too much for her age.

Solay hugged her. 'Don't worry. After I'm wed, we'll find a husband for you.'

Jane was stiff in her arms. 'I don't want a husband.'

'Of course you do.'

She shook her head and sighed. 'Is there no escape from being a woman?'

'Escape? What do you mean?'

'I want to be free. Like a man.'

Solay shuddered at the thought. How did men live with only the blunt instrument of power? Unable to bend, they were forced to break. Better to be pliant, to accommodate the ever-shifting winds of power. But Jane loved books and horses and had never enjoyed womanhood.

'None of us choose the lives the stars give us,' Solay said, running her finger over the cut-velvet cover of her mother's Book of Hours with the charts of the planets in it. Now that it was forbidden, it called to her more than ever.

'No more than we can choose our parents,' Jane sighed.

'Nor our husbands.' Solay picked up the book. 'Perhaps

Mother will let me take it with me. Would you mind?' She had taught Jane to read, but her sister had become more the scholar than she.

Jane shook her head. 'It should be yours. You are the student of the stars.'

'A poor one.' But perhaps better than she knew. She had discovered something about the King's birth even he did not know. And something about her own. 'Jane, I found out when I was born! It was St John's Eve.'

'What about me?' Jane asked, finally smiling. 'When was I born?'

The question broke her heart. The girl would rather have a birth date than a husband. 'I don't know, but I'll find out.' Perhaps Justin's mysterious laundress would have Jane's answer as well. 'I promise.'

Five days later, Solay held out the velvet-covered book as her mother laid the last of her few dresses into the trunk. 'May I take it with me, Mother?'

Her mother, never one to cherish books, nodded. 'If you like, but guard it well. The books and the jewels are easy to carry and easy to sell. This one could fetch nearly a pound, should we need it.'

But her mother's hand stopped hers as Solay lowered the trunk lid. 'The brooch was to be yours,' she said. 'I will keep it as long as I can.'

Solay nodded. The brooch would have to feed them, if Solay's husband could not.

'You must keep the favour of the King and your husband. We will need them both in the year to come.'

Dread knotting her stomach, Solay met her mother's eyes, hard with experience. A child no more, she must not expect to be taken care of like a child. 'This man, he is not like others.'

'All men are alike. Even a King. Discover what this man wants and give it to him.'

'How am I to do that?' *How did you?*

Her mother gazed out of the window, as if seeing the past in the clouds that scuttled over the winter brown grass that poked through the snow stretched across the flat Essex land. 'When the Queen was dying, the King needed nurturing, but he wanted people to see him as a warrior still. So it was necessary for me to…' she paused, searching for a word '…portray a desirable woman.'

Solay wondered, suddenly, whether she and her sister existed merely to prove that the King had been in her mother's bed. 'What did *you* want?'

Her mother brought her gaze back squarely to Solay. 'I got what I wanted. He made me the Lady of the Sun.'

And what do I want? Solay wondered, as she hugged her mother and sister goodbye.

No answer came as the cart pulled away, loaded with a trunk carrying her only possessions. It was just as well. What she wanted for herself was unimportant. She must provide for her family.

Yet for just a moment, she wondered what the stars might predict for her own life. She let the wind blow her wish away. The heavens gave answers for countries and Kings. Astrologers read their grand designs to find hints of Christ and the Apocalypse, of comets and eclipses and wars, not to comfort puny individuals.

Right now, her fate was firmly entwined, at least until Easter, with Justin Lamont's. That was all she needed to know.

Chapter Seven

Justin listened, grimfaced, as the first banns were read in Windsor Castle's chapel after the sermon on a sunny Sunday late in January.

Even though he had made his condition clear to the priest, a *frisson* of uncertainty rippled through him as the curate pronounced his name and parentage.

The last time his name had been called out with a woman's in a parish church, his family had stood beside him. This time, his family was not with him, even in spirit.

With the King's urging, familial negotiations that usually took months had been concluded in weeks. He would not assume her mother's debts. She would bring no dowry and make no claims on his family's land. It was almost as if the stars, that fate she so believed in, had brought him here.

Next to him, the shiny curl of her dark hair tempted his fingers. If he could push it away from her neck, he could kiss the pale skin—

He turned his eyes away from the dangerous vision. Being near her lured him into dreams of a home and a family— things he would never deserve.

Why didn't you refuse? she had asked.

I should have.

Solay stood serenely beside him, her back straight, never looking to Justin for comfort as the priest stumbled over the name 'Lady Alys of Weston' and that of her mother's ostensible husband. The congregation coughed.

As they left the church together, the tolling bell clanged like the door of a donjon cell. Solay was swaddled up to her neck in velvet and ermine, her cloak an extravagant gift from the King that Justin would no doubt find listed as an official government gift in the household expenses.

They were seated together at the *noonmeat* meal, sharing a trencher of chicken stew, while the rest of the Court tried to watch them without staring.

'When shall we travel to visit your family?' she asked, finally.

The hope in her voice made him wish he could dissemble. He had visited home last week, as she had. Like most of the Court, his brother and his wife had snickered behind his back, unsure whether to be insulted because she was a whore's daughter or honoured because her father was a king. 'There is no need for that.'

'But I was looking forward to meeting your parents.'

'My mother is gone,' he said.

'Oh, forgive me. I did not know. I'm so sorry.' She touched his arm, her eyes full of fake compassion.

He pulled away, wanting neither her touch nor her sham sympathy. 'It was years ago.' Half his life ago.

'That must have been hard. I cannot imagine losing my mother now, but to lose her as a child…'

Startled, he watched her blink back tears. Could she really love a woman the whole world reviled?

'What was she like?' she continued.

Nothing like you, he wanted to say, but he was no longer so certain that was true. 'Wise. Strong. Forgiving.' *And she loved my father very much.*

'And your father?'

Her examination made him uneasy. She already knew he had been dead two years and his older brother held the title. 'What about him?'

'What was he like?'

He had no ready answer. 'He was a judge.' It was more than his profession. 'He taught us to reach our own conclusions.'

'No matter what the King thinks?'

'No matter what anyone thinks.' Yet the words were hollow. He had let the King force him into this betrothal.

No, do not blame the King. It was not he who persuaded you. It was the lust-filled stones between your legs.

Looking at her profile, he fought the lure of her flesh. He had barely touched her since that kiss forced by the Lord of Misrule, but he could still taste her wine-tinged lips, feel her soft breasts against his chest. And if he relented for a moment too long, all the conditions in the world would not save him.

Consummation would mean consent.

'Would you visit mine, then?'

He stared at her, realising he had lost her meaning. 'What?'

'Would you come to meet my mother and sister?'

He blocked his curiosity about the Lady of the Sun and the sister with no name of her own. He refused to be dragged into her world or to insert her into his. It would only make the parting more difficult.

'Yuletide is over. I must return to my work.'

She put down her chicken without tasting it.

If he were a flatterer, he would say that a visit would be more convenient at another time or that the weather would make travel difficult.

But that would be a lie.

Around them, pages from the kitchen carried in dishes chilled from their journey through draughty stone corridors. He pushed a fried almond towards her side of the trencher, a poor apology for his rudeness.

She smiled and picked it up. 'Justin, which laundress was it? The one who knew of my birth?'

'Do you think to punish her for revealing your secrets?'

She lifted her chin and he saw the flash of pride defying his pity. 'I hoped the woman might remember my sister's birth as well. 'Twas no great thing for me to know my birth date, but my sister is still young and cares about such things.'

His anger at the King's whore flared anew. 'Your mother doesn't know?'

'A woman in the throes of childbirth cares little for dates and times. She remembers it was cold and the Queen was dead.'

'My mother could tell you how many roosters crowed the morning I was born.' He had always taken that for granted. 'She made me a tray of comfits each year to mark the day.'

'And what day was that?'

He squashed a vision of Solay bringing him sweet cakes on his birthday. 'You will not need to know.'

She made no more attempts at conversation, chewing her red-spiced chicken in silence.

His mother would have scolded him for his harsh words, he thought. Whatever Solay might be, nothing she had done today deserved his rude replies.

He cleared his throat. 'Your sister. Her name is Joan, too?'

'No,' she answered softly. 'My sister's name is Jane.'

'But…' Gloucester had said they were both Joan. Was every 'fact' about Lady Alys so wrong? 'The laundress is the heavy one. With her front teeth missing.'

The smile that blessed her face was the first honest joy he'd seen from her. It tempted him more than her kiss.

Bad enough her body called to his. He would allow no tender feelings to take root. In just a few weeks, Easter would come and he would be quit of her.

Chapter Eight

With the Yuletide log extinguished and Windsor emptied of guests, cold seeped through the very stones and crept into every corner.

There were not enough trees in all England to keep the castle warm, Solay thought, as she and Agnes huddled close to a fireplace in their chambers, burning a few sticks of hoarded wood and trading stories.

'I envy you,' Agnes said. 'Betrothed with the blessing of the King.'

She had not shared the King's reasons with Agnes. 'At least you have a lover who does not leave the room when you enter.' Envy bit her. What would it be like, to be loved so?

Agnes shook her head. 'He is not mine. He is only borrowed.'

'But you make him smile, you make him laugh. He can't wait to be with you.' Hibernia's wife had fled the court as soon as the Yuletide festivities ended and Agnes could smile again. 'Everything I say or do makes Justin angry.'

'So you envy me, too?' Agnes reached for her hand and squeezed it. 'Ah, we are a pair, aren't we? What are we to do?'

Agnes's sympathy touched her. She had never had a friend

outside her family. No one had ever cared what she thought and felt. But with Agnes, she might at least confide her heart's foolishness, if not the King's plans.

'How am I to persuade him I love him?' She sighed.

Agnes chuckled. 'You are a woman. He is a man. It is not so hard.'

'He is not like other men.' Any other man would have been easier to fool.

Agnes put down her needlework. 'And your marriage will not be like other marriages. He must not suspect you report his every move to the King.'

The little heat left in her body drained away. She looked behind her, relieved to see the room's door closed. 'Hibernia told you.'

'Of course.'

She regretted her moment's candour. Agnes might act the friend, but the shared whispers of lovers respected no boundaries. What Solay said to Agnes might reach the King's ears through the same channel.

Yet knowing all, Agnes was the only one who could understand why she must succeed. 'Please. Help me. Tell me how you please Hibernia.'

Agnes's cheeks turned pink. 'Beneath the sheets, everything pleases him.'

No doubt. Between Justin and her there was no lack of fire. All the more reason, she suspected, that he avoided her. There must be some another way. 'But before that, how did you attract him?'

'It was over a game of Merrills. We were close over the board, our hands touched, I looked into his eyes…' She smiled, remembering.

'You make it sound so simple.'

A dimple flashed in Agnes's cheek. 'I let him win every game.'

Solay laughed. Of course. She had been too forward, even asking to visit his family instead of waiting for him to suggest it. Justin struck sparks that made her want to spar with him, no attitude for a wife. 'I'll try it.'

If only she could concentrate enough to lose.

This was what came of misguided politeness, Justin thought, setting up the pieces on the Merrills board for the game with Solay. He should have refused to play, but the rest of the Court seemed party to a conspiracy to leave them alone together.

And as much as he tried to resist temptation, he craved her physical nearness. Her dark hair and her pale skin drew his eyes. His gaze traced the subtle curve of her lower lip as she tapped it with a finger, contemplating the board.

He made a move and took one of her pieces, realising too late that he had put his man directly in line for her to take on her next move.

Instead, she made a move that put her piece directly in harm's way, then looked up at him with a bland smile, hiding all the intelligence behind it.

He knew, clearly as if she had spoken, that she was trying to lose, pandering to her perception of what would give him pleasure.

He leaned back and crossed his arms, smiling to himself as he looked at her pleasantly expectant face. Two could play that game.

Instead of taking one of her pieces, he moved his stick out of position.

She looked at him sharply and opened her mouth as if to question the move, then shut it.

He had left her in a quandary. Her only move would take

one of his pieces. Struggling to keep his mind on the game, he watched her study the board, looking for a way out.

The thicket of her black eyelashes shadowed her fair skin and, although her sleeves nearly reached her hands, he could see the pale skin of her inner wrist and wondered how much paler it would be below her navel when he—

'Your move.'

He started. She had succumbed to the inevitable and taken a piece of his. 'You play well,' he said, goading her. 'You may be the victor in this game.'

'Oh, no. It was a lucky move. You are by far the better player. Perhaps your mind is not on the game.'

His mind *wasn't* on the game, but her voice was too innocent to suggest that she knew where his mind was. He nudged another piece into harm's way.

This time, she protested. 'Are you sure you want to make that move?'

He grinned. 'Can you suggest a better?'

'Oh, no,' she said, flustered. 'I would not know a better one.'

Boxed in by his play, all her available moves would take one of his pieces. All but the one she made.

'Are you sure you want to make that move?' he asked. Reaching over the board, he touched her hand and moved it to one of the other pieces. 'Instead of this one?'

She froze, looking at his eyes, then laughed, a high-pitched trill. 'How foolish of me. You are so much the better player. I hadn't thought of it.'

He could swear she batted her eyelashes. 'You not only thought of it, you took time to think of every possible move trying to avoid it.'

'I need time to think because I'm not very good at the game.'

'On the contrary. You are deliberately trying to lose.' He grabbed her hand again, her fingers cold in his. 'Why?'

She met his eyes, taking his measure, then sighed. 'How did you know?'

He let go of her hand, savouring her moment of honesty. 'It can take as much intelligence to lose as to win. You must be a good player to make so many moves that lead directly to my strength.'

A genuine smile lit her face. 'My sister and I played often at home.'

'Then play as if I were your sister.'

Confusion dented her forehead. 'You won't be angry if I win?'

'I will be angry if I'm given a victory I have not earned.'

The smile that danced around her lips put him in mind of kissing. 'Then we shall start a new game.'

The game's pace quickened as both played to win. She let her cloak fall off her shoulders; more than once, his fingers brushed hers as both reached for the next move. He liked the Solay who played her own game; when she bested him, he laughed with her.

When he rose and put the game away, the hall was empty and the fire burned low.

Solay pulled her cloak around her shoulders and stood, smiling, a sparkle in her impossibly purple eyes.

Her lips parted, ready for him.

He touched them with an unsteady finger, her breath brushing his skin. One kiss, just one. But a kiss would not be enough—

His pleasure ended with the thought and he pulled away.

'So you do punish me for winning.'

He could not tell whether her pout was genuine. 'You know better.'

'Then what harm is a kiss?'

'It would lead to more.'

'And if it does? It's what both of us want.'

She was a ruthless, unrelenting opponent and the real game was not over.

'No. It's what you want.' The stiffness between his legs belied his words. He rued the day he had agreed to this Devil's bargain, yet he could only blame himself. He had told her he would not marry her, but he had not told her he would not marry at all. If she knew why, she would surely refuse him as well.

Her gaze met his. 'You pride yourself on your truthful tongue, but I wonder whether you speak it about yourself.'

Silent, he watched her leave the hall and wondered whether he might regret unleashing an honest Solay.

Yet it was easier to know the true face of his enemy. Besides, if he could force her to reveal herself, this enforced betrothal might be worth it.

He would not give her marriage, but perhaps he could give her herself.

And spare the world another Lady Alys of Weston.

Ask Mother whether two days after Candlemas sounds right, Solay wrote the next afternoon, glad the knowledge would bring some light to Jane's winter. Solay had found the laundress in the damp warmth of Windsor's wash room. The woman had a gap-toothed smile, a prodigious memory and fond recollections of Alys of Weston.

'She made him happy,' the woman said. 'A King deserves to be happy.'

And what about the rest of us? Solay wondered wistfully. Do we deserve to be happy? Last night, Justin had laughed. It was the first time he had looked at her and not been stern, or judgemental or angry. His smile rekindled her hunger for someone who could look at her without seeing her mother.

Someone who might make a special treat for her birthday.

She shook off her daydream. It was Justin's happiness that must concern her, not her own. She must make him as happy as her mother had made the King.

Childish shrieks from the quadrangle pierced the wooden shutters. Pulling her cloak tighter, she walked to the window and peeked through a crack in the wood.

Winter's first snow blanketed the ground, but instead of a peaceful white pasture, the castle's inner courtyard had become a battlefield. Three pages and a kitchen boy flung snowballs at each other, running, ducking and yelling in turn. Hurtling snowballs with them, like a boy of ten summers, was Justin.

The sight brought a twinge of pain for the boy he must have been and the child she no longer was.

A 'thank you' for giving her the laundress's name would give her an excuse to seek him out. She left the fire's warmth, hurried down the hallway and stood in the shelter of the doorway, watching the mock battle, reluctant to step into the cold.

Justin looked up from his game, grinning. 'Lady Solay! Catch!'

A snowball came straight towards her, splattering the red velvet cloak with a dead aim.

She brushed the soft fabric frantically, wet snow numbing her fingers. If the King's gift were ruined, he'd think ill of her.

Across the lawn, Justin laughed, a sound so boyish that she forced a smile and a wave. He grinned back, delighted at his aim, of course, not because of her.

The young boys ran towards the Round Tower, still hurling snowballs, their shrieks echoing off the stone walls. Justin walked over to her, smiling up at the first snow as if it were a gift instead of a curse.

His smile deepened the cleft in his chin and softened the hard lines of his cheeks and jaw. Big, damp flakes dusted his hair and shoulders, his chest rose and fell with leftover exertion. Despite the snowball fight, he wore no gloves.

Never had he looked more tempting.

'Here…' he grabbed her hand, his fingers warm despite the wet snow, and pulled her into the courtyard '…look up.'

Obediently, she tilted her head back and let her hood fall off. Snowflakes skipped down from the sky, swirling, confusing, filling her vision. Dizzy, she could not tell up from down, ground from sky.

She stumbled.

He caught her arm, his heat blocking the cold. It was the first time he had truly touched her since that kiss. Even his gaze warmed her. For a moment, she let herself rest in his smile.

His needs. Remember his needs. 'You like the snow?'

He nodded, an unforced grin lighting his face. 'I like to watch it fall.'

Safe in his embrace, she did not feel the wind or miss the fire. She leaned into him as he swayed towards her, his breath a whisper on her cheek, coming closer.

Now, she thought, her lips parting.

Abruptly, he let her go. 'You want a kiss, Lady Solay? Then trade some truth for it. Tell me—do you like the snow?'

'Of course.' She lifted her hood to ward off the flakes prickling her head. The cold chilled her eyes. 'It's beautiful. I like to watch it fall.'

The light left his eyes and she faced her enemy again. 'How strange, Lady Solay. That's what I just told you.'

The icy wind swirled inside her cloak. She hunched her shoulders, missing the warmth in his eyes as much as the heat of his body. 'Does it not please you that we both like the same thing?'

'It would please me if you would tell the truth. About anything. I asked whether *you* like the snow.'

'Wouldn't you prefer I like what you like?'

'I would prefer you know what *you* like first. Now, once more. Do you like the snow?'

What did it matter what she thought? No one in power had ever questioned her for agreeing with him.

Except this man.

'I don't know.'

He crossed his arms, blocking the door to Windsor's blessed shelter, unmoving as a block of ice. 'Then we shall stand here and experience it until you do.'

Anger heated her cheeks. Why couldn't he be content with surface pleasantries? No one else forced her to consider her own opinion. She fought back a frown as the icy flakes weighed down her eyelashes.

Winter was a long, dark, hateful time of numb fingers and growling bellies, with the Lenten fast conveniently placed after the Yuletide feast, just as there was no more food to eat until the spring.

Shivering, she narrowed her eyes. 'I hate the snow.' She would give him the truth and more. 'I hate all of winter: snow, cold, ice, long, black, sleepless nights, short, sunless days.' He raised his eyebrows as she slapped him with the words. 'There. You have my confession. Now, where's the kiss you promised?'

Surely he would not kiss her after she had disagreed with him.

But a smile deepened the corner of his mouth. Warmth… no, more than warmth, fire returned to his eyes. His palms cupped her cheeks and he bent his lips to hers.

His kiss made her dizzier than the snow. Head cradled in his hands, she felt at once vulnerable and protected. With the touch of his lips, strong and demanding, something below her belly caught fire.

Oh, for this, she would tell a thousand truths.

She slipped her arms around his waist, eager to steal his

warmth. Her breasts pressed against his chest, her hips matched his, and everywhere she touched him she found heat.

His lips moved over hers and she kissed back, hungry for the taste of him and more. His chest rose and fell, as it had when he'd run with the boys.

Her lips clung to his as he pulled, gently, away.

He cleared his throat. 'You see, Lady Solay? Truth is not so difficult.'

Looking up at him, she smiled, full of the tender weakness the poets described. Now. Now, if she told him, surely he would believe her. 'I love you.'

He stepped back and his face became as ice. Snow fell between them again. 'You learn nothing. I weary of your lies.' He turned his back and walked towards the door.

She cursed herself for letting the words slip. She had badly miscalculated. No, she had not calculated at all. To be in his arms, to feel his kiss was so right that she had wanted to stay there always. It was just three words, three words she thought would keep her there for ever.

She ran after him, touching his back when she caught up. 'Wait, please. I wanted to thank you.'

He turned, eyes cold as dead ashes. 'What for?'

'For telling me about the laundress. She knew when Jane was born.'

A faint smile softened the harsh lines in his face. 'What was the day?'

'Two days after Candlemas.' She smiled. In little more than ten days, Jane could celebrate.

'And Jane loves the snow.'

'How did you know?'

His smile was not the one of boyish joy, but a thin line of triumph. 'You were born in summer and they call you Solay.' He turned back to the door.

'Wait!'

He did, blocking the door, as if happy to stay in the cold. She shivered, wishing she had followed him inside to talk. 'Would you like a game of Merrills tonight?'

He shook his head. 'I leave for Westminster tomorrow.'

She cringed at the very name of that dreaded palace. 'How long will you be gone?' Every day apart was a day of persuasion lost.

'Far past the end of Lent.'

She smiled to hide her fear. 'I would like to come with you if the King agrees.' Of course the King would agree. The King expected her to report on Justin's every move.

'You just flinched when I mentioned Westminster. You have no desire to come with me except to continue this futile effort to persuade me you can love. Stay here and find a husband you can keep.'

How could he read her so easily? 'I merely blinked to avoid a snowflake. I want to come, truly.'

'No, you don't. You think you *should* come.' Under the strong, dark brows, his eyes weighed her and found her wanting. 'I don't know who you are or what you want. And neither do you. Better discover who you are before you profess to love someone else.'

He closed the door behind him and left her shivering in the snow.

Chapter Nine

I don't know who you are or what you want.

Two days later, Solay woke with Justin's words still echoing in her head. *I have no right to want something for myself,* she argued back, full of truth as long as she did not speak aloud.

Did he think she should abandon her family for a selfish whim? For, for…for what? She could think of nothing selfish she might want this morning except to break fast.

Stomach growling, she rolled over in an empty bed, hoping Agnes would be back soon to help her decide what to do next. Justin was a hard day's ride away. How was she to woo him?

Want tangled with necessity. His judgement hurt in a way that the cruelty she had met from so many did not. He seemed to expect her to do something more, be something more.

The only man who is free is the man who answers only to himself.

A man such as Justin.

There could be no greater freedom than not to care for the opinion of others.

Yet he cared whether she loved him.

Fa! Head spinning with confusion, she forced herself out of the warm bed and into her dress. Love was only a word for poets to swoon over. If he looked at the evidence as the lawyer he was, he would know it did not exist. Marriages were made for money, power, position. As for other couplings—well, the connection of bodies was much more elemental than some invisible emotion.

The door opened and Agnes tiptoed in, carrying two smuggled sops from the kitchen to break their fast.

'Oh, thank you!' Solay savoured the wine-soaked bread, a secret little ritual they now shared each morning, despite the King's disapproval. The King believed that breaking fast before the midday meal was a weakness of the lower classes.

'The King has new plans,' Agnes said. No need to ask how Agnes knew the King's plans. 'We'll be travelling north within a fortnight.'

'And leave the Council in Westminster?'

Agnes smiled like a cat. 'Exactly.'

'Is that legal?' She surprised herself with a question that Justin would have asked.

Agnes tilted her head, as if she did not understand the problem. 'He's the King. He goes where he pleases. Won't it be wonderful?'

Wonderful for Agnes because the freedom of travel would leave her plenty of time with Hibernia. But what did it mean for Solay?

A knock interrupted them and Solay opened the door to the King's page. 'His Majesty summons you.'

Solay grabbed her cloak, brushing the mark left by the snowball, and picked up the letter she had written to Jane. She had asked the King if he could spare a messenger to send it to Upminster in time for her birthday. He must have decided to say yes.

* * *

She entered his chambers, expecting him to smile at the cloak, or at least at her deep curtsy, but instead, she faced a frown.

'Why have you brought me no report of the Council's activities?'

She swallowed, her throat dry. 'I have not seen him since he left for Westminster, Your Majesty.'

'You saw much of him in the Upper Ward right before he left, Lady Solay.'

She shifted uneasily. Who had been looking out of a window and into their lives? 'We were speaking of other things, Your Majesty.'

'I've heard he's developing new charges against members of my household,' he said, glancing at Hibernia. 'Is it true?'

She assumed a serious expression, wondering who else was spying for the King. 'I believe so, but he did not say specifically who would be charged. I did not want to bring Your Majesty incomplete information.' She let the answer lie, hoping it would satisfy him.

'Did he say what the charges would be?'

She shook her head.

'Or how many would be named?'

'He was not precise.' How many might he charge at one time? 'No more than two or three, I think.'

'You know no more than I.' He looked down at her, standing before him, letter in hand. 'I can spare no messenger today.'

His threat was clear. He could remove more precious things if she did not fulfil her part of the bargain.

'Perhaps I should visit Westminster,' she said, subduing her hatred of the place. Justin would not welcome her, but she could learn nothing more here. 'I'm sure I could discover something else.'

'An excellent idea,' Hibernia chimed in.

Of course he would think so. If she were gone, he could share Agnes's bed at any time.

The King nodded. 'Go. They are plotting against me. I know it.' A small smile came to his lips. 'They think they have the upper hand, but all their legal tricks will come to naught.'

She stifled a shudder, not sure whether she feared the King or this trip more. But now that she had promised, she must not return empty-handed. What could she offer Justin to build his trust in her?

Something about the King. Something he doesn't know. Something that would convince him I am on his side.

Some small betrayal.

Justin moved closer to the west window, trying to catch the last of the faint winter light on the document before him. Through the cracks in the shutters, he saw snowflakes heavy as raindrops hurtling towards the frozen ground.

Safely back at Westminster and away from temptation, his days had been feverish with activity. Messengers rode daily between the two palaces by the Thames, returning from Windsor with the King's reluctant signature over the Council's seal on the endless flow of documents needed to run the realm.

Yet even the hectic pace could not keep his mind off Solay.

Fool. You knew better than to touch her.

Their kiss had released all the passion he had sensed from the first, along with something more. A hum in his veins of possession. Of knowing that she could be his.

Yet if he let his lust rule, they would share not only a bed, but a life and he'd find himself married to another woman of lies.

Still, none of that seemed to matter when he touched her. He had even hoped for a moment, that her kiss and her words were real.

I love you. Meaningless as *I like to watch the snow fall.*

Such desperation raised an ugly suspicion. What if her urgency came with a babe attached? He should have thought of that before. It was the way of women, he knew too well.

He looked back at his document, surprised that his quill had not moved and irritated that she would not leave his mind. It seemed as if he could smell roses, just by thinking of her.

A knock interrupted. 'Come,' he called, welcoming the distraction.

Solay paused at the threshold. The snow she so hated dampened the flowing red velvet cloak. She had thrown back the hood and her dark hair cascaded riotously over her shoulders. And, despite his distrust, when he met her eyes the very air in the room shimmered and his tongue seemed useless.

'Why are you here?' he said, finally.

Rude as he had been, she smiled. 'May I warm myself by the fire?'

'As you like.' He shrugged off his unease at her nearness and watched her cross the room. Her cloak covered everything.

It would even hide a change in her belly.

He looked down at the near-finished writ before him, the words now gibberish. The fire warmed his chest, but an inner heat smouldered as she walked closer. She dropped her hood and stood behind him, her hands caressing his aching shoulders. Her scent crept into his pores.

Refusing to face her, he shook off the comfort of her touch. 'You would have done better to stay at Windsor. I have no time for pleasantries.'

'The day is near over. Is it not time to rest?'

His shoulders sagged at the thought. He had not rested in years.

Always, his father had demanded one more task, one more achievement he could never quite attain. He had become a sergeant-at-law in thirteen years instead of sixteen, then joined the household of the Duke of Gloucester, finally rising to serve the Council itself. Yet after his mother's death, there was no one to soften the judgements or celebrate the triumphs.

Now, the year of the Council's charter stretched endless before him. 'Time enough for rest when the Council's work is done.'

Her hands soothed his knotted muscles. She leaned closer. 'What can be so important?'

Work seemed a safer topic than the scent of her skin. 'A subpoena.'

'A subpoena? What's that?'

Beneath her fingers, his shoulders sagged, relaxed. If he leaned back, his head would be cradled on her breasts…

He woke from his trance and sat up to escape her touch. Her interest in the law was feigned, no doubt. 'I am not at liberty to discuss the Council's business.'

She sat on the bench beside him. 'But I came to tell you something the Council should know.'

He shifted away from her, suspicious. 'What?'

'The week after Candlemas, the King will leave Windsor and he won't return until Eastertide.'

Absent from Windsor or Westminster, the King would be conveniently away from the Council's supervision, free to spend as he pleased. 'Where is he going?'

'He has not said, though some talk of Nottingham and Lincoln.'

If Hibernia escaped to the north, it would take an army to bring him back, not a piece of parchment. 'He's trying to sabotage our work,' Justin said, wondering whether the King already suspected their plan.

'What if you came along with the Court? You might serve as a link between the King and the Council.'

'The Council must work at Westminster.' Parliament had so stipulated in the law. 'The King knows that better than anyone.' No doubt that was the reason for this gyration into the countryside.

'Staying at Westminster seems a legal nicety.'

Nicety. As if the law were no more important than the King's protocol. 'We cannot follow only the laws we like.'

She pouted, which put him in mind of her kiss, a distraction he did not need. 'You are not a member of the Council. Surely Parliament would not object if you travelled with the King. Council business would be more smoothly conducted.'

Although he hesitated to take her at her word, her reasoning was sound. He reached for a clean parchment and dipped the pen into the ink. If he could not compel Hibernia into testimony, at least he could keep an eye on them both. 'I'll inform Gloucester in the morning. Take this demand to Windsor tomorrow.'

'No!' She gripped his hand.

Her cold fingers burned his skin. He stared at the moving shadows cast across their fingers by the fire.

'Why not?' The words struggled up from his throat. He forced himself to face her eyes again. 'You just said—'

'Don't you think it would be better if the King thought the idea his own? A demand from the Council might be ill received.'

An understatement. 'But now that I know he's leaving, I must act.'

'If you do, he'll know I told you.'

And Solay would bear the brunt of the King's displeasure. 'So you have a different plan.'

She nodded. 'If someone he trusted suggested it to him, he would surely agree.'

'Who?'

'Let me talk to a friend.'

This was what he hated about the Court. All was whispered behind closed doors. Arrangements were made in secret, for reasons that he could never quite understand. 'It is a simple matter, not a Court intrigue.'

'Not so simple as you make it sound.'

He wanted to protest, but she was right. If the King's objective was to avoid the Council, it would take delicate persuasion to allow a representative to travel with him. 'Why are you helping the Council? The King holds your loyalty.'

'You challenged me to prove I love you. The task will be impossible if we are separated for the rest of Lent. Do you intend for me to fail?'

Eyes wide, she waited for his answer.

He did, of course, feeling a guilty pang. At least she had asked an honest question. 'All right. Return to Windsor tomorrow. If I don't receive an invitation from the King within the sennight, he'll get a formal request from the Council.'

'Tomorrow?' The desperate edge returned to her voice. 'I had hoped to spend more time with you.'

First she wanted to talk to the King. Then she wanted to stay. Where was the lie here?

In the babe.

He struggled against black memories.

If she was with child, she would need to bed him quickly. That, he would not allow. Never again. 'We'll have time aplenty on the road.' He rose, a dismissal. 'The chamberlain will find you a room.'

And the farther from his, the safer he'd be.

Huge and oppressive, Westminster closed in on her as she wandered the halls, seeking the chamberlain to find her food and a bed. Solay had always hated this cavernous palace that the King shared with Parliament. Here, when they prayed, portraits of the King's wife and his nine legitimate children peered down at them from the walls of the chapel.

And here, her mother had faced the judgement of Parliament and lost.

Now her long, frozen trip to this gloomy place seemed for naught.

Agnes would persuade Hibernia to persuade the King to invite Justin on his gyration, but only if Solay could use him to gain information. The King already doubted her. She must discover some new titbit.

Something more about the document he was writing.

She tried to puzzle out a plan, yet the weak-kneed want she felt in his presence muddled her mind. Instead, she felt again the breadth of his shoulders and the power of his muscled back against her palm.

Stop brooding, she told herself as she ate the hearty cabbage soup the chamberlain found for her. If my want for him is a weakness, so is his for me.

It was in every breath he took in her presence. It was in his eyes that seemed to devour her. Justin might resist kisses, but if she bared her body, surely he would succumb. And afterwards, he might whisper secrets.

She put down her spoon and rose.

You must save your maidenhead for your husband, her mother had warned. *It may be your only currency.*

She ignored the voice. Banns had been read. Once she unleashed his passion, he would be her husband in truth. There would be no more talk of conditions.

Now. Tonight. She must not return to the King empty handed.

Chapter Ten

After the castle was well abed, she crept through the echoing halls. Justin's room, the chamberlain told her, was well away from the smell of the river, in the shadow of the Abbey's towers. Faint firelight still showed underneath the door.

Heart pounding, she trailed her fingertips across the rough wood, afraid to knock.

Make his body want you and you can convince him of anything.

The door moaned as she pushed it open.

With his back to her, Justin stood before the window, staring out at the falling snow. She crept up behind him, slipping her arms, seductively, she hoped, around his waist and resting her cheek on his broad back. 'Husband.'

He slammed the shutters shut and pulled away from her. 'I am not your husband.'

Something hot, more than the fire's reflection, burned behind his eyes despite his harsh words. A muscle moved near his cheekbone.

So, he was fighting his desire.

She gentled her expression. 'Can you not spare me a word?'

'Talk.'

She turned away to compose her thoughts. Before her, his bed loomed, soft with a feather-stuffed mattress, deep blue curtains open to catch the fire's heat. Behind her, a log landed with a chunk. The fire licked it with a hiss, then it crackled into flame.

What must she do now?

Remember, her mother had said, *a man lusts with his eyes. He is helpless against what he sees.*

She did not understand how this could be so, but she knew when he touched her she was helpless. If seeing her would weaken him like that, surely he would bed her before dawn.

Back still to him, she reluctantly removed her cloak and draped it on top of the bed, grateful for the fire's heat.

Behind her, she heard nothing.

She shrugged out of the sleeveless surcoat, letting it slide to the floor to reveal her cote-hardie.

Nothing stirred except the snapping fire. Did she feel his eyes on her or was it only hope? She had expected him to touch her by now. Could she have been wrong? Perhaps he didn't desire her.

No. That was not true.

She tugged her front laces free.

Behind her, his breath turned ragged.

He was watching, then. The thought sparked an inner fire. Slowly, she threaded her fingers through her hair, then shook it down her back.

A sound, not quite a moan.

Her breath quickened as a plume of desire slithered up from her centre.

She squeezed her thighs against the weakness, waiting for his touch.

It didn't come.

What was she doing wrong? She thought she knew enough

to fan his lust. It had never sounded hard. Men were all helpless that way, led by their staffs to drink at a woman's well, else how would a woman live?

She fumbled with the last of the laces and shrugged off her final gown. Now, covered only with the thin linen chemise, the fire still warmed her back, but chill air snaked across the floor and curled up her legs.

What was he doing? When was he going to touch her?

She had only one more layer to shed.

She bent to reach for the hem of the chemise.

'Solay, stop.' Hard anger and rough desire clashed in his voice.

She dropped the hem and turned. Sitting by the fire, one leg flung over the arm of the chair, his legs spread wide enough that she could see his arousal.

Their eyes met and, for a moment, they breathed together.

He blinked, finally, breaking the spell.

'A pretty performance, Solay. No doubt you have used it successfully on many other men. Perhaps even on the father of the babe you carry.'

She crossed her arms over her shivering breasts. So that was what he feared. She should have realised.

'There is no child. Take me to your bed and you'll discover I'm a virgin.'

'If I take you to my bed, it will no longer matter whether you are a virgin.'

'If I had been so urgently in need of a husband, I would have asked the King for one. You were the one who suggested marriage, not I.'

Despite his frown, it could take little more, surely. She curved her lips in a slow, deliberate smile, knelt before him and reached for his staff. Perhaps he would like her to put her mouth on it. Men did, Agnes said.

He grabbed her wrists before her hands could reach him and held them apart. Now he was in control, his eyes taking in everything she had teased him with, forehead to toes, barely shielded by her linen shift.

She felt herself softening, aching for him to hold her.

No, no. There is no time for your wishes. You must satisfy his dreams.

She squeezed her thighs together as he stared at her belly. She knew her looks pleased him. If she leaned closer, surely—

He raised his eyes. 'You are so determined to display yourself. Let me watch you.'

As he stared at her, her mouth turned dry and her centre wet. 'What do you mean?'

'Don't pretend innocence. You know how to make a man covet you.' His glance fell again to the space between her legs. 'I'll be a willing audience.'

A hot, wild craving burned below her belly. She lifted her head with a seductive smile. Their eyes locked together and she felt the heat creep up from her centre, up through her breasts. Want muddled her thoughts. 'What would you have me do?'

He laced his fingers in hers and squeezed, his unyielding ring biting her flesh. 'You have needed no direction from me so far.'

'I don't know what you want.' she whispered, tilting her head, craving the kiss that must come. 'Show me.'

His ragged breath brushed her lips. A moment more and she'd have the kiss and whatever came next.

She pressed her lips against his.

He dropped her hands, threw her away from him, and stood. Without the balance of his touch, she fell, the cold floor raising bumps on the flesh of her thighs.

Towering over her, he wavered, swaying towards her, then pulling back.

The closeness she craved lay just out of reach. For ever out of reach.

She scrambled to her feet and clutched the soft wool of his tunic. She was so close, she must not let him slip away now. 'Don't you want me?'

He grabbed her hand, pulled her to her feet, and held her close, her breasts hot and full against his chest.

'Want you? I want to ravish you. I want to hear you cry out for me and I want to plunge into your body until the fire is ash and dawn lights the sky.' He let go and stepped back, shaking, as if his body were barely under his control. 'But I won't.'

'Why?' Panic edged the word.

'Because I will not trap us into this marriage.'

'It is not a trap. We agreed. Both of us.'

'I told you not to let anyone force you. I won't be forced either.'

'Loving is pleasure, not force.'

'Not when your body alone consents.'

'But you said I had to convince you of my love. That is what I am trying to do.'

'If you think a swift coupling will convince me of your love, you know nothing of lust or love. I told the King I would not marry you unless you were willing. I did not mean willing to lie with me. You've demonstrated that amply. To me and to how many others?'

'No others. There have been no others.'

'I don't believe you.'

'I am giving you the truth you asked for.' *And still you do not believe.*

'Regardless,' he said slowly, 'giving me your body will not convince me of your love.'

She gathered the remaining shards of her pride, stepped away and wrapped the King's cloak around her nakedness. What was left of the royal temper shot through her veins. 'You would not speak so to me if I were the King's legitimate daughter.'

He laughed, a hollow sound that fuelled her anger. 'You think not? I've insulted the King himself.' He waved towards the curtained bed. 'Take my bed. I'll find another.'

She bit her lip as her future walked towards the door. Stupid, stupid to let anger betray her. If he left now, what would she tell the King? She knelt and grabbed his leg, her body still pulsing to hold him, hoping the deference that pleased the King might work. 'Please. Stay. I will not try to tempt you again.'

He paused, eyes burning with want acknowledged. 'Do you believe that would make a difference?'

And then she realised she had not even needed to remove her cloak.

Wordless, she released him.

'Love demands more than your body, Solay. You must give your heart.'

After the oak door shut, she mourned alone before a fading fire, frightened at his words, for she had no heart to give.

He left the room, staggering, because he knew if he stayed he would take her. Take her and take her and take her again until every precious seed he had would be inside her and they would be married, never to be put asunder.

Clearly, she would say or do anything to hold him. Yet knowing why she had flaunted her body did nothing to bolster his resistance. His tongue craved her taste. Her soft skin tempted his fingers.

He was beginning to understand the old King's obsession.

He stepped outside, welcoming the blowing snow to chill the heat she had stirred in his veins.

He would not sleep tonight, knowing she lay in his bed. He only knew he must not touch her again.

But if he had any eyes at all, she had been honest about one thing. Virgin or not, her flat belly hid no babe.

He suddenly realised he had followed the path to the Thames, where the swirling waters rushed towards the sea. Cold. Dark. Final.

Please. Stay.

Desperation tinged her words. Beneath her scheming lay a deeper pain, the one he had sensed the first time he saw her. Would his rebuff turn Solay to melancholia? Or something worse?

If so, it would be his fault. Again.

Please, the other woman had said. *Let me go.*

He turned away from the river's memories.

He must not let Solay return to Windsor until he could be sure she had not descended into despair. That would mean taking her to London with him tomorrow so he could watch her. The masters at the Middle Temple would raise their eyebrows to see a woman, but he dare not leave her alone. He must keep her close for at least a day and keep her mood jolly.

Unknowingly, he had become responsible for her. He should call it off now. Before it was too late.

But he was beginning to fear it already was.

Chapter Eleven

Alone in Justin's bed the next morning, Solay lay half-asleep, imagining he lay beside her.

Wrapped against the cold, she would snuggle into arms strong and protective. When he opened his eyes, they would smile to see her. His lips would take hers in a sleepy kiss that would deepen until…

She opened her eyes to the dead fire, startled to realise she had been dreaming of love.

A gust of wind rattled the shutters and shook the thought from her head. She must have borrowed the foolish fancy from Agnes, mooning in hopeless passion for Hibernia, yet smiling from dawn to dusk.

She reached for her surcoat and dressed under the covers. Tugging her fingers through tangled hair, she assessed last night's disaster.

His want was plain enough. Strongly as he fought her, inexperienced as she was, she knew that.

But he was stronger than his want. What other man could have refused her protestations of love, refused her very body?

But then, as Solay climbed out of bed and opened the

shutters to the soft pink echo of dawn behind the Abbey's towers, she remembered the worst.

Please. Stay.

The daughter of a king did not belong on her knees before a lawyer.

She left the window and stabbed the embers until a flame burst free. She must bury last night's humiliation and speak of it no more, but first, she must prevent Justin from sending her back to Windsor.

She opened the door and tripped over Justin, stretched out across the threshold.

He scrambled to stand, holding something behind his back, and stifled a yawn. Sleeplessness shaded his eyes, but when he looked at her the very air hummed between them.

She squashed the feeling. It was no good to her now.

'How are you? Did you sleep well?' He tripped over the courteous words, as if his tongue were unused to pleasantries.

'Oh, yes.' She covered her stomach to muffle the growl of hunger. She had barely slept at all.

'I thought you might be hungry.' He entered the room and held out a wine-darkened slice of bread, wrapped in a kitchen cloth.

Shocked, she took it, muttering her thanks. 'I did not think you would approve.'

'The law does not forbid it.' He smiled. Deliberately.

Surprise set off a giggle. 'Did you mean for me to laugh?'

'That was my intention.'

She did laugh then, a long, slow chuckle that warmed her whole body. Was this the same man who had left the room last night?

'The weather has cleared,' he said, adding wood to the fire. 'I have to go to the City.'

Her smile faded. Next, he would say he had made arrangements for her to return to Windsor. Instead of bringing the

King whispered secrets, she had only the strange word subpoena. She needed at least another day.

She leaned against the bed, clutching her belly with her free hand. 'I don't feel well.'

Instantly, he stood before her, pressing the back of his hand against her forehead, then her cheeks. 'Have you pain? Fever?'

She shook her head, surprised that her mild statement had sparked such strong concern. 'But I'm not sure I should travel.'

'Then we will stay here.'

'We?'

'I thought to take you to London with me.'

She swallowed her last bite in surprise. Last night, she could have sworn the man would never again seek her company. Had her words convinced him to give her another chance? 'What takes you to the City?'

'Council business. And there's a house for sale I must inspect. But if you feel unwell…'

'Thank you.' Surely she could learn something for the King by going. 'I would enjoy the trip.'

'But you just said—'

She wiped her fingers on the cloth and smoothed her skirt. 'I must just have been hungry. I'm feeling quite well now.' She pulled her smile wide.

He looked at her keenly, gave a curt nod and put his hand at her elbow. 'Come.'

Shortly thereafter, Solay stood on the jetty at Westminster. A cold winter sun melted yesterday's wet snow at the river's edge as the boatman pushed off.

Justin gripped her hand firmly as she stepped into the boat. He had not let her out of his sight all morning, except when she visited the garden-robe. The man who vowed not to touch her kept his hand on her back or at her elbow, even when he went to his work room to roll and tie the document he had been working on yesterday. Once they were in the boat, his hand hovered near her arm, as if he wanted to be ready to snatch her at any moment.

Perhaps this change of heart meant he would speak more of the summons he carried. She dared not ask directly. Yesterday, that had raised his suspicions. Instead, she would babble nonsense while she pondered how to approach the subject.

'You wanted to know things I like,' she began. 'I like being on the water.' As a child, she had loved riding on the river-boats. How could she have forgotten?

Instead of coaxing a smile, her words made him frown. 'Why?'

'Why must there be a reason for what a person likes?' As the stars gave her hope and the sun courage, the water seemed to bring her peace. She smiled. 'Don't you like the river?'

'No.'

She did not ask why, not wanting him to dwell on a painful subject. Perhaps he did not have a boatman's stomach. 'The trip is so much easier than on land. And we enjoy this beautiful view.' As they rounded the river bend, London stretched before them, just as it had when she was a child ferried to her mother's house. 'I always loved the trip from Westminster to our house in London.'

'You told me you lived at Windsor.'

She gritted her teeth against his implication she had lied. 'We lived where the King lived, but Mother had a house in London.' When the court was in residence at Westminster or the Tower, she and Jane were shuffled off to the house by the river. She had not thought of it in years, but now she remembered the rush of the river, lulling her to sleep.

'Where was the house?'

'Near Cannon Street.' She rested her arms on the side of the boat, peering ahead. 'Look! We can almost see it.'

She leaned forward, hoping for a glimpse.

He grabbed her, nearly making her fall forward. The boat rocked, and the boatman yelled at them to keep low and to the centre.

His grip squeezed the air from her chest as he pulled her into his lap, his arms like iron chains.

'What are you doing?' he snapped. 'You nearly fell in.'

She gasped for a breath and smelled his scent, like fresh-cut wood, mixed with the crisp air and the tang of the river.

'I've never fallen overboard in my life,' she said, when she could breathe. 'I was just trying to see my old house.'

But he kept his arm locked around her until the boat docked at the city gate and Justin relinquished his sword to the gatekeeper.

The river's edge usually harboured the rough side of society, yet beyond this gate they walked up a sheltered street surrounded by snowy gardens. Instead of sailors and strumpets, the street was filled with educated men arguing, many followed by servants.

'This isn't London as I remember it,' she asked. 'Where are we?'

His smile was genuine. 'The law may be made at Westminster, but the lawyers are made at the Middle Temple.'

She looked again, expecting to see horns and tails.

He didn't wait for a question. 'We eat, sleep, study, argue, work and live here. It is university, home and workplace.' Affection warmed his voice. 'Here, we speak of what matters.'

'What could matter more than the King's will?'

'Truth and justice. Right and wrong.'

What could she say that would please him? He understood

nothing. Where was the justice in losing everything that should be yours by right? What was true except the need for food, clothing, shelter?

A young man, well dressed, walked by them, grinning. 'Your fine will be stiff for that one.'

'What does he mean?' she asked, glad to be spared from answering Justin.

His face reddened. 'The only women who come here are plying their trade. The fine for fornicating in chambers is six shillings eight pence.'

Her cheeks burned, thinking of last night. If he had been willing, the fine would have been worth a yard of russet wool.

He pointed out the hall, the chambers, the church, and she pretended interest in which ones were used to teach dancing, which for common meals, and which to learn the law, all the while wondering how she might get him talking about the Council's business instead.

They paused, finally, before a stone gate. London lay just beyond this private, orderly, serene world. And like a warning of what lay on the other side, black soot marred the stone, streaking upwards from dead flames.

'What caused that?' she asked.

'It happened during the rebellion.'

She had been safely away from London when the peasants rioted in the streets, yet she had hidden beneath her bed when angry voices echoed across the countryside, afraid they would come for her next. 'What happened here?'

'The peasants planned to hang the lawyers. When they couldn't find any, they burned the books instead.' His face was grim. 'We leave it as a reminder of what happens when there is no respect for the law.'

Solay nodded, for once in agreement. 'You dislike the King, yet it was Richard who calmed them.' It was a well-known tale, the fourteen-year-old blond King riding fear-lessly out to the mob and telling them he was their king, too. 'He was the one who restored the rule of law.'

'And then ignored it.'

'What do you mean?'

'Do you not know? He promised justice and freedom for the serfs, but afterwards, he hanged all the leaders and forced the peasants back to their lords.'

The King had given her his word, too. Would he ignore it so easily? 'But whatever the King wishes, that is the law.'

'It is power, not law. And certainly it is not always justice.'

Here was a hint of Justin's plan, but not yet enough to help the King. 'Have you come here today for justice, then?'

He ignored her question as they entered one of the buildings. At the door, Justin greeted a grey-haired man with a hearty handshake.

She peered beyond to a great hall, full of young men dining.

'Stay here,' Justin said to her, starting up the stairs. 'I'll not be long.'

Whatever reason he had come lay up those stairs. 'Can I not come with you?' She nodded towards the hall where several of the students had discovered her presence. 'Some of these young men look quite ready to pay the fine.'

'William will see you come to no harm.' Justin turned and mounted the stairs. 'And, William, see if you can find us some food.'

She watched him disappear, drumming her fingers in frustration. How was she to discover anything now?

'I am not accustomed to ladies in the house. Would you care for ale, milady?'

She started to shake her head, then realised William might have useful information. 'Yes, thank you.'

When he reappeared from the great hall, she put on her

most dazzling smile. 'Justin neglected to introduce us. I am his betrothed. You must be an important man here.'

He preened, handing her a battered pewter goblet. 'The most senior masters of the law live and work here.'

'You mean the justices?'

'Oh, no. I mean the professors.'

'Ah, of course,' she said, nodding as if she knew what he meant. What could a law professor have to do with a writ? She should have paid more attention to her mother's longwinded stories about her legal affairs. Her mother had a keen mind for how the law might be used. And abused. 'You must know much of the law yourself.'

He smiled. 'I am no scholar, but I have learned many things. I have been here since King Edward's time.'

She could not resist the vision of Justin as a young man. 'Did you know Justin as a student?'

'Oh, yes. He had a special talent even then. He became a sergeant-at-law more quickly than anyone ever has.'

A surprising surge of pride brought on a genuine smile. 'Who does he visit today?'

'He still takes counsel with the master teachers when he has a particularly thorny issue.'

'He's mentioned working on a subpoena,' she said, then looked at the man with wide eyes and a smile. 'You probably know what that means. I feel so ignorant, but as his wife, I will need to understand such things.'

Would he take the hint and share his knowledge?

'It compels a man to appear before the jury and give evidence.'

'Ah, how interesting.' She nodded and took a sip of ale. She opened her eyes wider, tilted her head and smiled. Who would Justin force to testify? And about what? If a man was forced to tell all he knew to the jury, he might convict himself and many others before the questioning was through.

Justin came down the stairs, no longer carrying the document, took the bread and cheese William had found, and led her outside. They sat on a sun-warmed bench to eat.

'You forgot the document,' she said, as if she had just noticed.

'No. I left it with my old professor.'

'I thought you were through with training. Do you still need the approval of your professor?'

'Just because a man seeks counsel does not mean he needs approval.'

Now what could she tell the King? He took a document called a subpoena to an old man and left it? 'What sort of advice does he give you?'

'You have a new-found interest in the law.'

'Of course I do. It is your life.' If she were not careful, he would suspect the motive for her curiosity. She braved the feel of his bare skin to touch the gold ring on his left hand. 'It is even the ring you wear.'

He pulled back his hand, twisting the band without looking at it. 'My father gave it to me when I was called to the bar.'

His father. The judge. 'What does it say?'

'*Omnia vincit veritas.* Truth conquers all,' he translated.

She must not forget. All the untruths ordinary people needed to survive were nothing against this touchstone.

No wedding vows would bind him more tightly than this.

'Well, the law seems a tedious, slow-moving business,' she said. 'I had no idea it was so complicated.'

'Sometimes,' he said, 'the law is much more complicated than justice.' His stern expression softened. 'You've been patient this morning. You spoke of your old house. Would you like to see it again?'

A little flood of happiness surged through her and she squeezed his arm. 'The house by the river? Oh, yes.'

Even if he was being suspiciously solicitous, the law, and the King, could wait.

Finding the house again was not easy. Forgotten memories guided her as if she were groping through a dark room. Conscious of Justin's eyes on her, she turned down more than one dead end in the maze of streets.

Gradually, things seemed more familiar. A house with a dragon's head over the window. The smell of the river and then, at the corner, she saw it, the small white stone house, just as magical as she had remembered.

When had her mother lost this home? Of all the properties, this one and the one at Upminster were the only ones she cared about.

Here, her mother even played with them, sometimes.

'We had a boat,' she said, drawn towards the house. 'The servant would take us for rides on the river.'

She gazed at the door knocker, the familiar head of a lion, a subtle reminder of the King's coat of arms. If she opened the door, could she walk back in time to the days when she had played barefoot on the jetty?

She raised her hand to knock.

'Solay,' he called, 'are you sure—?'

She knocked, for once not asking his permission.

A plump woman answered the door. A small boy hid behind her skirts and glanced from Solay to Justin. 'What do you want? If you are looking for the Lincoln family, they moved.'

'No, we're… I mean, I used to live here when I was a child. I was hoping to look inside again.'

'Are you one of the Lincoln girls?' The woman squinted

with a suspicious eye, still blocking the door, shifting her gaze from Solay to Justin.

'I'm Lady Joan Weston.'

The woman frowned. 'One of the harlot's girls?'

'What did you say?' Justin moved towards the door.

Swallowing her anger at the insult, Solay held him back, nodding.

Wary, the woman looked at him. 'Are you here to force me?'

'No, but—'

The door slammed.

Solay choked back the burning in her throat. The wooden door blurred before her eyes. There was no room for happy memories in the real world. She blinked, refusing to turn until she could see the lion-headed knocker clearly again.

Justin put a hand on her shoulder and reached for the heavy iron ring. 'I'll see that she lets you in.'

'No, please.' She shrugged off his hands and looked past the house to the river one more time. She should not have confessed her affection for this house. Honesty only made your disappointments obvious.

She pushed the sadness deeper into her chest. 'It really isn't much of a house compared to Windsor, is it?' She smiled, making sure her teeth showed. 'Shall we go?'

Justin's heart slipped when the door shut in her face. As her head drooped forward on her slender neck, he glimpsed the ten-year-old girl, thrown out of her home.

If this was what her life had been like, it was a wonder she had not fallen into melancholia years ago.

He had no words of comfort. Groping for some childhood memories, she had been judged for her mother's sins. No wonder she tried so hard to please. Her very existence displeased.

Yet she squared her shoulders and put her brave smile back

in place. As they walked to the dock, she talked easily, as if the last few moments had never been, asking him anew about the intricacies of the law. And he answered, hoping it would distract her.

Back in the boat, he kept his hand firmly on her arm, fearing this fresh humiliation had saddened her anew. As he peeled back her disguise, he faced a real person and he saw again the pain he had seen from the first.

It frightened him.

The last time he had cared for someone like that, he had killed her.

Chapter Twelve

◦⟋⟍⟋⟍⟍⟋⟍⟍◦

Steadied by the oarsman's hand, Solay stepped into the rocking boat, burying her hurt next to her late-day hunger. She refused to mourn. Besides, her pain had an unexpected benefit. As they pushed off, Justin's arm circled her waist again, more gently than on the morning journey, and he answered all her questions about the law.

By the time Westminster came into view, she knew subpoena was Latin for 'under penalty', that it could compel a man's testimony and that the fine for failure to appear was one hundred pounds, a sum to make even a King think twice.

She still did not know whose name was on the writ.

Better to change the subject to frivolous things so he would not suspect her questions were more than idle curiosity.

'What colours do you like?' she said.

'Colours?' he asked as if he did not recognise the word.

'Yes.' She stroked the tightly woven wool of his tunic. 'This beautiful deep blue, for example. Is it your favourite?'

'It was the plainest the mercer had. The rest were gaudy enough for the King's fool.'

'And what foods do you like?'

'Good, plain food and drink.' He shrugged, as if he cared no more for food and drink than cloth. 'No need for it to be sugared and spiced.'

The oarsman's steady dip filled the silence. Plain dress, plain food. The man scorned comforts of any kind. No wonder the King's ways grated on him. 'Did you have a pet as a child?'

He pulled back and searched her eyes. 'Why all these questions?'

She fought a laugh. He had not wondered when she asked about the law. 'How am I to love you if I do not know you? As your wife, I will need to please you with meals and wardrobe according to your tastes.' She smiled, to forestall his objection. 'Yes, I know, you have not yet agreed to wed me.'

'Then talk of yourself. Did you ever have a pet?'

The sudden joyful memory did make her laugh. 'I had a popinjay.'

'A parrot?' He smiled. 'Did he talk?'

'I jabbered nonsense and he replied,' she remembered. They had kept each other company, the bright green bird half a world away from home and the lonely little girl who lived in borrowed houses. 'I think we taught each other to talk.'

She glanced at the boatman, then whispered, so he would not hear her naughty deeds. 'Once, I took him outside and it started to rain. He was so mad! He just kept squawking.'

She shook her head and raised her shoulders like a bird with ruffled feathers, then shrieked, 'Baad, baad', mimicking the parrot's cry just as well as she used to, when her imitation could fool Jane.

The boatman stared, round-eyed, and she started to giggle.

Justin's face, stiff with shock, dissolved into laughter, an easy rumble that came from deep in his chest. 'You sound exactly like a bird! What happened to him?'

Her laughter faded. 'We had to leave him behind.'

When the old King died, they had fled the palace in the middle of the night, jewels scooped up in darkness. There was no time to bring a useless bird to comfort a child. Only a King could waste money on such a trifle.

'I'm sorry,' he said.

She stared at him, unable to believe the word. No one had ever been sorry before. Many, like the woman at the door, had been hostile. Most had simply whispered and stared.

'Thank you,' she said, finally.

Hesitant to break the fragile peace, she sat in silence as Westminster came into view.

The boat touched the jetty and Justin stepped out, then gave her his hand. His touch coaxed some inner warmth, mixed with an ache for more.

Don't succumb. The King's velvet and ermine will warm you and your family long after this man turns cold.

Steadying herself on land, she slipped her hand away. She had enough to spin a story that would satisfy the King. 'I will leave for Windsor at first light.'

He looked at her sharply. 'You are feeling well enough?'

Puzzled, she finally remembered her feigned illness of the morning. 'Quite well now, thank you. You should receive your invitation to join the Court within the sennight.'

'If I do not hear from the King by Candlemas, he'll hear from the Council.' He walked beside her. 'Who else goes on this gyration? Hibernia?'

And suddenly, Solay feared she knew whose name was on the legal document left at the Inns at Court.

She shrugged, avoiding his eyes. 'I do not know,' she lied. 'I thank you for taking me to London,' she said, huddling beneath her cloak. 'I learned so much about what you do and I'm so interested. That subpoena, for example. Whose name is on it?'

Suddenly, Justin knew why the visit, why the 'wifely'

concern and the endless questions about his work. What a fool
he'd been to be tricked by sad stories of lost parrots and
houses by the river. 'Tell the King he'll find out soon enough,
Lady Solay.'

She looked at him, eyes wide with imaginary innocence.
'What do you mean?'

He ignored the pain in his stomach. What had his truthful
tongue let slip that the King need not yet know? All because
he had thought, just for a moment, that her interest in the
workings of the law was sincere.

'You did not drag yourself across the countryside in the
snow for the pleasure of my company.' Anger burned in his chest
that she let herself be so ill used. That he let himself be so ill
used. 'You are here on the King's business, not your own.'

''Tis not true,' she said. 'I came to let you know about the
King's gyration and to help you arrange to go with him. Why
do you doubt me?'

'Because the King's desires rule your life, not your own.
And certainly not mine.'

She faced him, then, eyes steady, though the wind
whipped her dark hair behind her. 'The King's desires rule
all our lives.'

'Not mine.'

She smiled a woman's smile, then. One of those that said
I know truths you never will. 'Yes, at the end, even yours.' She
pulled her cloak close and turned to go inside.

He wanted to argue, but as Gloucester came out to meet
him, he realised that, every day he worked to restrict the
King's power, his life, too, revolved around Richard.

Gloucester joined him, leering over his shoulder at Solay.
'A strange choice you've made for a wife, Lamont. Is she as
good as her mother was?'

The vision of her skin, licked by firelight, warred with the haunted shadows in her eyes. She was the King's spy and, still, her smile seduced him. 'She is not yet my wife.'

Gloucester raised his brows, but let the statement lie. 'So where's the writ?'

'It's under review. We have only one chance. We can afford no errors.' No one had ever tried to compel a Duke into a court of law. A judge, even a brave one, would need an ir-refutable case.

'Your endless details are costing precious time.'

'I'm aware of the urgency,' he snapped. 'The King is rumoured to be leaving Windsor soon.'

'What? How do you know?'

'The Lady Solay told me. Unless we serve Hibernia first, the writ will be useless.'

'Then let's take him. Now.'

'The other lords will never move against one of their own without cause.'

'He's not one of ours. He's an upstart whom the King has raised beyond his station.'

'He's a Duke. To take him without a reason would set a precedent. You could be next.'

Gloucester slapped his gloves against his sleeve as they entered the castle. 'Use what legal tricks you must, just get him out of the way. We must be in control and ready to rekindle the war against France by spring.'

Justin hoped it was only the man's temper speaking. 'Par-liament charged us to investigate internal scandals. War remains the King's prerogative.'

'I will not sit idle while Richard loses land my family has held for centuries.'

'His behaviour is no excuse for us to violate our charter.'

Gloucester's look carried all the menace of his nephew's. 'Don't argue the letter of the law with me. Do what I need or I'll

find someone who cares more for results than legal pleasantries.'
Gloucester raised his eyebrows. 'An army makes the best law.'

As Justin made his way back to his work room, Solay's deception mixed uneasily with the knowledge that, if the legal path failed, Gloucester would forsake it for something more direct.
And violent.

Chapter Thirteen

'He's done what?' The King's shout echoed off the stone walls of his solar. He raised a fist.

Solay cringed, expecting the blow to fall on her for bearing bad news. 'He wrote a document, Your Majesty, and took it to the Middle Temple Inn.' It was a titbit of truth, but she hoped it would satisfy.

The King slammed his fist into his palm and started pacing.

Hibernia took over the questioning. 'What did it say?' His patience with her had grown because she was Agnes's friend.

She raised her shoulders, palms open, to convey the confusion of a simple woman. 'I know little of the law.'

The King glared at her, narrowing his hard blue eyes. 'And where is this document now?'

'I don't know.' That was true. She didn't know which professor had it.

Hibernia shook his head. 'Best we start our journey now and leave Lamont behind.'

Solay gasped. Moments before, as she and Agnes had planned, Hibernia had suggested to the King that Justin accompany the court. 'But if he comes, I can watch what he does.'

'Lady Solay, if you cannot tell us something more useful than you already have, there will be no need for either of you to come with the Court.'

Useful. It would be useful to tell them Hibernia's name was on the writ, but, if she was wrong, she would suffer the consequences. If she was right, Justin would. 'I'm sorry I know so little. There were many words I could not read. I think he called it a "sup" or a "sub" something.'

'A subpoena?' Hibernia asked.

She rolled her eyes heavenward, as if trying to think. 'Perhaps.' How had he known so quickly?

The King exploded. 'He's coming after my household! This is treason!'

She swallowed and found her mouth dry. Justin Lamont would do nothing that was not by the law of the realm. Of that, she was certain. 'All the more reason for him to accompany the Court, as the Duke so wisely suggested. If he is left alone, he could cause mischief—'

The King interrupted. 'You expect me to allow him to travel beside me while he's trying to destroy me!'

'I'm sure Your Majesty can protect your household from a piece of paper,' Solay said. Justin himself could not take Hibernia physically with the King's soldiers all around. 'His legal demands can wait upon the King's pleasure.'

She held her breath, hoping flattering words would work.

'My pleasure!' the King snapped. 'My pleasure would be that he leave us alone until pigs fly backwards!'

Hibernia laughed, flapped his arms and walked backwards, snorting like a swine. That set the King laughing until they both doubled over and Richard was forced to use his little white cloth to wipe the laughter that had come through his nose.

And she suddenly saw why the King had raised him so high.

A King had no peers. No one to trust. No one to laugh with. Yet with this man, for good or ill, Richard could be himself.

'No law clerk can best a King,' Richard said, in a better mood. 'The King *is* the law.' He put a hand on Hibernia's shoulder. 'Lamont may follow us to verify my seal on the endless documents that Council seems to generate.'

Solay released a breath of relief. The King, jollied, offered to send a messenger to her mother in Upminster with a letter explaining that Solay would be travelling with the Court, along with a gift of a cask of wine.

The Duke nodded at her, a sign of dismissal, and she curtsied, backing out of the room.

Everything was working out as she had planned, except that she seemed to have developed a foolish desire to protect the King's enemy.

As Solay had promised, Justin's summons arrived within the week. Now, as he entered Windsor through the towered gate where he and Solay had watched the stars, he wondered what she had said of the writ and his visit to the Middle Temple. Before greeting the King and Hibernia, he must know.

He found her huddled before a fireplace, studying the pages of a red velvet book. She raised her violet gaze from the page and she looked glad to see him. Doubtless another whore's trick.

'Justin—'

'What did the King say when you told him about the subpoena?' he began, without preamble.

Whatever fleeting expression he had seen disappeared. She closed the book and rose, her bland smile unwavering as she dipped before him in submission. 'Welcome, husband,' she said, in the tone that lied.

'Cease your pretence.' If he could see her eyes, would he

recognise a lie from the truth? He grabbed her arms and pulled her to face him, immediately regretting it. The soft rise and fall of her breath tangled with his own, threatening to make him forget his distrust.

She lowered her lashes and ran her tongue over partially open lips. He gripped her harder, trying to hold on to his control instead of taking the kiss that tempted. 'What did you tell him?'

She shook off his hold and he let her, relieved when she stepped away. 'I simply told him you had a document.'

Did she lie still? 'What kind?'

She laughed then, a high-pitched tinkle that grated on his ears. 'Am I a lawyer to remember what the silly thing is called?'

'You remembered in London. In fact, for someone who despises the law, you seem to know a great deal and what you didn't already know, my flapping tongue told you.' He forced her chin up to face him. 'So he knows I am working on a subpoena. What else did you tell him?'

Her calm could have held truth or hidden lies. 'I told him you took it to the Middle Temple.'

He gritted his teeth against the disappointment, sorry to have been proven right. 'Nothing else?'

'What else was there to tell?'

He could not ask whether she told him Hibernia's name was on it. Hope remained that she did not know.

He let her go, wondering whether she told the truth. A creeping chill gripped his back. If the King knew about the writ, and suspected more, there was only one reason he would allow Justin to accompany the Court, a fact so obvious Justin was surprised he had resisted it so long. 'You are to spy on me as we travel.' The truth tasted surprisingly bitter.

She blinked, as if startled. 'Spy? What need is there to spy?' Her words held a practised lilt. 'You are here to keep the King informed, are you not?'

He consoled himself with congratulations that he had been clever enough to leave himself an escape from marriage to this woman. 'You are more than a simple flatterer. You would gladly see me in the Tower if it pleased the King.'

'How can you think so? You are my betrothed. I would do well to look after your head.'

'I am your betrothed for the nonce. Abandon hope of persuading me you are capable of any feeling for me.'

'Why do you still doubt me? I did as I promised and arranged for you to accompany the Court so you could mind the Council's business. These are all things of use to you, not the King.' She leaned against him. 'Do you not think you might enjoy the trip?'

At her touch, his blood again raced throughout his limbs. Her body had beckoned him from the first, but now that he had seen her, he seemed to be ever hard between the legs.

'Enjoy is not the word I would use.' Now that he'd vowed never to touch her, her nearness taunted him all the more. He could see few curves in a body bundled against the cold, yet the clothes that cloaked her mattered not. He saw her as she had been that night by firelight—her breasts peeking out from her dark hair, her skin, fair and smooth, the dark triangle hiding the sweetness between her legs.

'What word would you choose, then?'

He gritted his teeth. 'Torture.'

The damn vixen laughed. ''Tis torture easily ended.'

'Yes. I shall end it when Easter comes,' he said, leaving the room.

Tricked by a glimpse of false pain, he had let down his guard and stepped in like a chivalrous Galahad, thinking she needed rescue from the King.

It was obvious that she did not. In fact, he was the one in danger.

Her mother had shown no respect for marriage and

neither did she. Perhaps she did not even realise what marriage should be.

Perhaps it was time he taught her.

As the Court prepared to leave, two grooms hoisted Solay into the sidesaddle Queen Anne preferred. Instead of riding firmly astride the horse, she perched precariously on a little chair with a footrest, balanced as uneasily as she was between Justin and the King.

Still, February's false spring lifted her spirits as they rode north towards Nottingham. She and Justin travelled with the Court. Jane had celebrated a birthday for the first time. Perhaps things could work out.

Without a clear place in the royal household, she and Justin also rode awkwardly between the riding household and the walking household staff. Behind them, moving slowly, followed servants, yeomen, household officials. Then lumbered the carts full of linens, clothing, beds, plates, musical instruments, vessels to celebrate the Mass, and hundreds of other items the royal household needed.

Before them rode the King and Queen, Hibernia, Agnes and the other gentlewomen, and a gaggle of footmen, grooms and armed men. Impatient, the King charged ahead at break-neck speed, catching the trumpeter heralding their approach. Soon, the monarch was a tiny figure in the distance, dwarfed under a clear blue sky.

The sky did not diminish Justin, she thought, as he pulled his horse up beside hers. The smile she had cherished had disappeared, replaced by a scowl of disapproval as he watched Agnes and Hibernia ride side by side.

'His wife would weep to see them thus,' Justin said. Tired of humiliation, Hibernia's wife stayed in their castle in Essex. 'It sours my stomach.'

'They do no more than the rest of the Court. Why do they disturb you so?' she asked, genuinely curious.

'He violates his vows,' he said, his tone a warning.

Her horse shifted from side to side with each step, and she clung to his mane, hoping she would not fall. 'What wife expects a faithful husband?'

'Mine.' The possession in his voice sent a rush of heat through her.

First he demanded love. Now he promised to be faithful. What kind of man expected such passion within a marriage? Marriage was about property and protection. Passion, if you found it, came outside the marriage bed.

'Then I shall have an unusual life,' she answered, trying to steady her voice. 'Even the poets write odes of love to the wives of other men.'

'Not only will I be faithful, I will demand a faithful wife.'

'Then of course I shall be,' she answered, by rote.

He grabbed the reins and her horse stopped, nearly throwing her out of her seat. 'Do not speak those words lightly.' A breeze whipped strands of his dark hair around his forehead. His eyes held her captive.

A frown creased her brow too quickly for her to stop it. All her efforts to please had failed and still he piled on new demands.

She grabbed back the reins and the horse walked again. Fresh air and an unfamiliar sense of freedom loosened her tongue. 'First, I must convince you of my love. Now, I must be ever faithful. Is there no end of conditions that I must meet?'

Justin raised his eyebrow and studied her. 'If you meet my first condition, the second will be no trial. How could I expect you to be faithful unless you come out of love?'

A flash of longing shook her, a leftover dream of love. 'A lawyer who demands proof of all things. What evidence have you seen of love in marriage?'

A smile softened his hard expression. 'My parents.'

Jealousy sharpened her tongue. 'Your parents were an exception to the rule. My mother's marriage served one purpose and it was not love.'

'How so?'

'You do not know the story? As a legal scholar, you would find it an interesting case, though a lengthy tale.'

'Tell me. The road is long.'

She looked around. The riding household had pulled away. The walking household was falling behind. No one would hear.

'After the King died,' she began, 'Parliament tried her as a *femme sole*, responsible for herself.'

'I know what it means,' he said.

She swallowed her resentment. 'They found her guilty, of course, of some imagined charge.' Telling the tale anew, anger sharpened her voice.

He opened his mouth as if to argue, then shrugged. 'The tale is yours. What then?'

'The sentence was banishment.' Remembered fear gripped her stomach. Her mother, four-year-old Jane and herself, nine, would be abandoned with nothing on a beach in France, at the mercy of predators with four legs. Or two. 'It was at that happy moment that Weston reappeared and claimed her as his wife.'

'Did he have proof?'

'What proof did he need? No one disputed his claim, least of all my mother. As his wife, her life and all she owned was his. Parliament promptly handed him her property and her person. He took the property, we took our lives, and he happily spent everything we had and more before he died.'

It was a fair trade, her mother had always said, without ever revealing whether Weston's appearance had been his idea or hers. Either way, no love had been exchanged.

He shook his head, frowning. 'With such an example, I'm surprised that you want to marry.'

'What else is a woman to do? The only women who do not serve men are those who serve God and even He requires a dowry.' Wife, nun, whore. Those were her choices. 'A woman must please either one man or many.'

He pulled her horse to a stop and leaned forward, his eyes demanding. 'Look at me and understand, Solay. Marriage is no game. Should I choose to wed you, you will please one man and one man only.'

Already she had bared her body, but his gaze demanded something more. It was as if he wanted to expose her secret self, the painful parts she would never share with anyone.

'Marriage is no game to me.' She met his eyes, trying to still her shaking hands. Somehow, she had never truly faced what it would mean, spending her life tied to this man. 'It is a matter of life and death.'

She pulled the reins away and rode on, hoping again that she would be able to escape being wed to this frightening man.

Agnes's laughter floated on the breeze and tickled her ears.

Chapter Fourteen

The next night, in one of the guest rooms of an overfull abbey, Solay lay awake, listening to the snores around her, and puzzled over Justin's words.

One man and one man only.

As a woman, her only weapon was her body. The promise of it was all. Wisely used, concealed and revealed, she could tempt and tease until she got what she needed from any man.

But this one had resisted her as if he knew that the joining itself would cast a spell. As if there were something more to the act than the simple satisfying of need. Of course, she knew the wanting itself made you dizzy, but after that, when the wanting was satisfied, wouldn't that be all?

Next to her, Agnes shifted on the straw mattress.

'Are you awake?' Solay whispered.

'I am now,' she mumbled.

'What's it like with you and… I mean, when you…?' She did not know how to ask the question. 'He has not tired of you?'

'We want each other more each day,' Agnes said with a sigh that could not be healed.

'When you come together, what is it like?'

The straw crunched as Agnes turned on her back. 'When I lie with him, such loving as we have opens up the soul. There is no hiding.'

It was as she had feared. After such a joining, after he plundered her soul as well as her body, she would look in his eyes and see disapproval every morning for the rest of her life.

She pulled the King's cloak, spread over her like a blanket, up to her chin. 'Is there a way to be together without that kind of loving?'

'Oh, yes. That is the way with many marriages.'

Relieved, she turned on her side and pulled the cloak over her shoulder, muttering her goodnight. It was just as she had thought. Should she be forced to wed him, he would leave her bed soon enough to chase comfort elsewhere despite his threats of love and faithfulness. She would be left alone like Hibernia's wife, only meeting her husband on ceremonial occasions.

She ignored the little voice that kept reminding her this man was not like other men.

She had almost met sleep when Agnes's voice trembled beside her.

'Solay? Would you read the stars for me?'

The stars. Her days in the old astrologer's room seemed a lifetime ago. 'The King forbade it.'

Agnes turned over, whispering directly in her ear. 'Because he fears you may foresee his death,' Agnes said, in words she must have heard from Hibernia. 'But I am asking you to read my stars, not the King's.'

You would not ask me if you knew what a fraud I am.

Solay shook her head. 'I am not even a student.'

'Yet you told the King truths.'

'I had the old astrologer's notes.'

'But you found things he had not.'

Only because I was trying to please the King. She was lucky that her deception had stumbled on his real time of birth. 'Besides, the stars only tell of Kings and countries.'

'Please.' Agnes gripped Solay's arm. 'Help me. I love him so much. I must know whether there is any hope. If you look in your book, you might find something.'

In the urgent whisper of the woman who had been her only friend, Solay recognised the desperate need for something to cling to when there were answers nowhere. Hadn't she sought the same from the stars?

Well, what harm if she spun a little hope for Agnes?

'When we reach Nottingham, I'll try.'

Agnes bounced on the straw-stuffed mattress, stifling a squeal of glee. 'Thank you,' she said.

As Agnes's dainty snore began again, Solay lay awake, wondering whether the stars held any hints of hope for her friend.

Or for herself.

Halfway to Nottingham, the King's entourage descended on Beaumanoir Castle, commandeering the comparative luxury for a few days of rest.

Messengers on horseback travelled more swiftly than the King's household, so Justin spent the day reviewing the most recent documents from Westminster, then persuading the King, like a petulant child, to sign the most important.

Solay was never far from his thoughts. The more he knew of her, the less she was what he had imagined. Though he had glimpsed the long-buried, vulnerable child, he had discovered her pliancy hid strength of steel forged by pain and fuelled by anger. No matter how many blows were dealt her, this woman would not give up on life.

Unlike Blanche.

Yet her vision of life after the vows was more barren than

he had ever imagined. All the more reason to avoid being trapped with her.

Despite it all, he looked for a glimpse of her graceful walk as he went about his work and he was relieved at the end of the day when she suggested a game of Merrills.

He was silent while they played, trying to ignore the tantalising whiff of roses every time she reached across the board to move a piece. Before the fire's heat, Solay cast off her cloak to reveal the body he'd been trying to block from his dreams. Firelight highlighted the curve of her breasts and cast shadows in her lap. Desire surged again, but try as he did to blame her, he had to admit that since that night he had rejected her, she'd done nothing to encourage it.

Nothing but exist.

Laughing, Solay scooped up the last of his undefended pieces, besting him again.

He sighed. 'You are the better player tonight.'

'My sister's game sharpened mine.' He was jealous of the warm smile that beamed when she spoke of her sister.

'Tell me about Jane,' he said.

'You would approve of her.' Her gaze was neither guarded nor full of guile. 'She's not afraid to speak her mind to any one.'

'Is she is near an age to wed?'

She rolled a small round Merrills stick between her palms. 'That will be difficult.'

'Why?'

Solay glanced towards the fire.

He regretted the question. It was self-evident that Solay was not considered highly marriageable. It would be no different for her sister.

'I think,' Solay began, 'that Jane would have been happier born a man.'

He frowned. 'It is not so easy to be a man.' Particularly now, when he watched her breasts rise and fall with each breath and struggled to keep his own under control. The fire between them threatened to consume his reason. It warmed him every time he looked in her eyes, scorched him when he touched her hand.

'Neither is being a woman.'

'What makes being a woman so difficult?'

She lifted her brows and stood, acting out the words better than the cleverest jester. 'Jane calls it "mince and curtsy, twitter and cling".' She looked at him over a lifted shoulder with a silly simper, batting her eyes fast enough to blur her lashes.

He laughed. Only one so thoroughly a woman could ridicule her sex so completely. 'And you think your lot is more difficult than a man's?'

She shook her head, serious again. 'It is my nature to be a woman. I cannot imagine being anything else, just as you can only be what you are.'

He heard a trace of judgement in her voice. 'I am a man. What else do you mean?'

Instead of answering, she reached for his hand, running her thumb over the engraved letters of his gold ring. The whisper of her fingers on the back of his hand tempted him more than her fake kisses ever had.

'"Truth conquers all" you said. I think you have no choice but to believe that, even if it isn't true.'

He pulled his hand away.

Every minute with her was a lie. Not only was he hiding his past from her, he was withholding a truth of his present. Whether she ever loved him or not, he wanted her as he had never wanted another woman.

Their moment of closeness vanished along with the false spring. By the time they reached Nottingham, snow chased them across the drawbridge into the castle.

Solay saw little of Justin.

'Probably wandering through the snow, just to watch it fall,' she muttered, peering out of the window. Perched on top of a rock overlooking the city below, the castle caught the full force of the storm. Wind battered the shutters and screamed in the chimneys as it dropped fresh snow below and blotted out the daylight creeping longer into the sky.

Alone in the room she was sharing with Agnes, Solay moved closer to the fire, opened her mother's Book of Hours and stared at the pages.

The table of planets danced down the page, mocking her. Oh, she knew the names of all five planets, the twelve signs, and the twelve houses, but how was she to create meaning from this incomprehensible list?

She spread her paper on a table and traced a square representing Libra, Agnes's birth sign, in the middle of the chart, then added empty triangles on each side, not knowing how to fill them.

One by one, she tried to decipher which planet would go in which house, never sure she was right. In the fading daylight, she squinted at the chart, staring as if she might force meaning to appear.

If she was reading the signs right, there was a change coming in the seventh house. Did that mean marriage, a lawsuit or a war?

Her experience with the King's chart had unsettled her. In the right hands, the stars *could* reveal truth. As she looked at the stubborn square in the middle of Agnes's chart, she fervently wished she had the wisdom to discover it and the courage to tell it.

She shook her head. She had been listening overmuch to Justin. She could spin whatever tale she wanted and Agnes would never dispute it.

'I thought you had abandoned the study of the stars.' Justin's voice leapt from her mind to her ears.

He stood in the doorway, his strong eyebrows shadowing his eyes. She closed the book, but the evidence lay spread before his hostile glance. 'Please tell no one.'

He shook his head. 'Always you give me your secrets to keep.' Yet there was no longer any question that he would keep them. He came closer, stroking the volume's velvet cover, then tracing the silver binding. 'Who do you flatter now?'

'I seek to help a friend.'

He sat on the bench beside her. At his nearness, her breath grew fast and shallow.

'You talk as if you believe you can read the stars. Do you?'

She put the book on her lap, frustrated with her traitorous body. He still believed her use of the stars a ruse. Well, it had been, once, and her fragile hope that she might actually decode the heavens was too new to share. 'The King has forbidden me to read.'

He frowned. 'I did not ask what the King thinks. I asked what *you* believe. Think for yourself instead of parroting what you think others want to hear.'

Not content with the surface smoothness most men craved, he urged her to declare her own beliefs, even—no, especially if they contradicted his, or even the King's. Perhaps he intended to trap her. If he told the King that she'd been reading the stars again, there would be no marriage and no grant. That would suit Justin's purpose.

She tapped her lips with her finger, trying to think.

He dragged her hand away and smothered both hands in his. 'Solay, I asked a question. What do you think about astrology?'

The warmth of his grip travelled from his hands to the centre of her being. He wanted to see the parts she did not dare examine herself. 'What do you want me to think?'

'Whatever misbelief you choose, so long as it is your own.' His hands gripped as tightly as his gaze. 'Just tell me something true.'

Trapped by his hands, dizzy with the scent of cedar, badgered by his questions, she had no escape. 'I don't know what I think!' The words exploded from her. For one moment, they were true.

He squeezed her hands more tightly. 'How can you not know? What you think is who you are!'

'No, it isn't.' She ripped her fingers away from the cradle of his hands and rose, clutching the book like a shield. 'I am what other people think of me. Even you. You asked for something true and I told you, but you will not believe it. You've already decided who I am. Nothing I say or do will change your judgement.'

'That's because you've done nothing but lie.'

She sighed. A lifetime with this man would surely be the Seventh Circle of Hell.

'What is it like to have no doubts that you alone possess the truth?' she whispered in wonder. She could not imagine being that certain, that uncaring for the opinion of the world.

An old ache seemed to fill his weary eyes.

'I am not always right,' he said, finally. The admission seemed dragged through his throat.

'I've never heard you express a doubt,' she said, surprised. 'What opinion do you question?'

'I no longer know whether I am right about you.'

Her heart thumped in her ears 'What do you mean?'

He moved closer and she forced herself not to back away. He did not touch her, but the very air trembled as he studied her face as if seeing it for the first time.

As the fire warmed her back, she studied him. Between his brow, two permanent frown lines carved the immovable stone of his face. Implacable features confronted her: the brooding brow, the sharp curve of high cheekbones, even the cleft slashed into his chin.

He was an inflexible enemy of the King and he hated her, yet when she stood this close, none of that mattered.

'You bow to power,' he said, finally, 'yet in defence of family and friends, you stand strong.'

'And you are stubbornly wed to the illusion that the law creates justice.'

'You are as stubborn as I.'

'You accused me of parroting what others say, hardly the act of a stubborn woman.'

'I begin to think your pliability is a feint. In pursuit of your goal, you stand resolute.'

She heard an echo of warmth and wonder in his voice. For once, instead of making her angry, his words gave her a quiet certainty. 'And you believe in speaking your truth no matter what others say.'

He searched her eyes. 'And I would have the woman who is to be my wife do the same.'

She hesitated. She wanted more. Before she spoke, she wanted to know that he wanted not only to hear the truth, but to accept it.

'Tell me…' he touched her cheek, forcing her eyes to his, yet his voice was gentle '…do you believe you can read the stars?'

His breath brushed her lips.

What would it feel like, to tell the truth? Would the words taste sweet, like honey?

'I believe the stars can illuminate our world,' she began, surprised her throat did not close against the words. Instead, they triggered a rush that washed through her body, cleansing her of fear. 'I do not know whether I have the skill to discover their truths, but I have promised a friend I will try.'

He nodded and let go of her cheek. 'And what will you tell Agnes?'

She did not bother to deny the name of her friend. She had only one. 'Some things she wants to hear and some she does not.' Hibernia might be bad for the King, but Agnes's chart showed coming change.

'Is that a balanced answer meant to please?'

'No. It's the best I know.'

The hard lines around his mouth softened. 'Then I am proud of you.'

The warmth of his approval washed over her. Somehow she had pleased him without trying. She let his words rest in silence, not wanting to spoil this precarious moment of peace. Even the wind had quieted and outside, the snow muffled the world like a warm blanket.

I love you quivered on her tongue.

'Thank you,' she said instead.

'If you can tell Agnes the truth,' he said, 'why can't you be honest with me?'

His words shattered her peace and her fear fluttered free again. He wanted more. More frightening, she wanted to give it to him. To tell him that his condition only encouraged lies. To tell him she wished he would love her, too, just as she was. To tell him—

Putting down the book, she donned her teasing mask. 'I'll do for you what I'm doing for Agnes,' she said, lightly. 'Tell me your day of birth and I'll tell you what the stars say.'

'I have no wish to know.'

He had resisted the question before. She wondered at his reticence. 'It must be St Justin's Day, of course.'

'No.'

She rose to poke a fire already burning merrily. 'Then what day was it your mother remembered so clearly?'

He gritted his teeth and his lips moved, but he remained silent.

'You won't tell me?' She set down the poker and put a hand to her breast in exaggerated disbelief. 'Is there a truth Justin Lamont will not tell?'

She had expected him to smile and answer with the name of his saint's day. Instead, his face turned to stone. 'You have no need to know. We won't be together when my birthday comes.' Without a farewell, he left the room.

She stood unmoving before the fire, staring at the empty doorway. So Justin, too, was hiding something. While he was insisting she reveal herself, what did he fear for her to know?

Stomping around Nottingham's snow-filled inner ward, Justin filled his chest with icy air. He had acted like a petulant child, unable to tell a lie, unwilling to tell the truth. It did not matter whether his birthday was St Michael's, St Luke's or St Ann's. He should just tell her.

But he feared that, if she knew his chart, she could see into his past. Then she would know how unworthy he was.

His campaign to force her into truth was working. Gradually, so gradually, she was revealing more of herself.

God forbid she would ask the same.

No, he must keep her off guard. As long as she had to prove herself to him, he remained in control.

He must keep probing her, yet still make sure she got no closer to him. In just a few weeks, Lent would be over and he could end this betrothal.

What would the King do about her then? Well, that was not his problem. Despite the pain of her past, Solay would survive anything.

If only Blanche had been as strong.

Chapter Fifteen

After being trapped in the castle for days by the storm, Solay smiled to see a clear sky on midweek Market Day. After the main meal, King and Court went to inspect the progress on the new St Mary's Church, leaving the castle strangely empty.

No one asked her to join them.

Restless, she put aside Agnes's chart and wandered the halls, puzzling over Justin's reticence to tell her his birthday. Was he plotting more against the King than she knew?

She was surprised to find him in the Great Hall, staring out of the window at the melting snow. Focused on her own lack of welcome at court, she had forgotten that he would not be embraced either. The King had taken this journey to be surrounded by his favourites and away from the Lords Appellant. In this company, Justin was the outcast.

That, they had that in common.

'I have been trapped inside these walls for days and would see something of the city,' she said. 'Would you accompany me?'

He flashed a lopsided smile. 'Since you have been so forthright as to ask for what you want, I can hardly refuse.'

As they left the castle, melting snow slipped off the walls, splattering like rain. He put a hand on her arm to guide her. Startled, she stiffened, but did not pull away. Then, his warm, ungloved hand moved down to curl around hers.

The market swarmed with activity. Sellers of wood, water, leather and pottery hoped to supply the needs of the castle's hundreds of visitors.

'We shall have to move on soon,' Justin said, as they saw the King's overworked cook bargaining for onions. The Court had nearly exhausted Nottingham's hospitality—and its stores of food.

'Stop that boy!' a voice cried. 'He's a thief!'

A small boy carrying a loaf of bread ran right towards them, the bread seller chasing after. Several in the crowd reached for him, but Justin grabbed the boy's shirt.

Squirming in snow-soaked rags, the boy looked up at him. 'He took my coin, sir, 'n wouldn't gimme my bread.'

Solay touched the lad's shoulder, pleading to Justin with her eyes. It was easy to cheat the powerless. She knew the desperation of an empty stomach. Did Justin?

His stern frown showed no sympathy.

The round-bellied baker, panting, came close and reached for the loaf, but the boy clutched it to his chest. Justin blocked the man's hand, shielding the boy with his cloak.

Seeing the ermine trim on Solay's cloak, the baker recognised he faced members of the King's party. He stepped back and bowed to Justin. 'Thank you, sir, for catching the thief. I will take him to justice.'

Crushed between the boy's skinny arm and his tiny body, the offending loaf was in plain sight.

'Thief? Are you sure?' Justin said. 'We were just talking about the depleted stores for the King's table when the boy grabbed this loaf of yours. Perhaps we should see more of your wares.'

It was all Solay could do to keep her mouth from falling agape. The words, all technically true, spun with a lawyer's ease into a story that was, indeed, a lie.

The bread maker licked his lips. His belligerent expression became obsequious. 'For the King, you say? Well, I make the best bread in Nottingham.'

The crowd that had followed the baker on his chase drifted back to their shopping.

Justin pulled the battered loaf from under the child's arm and held it in his palm, as if assessing its weight. The broken brown crust nearly cut the round loaf in two. 'This seems light. Are you sure it meets the specifications in the Assize of Bread and Beer?'

The bread maker's face sagged. 'Well, yes, I'm— Well, I mean…'

Solay smothered her smile with a cough as the man babbled on. Only Justin would think to threaten the merchant with violating the King's laws regarding weights and measures.

'Well, if you're certain, we can just weigh it to confirm.'

The man put his hands on Justin's shoulders, as if they were old friends. 'No need for that, sir. In case you have any doubt, I'll just give it to you.'

A smile only she recognised twitched at the corner of Justin's mouth. The boy leaned forward, ready to run, but Justin's hands kept him close.

'How generous,' Justin said, 'that would be fair, since you've already received your payment.'

The man paled and backed away, his eyes never leaving Justin. 'You'll find it good bread and a fair weight.' He pointed to a booth with a green banner fluttering. 'Come to my stall and you'll find many others, all fit for the King's table.'

As the baker escaped, Justin turned the boy around, keeping his shoulder firmly in his grip.

The child's round eyes held both fear and worship. 'Thank you, sir.' His voice trembled a little and he licked his lips, looking at the lost loaf. 'I hope the King enjoys his bread.'

Justin handed back the dented bread. 'I think you will enjoy it more.'

Blinking with astonishment, the child finally had the courage to smile. 'Blessings on you.'

'Next time I shall not be here to save you.'

The boy clenched his fist, ready to fight again. 'But he cheated me!'

Justin crouched down and looked the boy squarely in the eye. 'I know he was wrong, but that doesn't give you the right to steal, even to get what is rightfully yours.'

The boy hung his head. 'Yes, sir,' he mumbled.

'Do you have a mother?'

The boy nodded.

'Then give her this.' Justin stood and dug out a coin. 'And tell her to buy some good wool, ale and a goose.'

The child knelt in the snow and clutched Justin's hands in thanks, then ran, bread in one hand, coin in the other.

Solay watched wide-eyed, uncertain whether the Justin she knew still stood beside her. 'You let him go?'

Justin shrugged and they turned back towards the castle. 'The man cheated him. The boy made it even and no more. It was just.'

'But the law would have said both were wrong,' she said, puzzled. 'I thought you would take both to trial.'

He stopped walking to look at her, his eyes showing a sense of astonishment that she could not see the obvious answer. 'Who would believe the boy?'

It was on the tip of her tongue to taunt him with the proof that power was stronger than the law, when she realised what he had done. 'It isn't just about the law for you, is it? It truly is about justice.'

He tilted his head, as if not understanding her words. 'Did you think otherwise?'

She no longer knew what to think about Justin Lamont. Was he a man of the law who would do nothing not written in the law? Or was he simply using the law to mete out his own idea of justice?

'What will you tell the King?' His matter-of-fact question assumed she would tattle of all that had happened.

She lifted her chin and met his eyes. 'The King has no interest in a stolen loaf of bread.'

His lopsided smile was her reward.

Solay's words burrowed into Justin's brain as they walked back to the castle and the setting sun turned the horizon gold.

It truly is about justice.

The amazement in her voice stung him. 'Did you really think me such a monster as to punish an innocent boy?'

She tilted her head. 'You pride yourself as the caretaker of the law's letter. I thought you would do no less.'

His father would have. His father would have punished them both. 'I did what was fair.'

Her eyes, painfully violet as the early evening sky, searched his face. He met her gaze, surprised to discover he wanted his answer to please her. How had it come to this? She was supposed to earn his approval, not make him long for hers.

'How do you decide when to substitute your judgement for that of the law?'

He opened his mouth to say 'never', but then remembered one time, maybe two, like today, when the situation was so obviously wrong—

Startled, he snapped his jaw shut. Life had been easier when she merely flattered him. 'Those occasions are extremely rare.'

'You made a decision about the boy based on your concept of what was right. Would you apply the same to your work for the Council?'

Unease prickled the base of his spine. The King might not be interested in a loaf of bread, but he would be very interested in the Council. 'Parliament has given us full authority.' More than that, Parliament had passed a law prohibiting anyone to disagree with what the Council did.

'But if you can substitute your justice for the law's, what is the difference between you and the King who substitutes his justice for yours?'

'I care about what's right,' he said, in tones too close to a mumble. 'The King cares only about his own power.'

They entered the castle and he pulled her into a sheltered alcove, trying to read her eyes. Her body tempted him and this time, he did not fight it. He wanted to reassert his power. Perhaps if he kissed her, he would know whether his words had turned her towards or against him.

He took the kiss without asking, not caring who might see them, wanting to reach something in her core.

Remembering her bare skin caressed by firelight, he hardened with want. He teased her lips with his tongue, wanting to taste all of her, wanting—

She stiffened in his arms, her lips tight as the night of their Yuletide kiss. He tightened his grip, pressed closer, but this time, she did not surrender.

He released her, relieved. If she ever truly surrendered, she would conquer him totally.

He cleared his throat and pulled his tunic back into place. 'You're upset.'

'Not upset. I'm…' She pursed her lips and smoothed her skirt. 'Confused.'

'So you will not kiss me.'

'I do not know you.'

'What I did about the boy today—it was right.'

'I know,' she said. 'But it was not the law.'

That night, her words haunted him as much as the memory of her body melting, just for a moment, against his. Why, after weeks of temptation, had she resisted him? Puzzling over that question kept him from wondering why, after weeks of resistance, he had tried to take her.

Waiting for sleep that would not come, he remembered lying in bed as a child, hearing his mother and father whisper in the bed next door. Her steady, loving voice had always soothed his father, when the judge's pronouncements began to sound like Moses's. Only his mother had been able to make him see another point of view.

After she died, there was no one to temper his judgements.

Now, he faced a woman who challenged everything he held dear, who would gleefully see him clapped in irons if it were the King's whim to do so. In probing his compassion for the boy, she had made him reveal a weakness that would undoubtedly reach his Majesty's ears.

He rolled over, pounding the feather pillow that gave disappointingly little resistance, cursing his candid tongue.

Her question had challenged him to be true to the words he had used to taunt her. Law. Truth. Justice.

He rolled out of bed and threw open the shutters, welcoming the cold air. He stared at the stars she so loved. Solay thought she might bring meaning to them. Could she do the same for him?

He pulled the shutters, closing out the sky. Lent was half over. The King's question would come soon.

There was only one answer he must give.

Chapter Sixteen

Solay loitered in the corridor outside Justin's room, listening to the voices, trying to understand the messenger's words.

The man had arrived, empty handed. His message must have been too important to commit to writing.

She bent closer to the floor, hoping some words would slip under the door. The King's urgency to know Justin's business had become her own. Despite Justin's prideful honesty, he had been tightlipped about his work since London.

Perhaps his justice and the law had parted ways.

She had known from the first that he opposed the King, but she never thought he would go beyond the law. If true, she must resist the tug of feeling he sparked in her. When he kissed her, she had fought the desire that welled within her, strangely grateful that he had left them an escape, that she was not tied to him yet. If he could lie about the law, could his kiss lie as well?

She retreated down the hall as she heard the men's farewells. Strolling towards the room as if she had just arrived, Solay smiled at the messenger as he left, then stood in the doorway, waiting for Justin to invite her in.

He didn't.

'What news did he bring?' she said, finally, ready to try the honest questions Justin claimed to prefer.

'I will tell the King myself if he needs to hear it.'

'The news might interest the King. Particularly if it concerns treason.'

His eyes darkened. 'Treason is no jest.'

Her heart pounded in her ears. He had not denied it. 'And that is not an answer.'

He leaned back, looking at her. 'Do you even know what treason is?'

'Yes, I do.' She smiled with relish, not needing to pretend. 'My father's law was clear on this. There are seven offences.' Her mother had drilled them into her head. There was a time her mother had needed to know. 'I shall list them for you. First, killing the King, the Queen, or his heir. Second—'

'Actually, it is "if a man compasses or imagines the death of the king".'

She nodded at his correction. 'Yes, even the planning is treason. But if imagining the death of a King is treason, how are we to prove it?'

'And how many might be guilty?'

Are you? She bit back the question and continued. 'Second, killing the Chancellor, Treasurer or Justice while he is attending to his duties. This implies that killing the Chancellor while he is hunting boar would not be treason.'

'Legally correct, Lady Solay.' His eyebrows raised in surprise. 'For someone who protests she knows nothing about the law, you seem well versed in its vagaries.'

'Only of this one.' She fought back a satisfied smile. 'Next, violating the Queen, the eldest unmarried Princess, or the wife of the heir.' Her mother had noted, jealously, that there was no treason in bedding the King's mistress. 'But if the Princess marry, there is no treason in bedding her.'

He frowned. 'You have the mind of a lawyer. It is a shame you haven't the heart of one.'

'I never knew a lawyer who had a heart.' *Until you.*

She recited the rest until she came to the worst. 'And finally, making war against the King or giving aid and comfort to his enemies.'

'The last recourse of lawlessness,' he said, then tilted his head in a bow of respect. 'You *do* know the meaning of the word. I trust you do not accuse the Council.'

'The Lords Appellant on the Council are men like any others.' Gloucester's jealousy, coupled with his royal blood, might lead him to aspire to the throne and bring along the others who hoped for their reward. 'I do not know what they might think or do.'

'But you know me.' He rose, forcing her to look up at him.

'Do I?' She searched his eyes. In all she had learned of this stubborn, impossible man, she would have sworn he would do nothing outside the letter of the law.

Until the boy.

'You know the law and all its tricks,' she said. 'The King takes you for an enemy.'

His grim smile brought no light to his eyes. 'Then do not fear for your life, Lady Solay. You have given me neither aid nor comfort.'

Turning his back, he returned to his papers.

She stood, watching him for a long time. Perhaps if she could look in his eyes again, perhaps if she could make him smile, then she might know his heart.

He did not turn.

What if the subpoena was just the beginning? What if he planned something worse? What would she do then?

* * *

The King summoned her to his chambers late in the day. She sank to her knees before him and acknowledged Hibernia with a nod.

'Well?' The King paced the room as rapidly as he galloped his horse. 'What happened today?'

'There was a messenger.'

'The gatekeeper could tell me so much.'

The red velvet cloak, the crackling fire, none of it warmed her icy fingers. She did not want to betray Justin, but if he planned treason, she could not stand by. 'I think he came from London.'

'What message did he bring?' the King snapped.

Anything I tell you will go straight to the King's ears. So, of course, she'd cajoled the answer directly from the messenger. 'He said the document was ready.'

'The subpoena?' The King was exasperated.

'The messenger did not say, Your Majesty. He brought nothing with him but the words in his head.'

'Whose name is on it?' Hibernia asked.

She looked at him and her heart squeezed for Agnes. 'I do not know.'

She would tell them later, in time for the Duke to escape. If she told too much too soon, it would be Justin at risk. Surrounded by the King's men, he could easily meet his death from an unfortunate accident and no one could prove otherwise.

'He's a traitor, I tell you,' the King muttered.

In his mouth, the words became a hangman's noose. Despite her suspicions, she did not want him dead. 'Surely not, Your Majesty.'

The King's scowl didn't fade. 'Find out what he plans. I'll decide whether it be treason.' He waved a hand to dismiss her.

She bowed her head and backed towards the door.

The King's voice followed her. 'The messenger from Rome will be waiting in Cheshire?'

'If the weather favours his journey,' Hibernia said.

'And the Pope our plea.' The King sighed. 'I am forced to deal with clerks to do what should be done on my word.'

Nodding at the guard, she lowered her eyes, pretending she had not heard.

What plea had the King made to the Holy Father?

When Agnes asked for the room to herself that night, Solay could not refuse. The King and Hibernia were leaving the castle tomorrow and Agnes longed for one night with her lover.

'You say you envy me,' Solay said, 'but I envy you. You have some happiness, even if just for the moment.'

'I may have even more than that,' Agnes answered, then hugged her. 'Thank you.'

A muffled knock announced Hibernia. He took Agnes in his arms, barely glancing at Solay as she left the room.

Agnes's moan followed Solay into the hall through the closed door. Desperate to escape the sound, she staggered down the dark corridor, but still it resonated, triggering a buzz of desire. Desire, that was all. Not love, nay, surely not that fickle, weak, emotion.

But desire, desire was not weak. Relentless, it gnawed at her resistance, conjured carnal dreams, and undermined her attempts to lead him on without losing herself.

She slumped against the wall, eyes closed, held captive by the growls and shrieks and gasps of love. What would it be like, that joining that seemed to wipe out everything else?

'What goes on there?'

She opened her eyes to see Justin, as if her wanting had created him.

He took her in his arms. 'Are you all right?'

Crushed against his chest, her breasts ached to feel his hands. His head dipped. Did his lips brush her hair?

The sounds of Agnes and Hibernia in heat echoed off the cold stone.

He lifted his head. She braced herself against his chest to stop him. 'Nay, you must not enter.'

An unmistakable squeal of feminine pleasure shook the walls. His arms tightened around her. 'You pander for them?'

'Why do you begrudge them their happiness?'

'Because he dishonours his wife. When we are wed, would I see you dally with every man who crossed your path?'

Amidst her dizziness, she heard *when we are wed*. 'No.'

'How can I believe you?' His breath, hot on her cheek, warred with his cold words.

He was hard with wanting. She was weak with it.

Once, she thought she would say anything to snare him. Now, she would do anything to keep him. No logic, no clever words could triumph over her body's truth.

She tipped her head back to meet his eyes. She steadied her voice. 'You are the first.'

He crushed his lips to hers.

And if a voice in her head whispered 'traitor', she did not listen.

She had always believed that woman tempted man, yet her treacherous body, urged on by the rhythmic sounds beyond the door, curved into his. There was nothing left in the world but quenching the thirst he raised in her.

'Now.' A word. A gasp.

She was not certain who spoke it.

Unyielding stone met her back and the night air still held a hint of snow, yet she pulled up her skirts gladly, baring her flesh to his searching hands.

He seemed equally wild, pushing his breeches down past

his knees, then straddling her. He was above her now and she missed the closeness of his hard, tender kiss, but the itch between her legs was more urgent. He teased her gently and she rocked, no longer in control of her mind or her body. Did all lovers feel this? No wonder it drove men mad.

And mad he seemed now, his lips close to her ears, his breath like another caress. And she could not tell whether the moan she heard was Agnes's or her own.

She started to spiral, empty, longing for him inside but consumed by what he was doing to that sweet, secret place. She was almost there, twisting, spinning to what? Her lips opened as if she could nearly—

Abruptly, he stopped.

She cried out at the sudden loss. Stripped of her clothes and his body, she dragged herself up against the wall and opened her eyes. He sat back on his heels, staring at the floor, clenched fist pounding his thigh.

Only one word fought its way to her tongue. 'Why?'

His chest heaved as if he had fought a great battle. 'You tease both of us too much, Joan of Weston.'

She sagged, unable to think, belly burning with a sort of hatred. It was not enough that she had begged him on her knees. He had used her desire to drag her to humiliation again.

She pulled her knees to her chest and covered her legs with her skirt, trying to catch a breath that was not a sob. 'You cannot blame me. You want me, too.'

He nodded, and when he met her eyes again, his looked sad, not cruel. 'I want more than a body.'

'More?' All the hot, wild feelings that had fluttered below her waist gathered in her throat. 'What more do you want?' He disdained her mother. Royal blood did not awe him. She brought no dowry. 'I am nothing. I have nothing except the body you've so forcefully refused.'

He shook his head and she closed her eyes against his pity. It had sounded so easy, to bare her body. Yet this frightening, immovable man had stripped her soul, then found it lacking. His bullying demands for honesty had ripped away the armour that shielded her from the world's scorn. Now, her heart lay naked, veiled by not so much as the thin linen that covered her nipples.

His fingers brushed her forehead, pushing aside the hair that had fallen across her face gently, as if the fury of the last few minutes had never been. 'Until you know who you are, you cannot love anyone else.'

She pulled her head away, angry at his insinuation. 'You know who I am. You have known from the first.' *Harlot's daughter.* Words too painful to speak. Would anyone ever look at her and see neither a harlot nor a princess, but simply a woman? 'That was what this tumble was about. For you to prove you were right.'

He shook his head, his eyes patient and sad. 'That's not true and you know it.'

'Do I?' She lifted her head, gritting her teeth to hold back the bile. She was the daughter of a King. She would not grovel. 'You are the one who claims to know all truth. Tell me what it is, then.'

Justin did not answer. At some point while they had grappled, Agnes and Hibernia had quieted and silence loomed, filling the hall.

She watched, shocked, as he seemed to be unable to speak, as if the truth were as hard for him as for other mortals. Unsteady, he rose to his feet and pulled up his breeches and hose, avoiding her eyes.

Finally, he faced her. 'The truth is this. If you knew me, you would want this marriage no more than I.'

He did not wait for her answer, but walked away, fist clenched. The flickering torchlight glinted off his gold ring.

Truth conquers all.

She hugged her knees and dropped her head. Truly, if she loved a traitor, the truth would defeat them all.

Chapter Seventeen

A few days later, Solay looked at Agnes's hopeful, round face and then at the chart spread between them on the bed. The King and Hibernia had gone to Lincoln so she could give Agnes's reading without fear of discovery.

If only she could decide what to say.

Despite her lack of training, the outlines were clear. The house of relationship was full of passion and there were signs of great upheaval. Was this change to come, or the upheaval when Agnes came from Bohemia with the Queen?

Just tell the truth, Justin would say. Yet while he spoke of truth he had hidden it as well. Since that night, they had not spoken a word.

Agnes clasped her hands, squeezing her laced fingers until her knuckles turned white.

'Please, proceed,' she said, with the slight quiver around the 'r'. 'You've found something good, yes?'

'Well, perhaps—'

'I knew it!' She bounced on the bed, giddy with happiness.

Solay's good intentions evaporated. If she stretched the truth to give her friend a little happiness, what harm could there be in that?

Agnes leaned forward, eager as a child for a Yuletide treat. 'What do the stars say?'

She gathered Agnes's hands in hers. 'I see a great change in your house of relationships.'

'So we are to be together?' Agnes held her breath as if her very life hung on the answer.

Solay nodded. It was not exactly a lie.

Agnes's eyes filled with tears and she stood up, tugging against Solay's hold. 'I can't wait to tell him.'

Solay tightened her grip, holding the girl back. 'No! You mustn't. The King forbade me to read. The Duke has no secrets from the King.'

'But he will be so happy. He will make the King forgive you.'

Solay jerked her to a standstill. 'Please. It would go ill for me. Just know in your heart that all will be for the best.' A vain hope, but all she could say.

'It will work, then,' Agnes whispered to herself. 'I had not believed it.'

She released Agnes and watched the girl twirl happily around the room, envying her joy. Perhaps for some, perhaps for Agnes, love was possible.

Until Justin's subpoena reached him and Agnes might find her lover on trial.

There it was, right before her, the disaster warned of in the stars. She had kept the information from the King, but Agnes was her friend.

Was she certain that Hibernia was named? Certain enough to tell Agnes? If she did, what would happen to Justin?

Agnes hummed and giggled, suffused with happiness beyond what Solay had ever imagined.

No, no need to tell Agnes anything yet.

'Oh, Solay, it will be so wonderful! The Pope will say yes and then we'll—' She bit her lip. 'I can tell you no more.'

If the Pope favours our plea. Could the messenger the King was expecting have something to do with Agnes?

Agnes knelt before her, eyes teary with joy. 'I will make certain you are rewarded when all this is over.'

Solay answered with a rueful smile. 'You could suggest to Hibernia that the King would be better served if I married someone other than Justin.'

Agnes nodded. 'Don't worry. The King will find you someone else. I'll make sure of that.'

Someone else. Someone who didn't hate her. Someone who didn't make her weak with desire.

She thanked Agnes and, as they hugged, waited in vain for a feeling of relief. Instead, she remembered a line she'd seen written in the old astrologer's notes.

The stars speak in riddles that we interpret as we wish, never seeing the true meaning until the time has passed.

Until it would be much too late.

The King and the Duke returned the following week. Hibernia approached her after the main meal and asked her to walk with him. Justin's frown and Agnes's smile followed them into the corridor.

Solay waited for him to speak. Dark and slender, the Duke was a perfect foil for the King's fair splendour. A small and merry mouth perched under a straight and handsome nose. Perpetually raised brows topped light brown eyes, ever moving.

She saw in him neither the threat that Justin did, nor the passion that Agnes did. He was, simply, a man.

'Agnes tells me you have been a good friend,' he said.

'And she to me, your Grace.'

'She tells me you want a different husband.'

She hoped Agnes had not put it so bluntly. 'The King's

wishes are mine. I simply hope my husband will feel the same loyalty to him that you and I do.'

'You speak of loyalty, yet you disobeyed his express orders not to study the stars.'

All heat left her body. Beneath the covers, lovers have no secrets. Well, too late to deny it. 'I read only hers, not the King's.'

'Ah, but in reading hers you read mine and in reading mine you read the King's more than you know.'

'I meant no harm.' The King might banish her from court, or worse, for such disobedience. 'Please—'

Hibernia held up a hand, smiling. 'Worry not. I can keep secrets that Agnes cannot. You gave her the courage to accept me.'

She murmured her thanks, certain again of one truth she had always known. Nothing was more powerful than a woman's words, whispered in darkness.

'When Lamont rejects you, who would you like the King to choose?'

Relief warred with a pang of loss. She struggled to picture the Earl of Redmon, but Justin's image rose instead. Surely after the betrothal was broken she would want another man. 'The King's choice shall be mine.'

A smile played on his lips. 'Of course it will. We would not tie such a faithful friend to an enemy. And you need not worry about garnering any more information from Lord Justin. We've taken care of that.'

She took no comfort in the thought.

After supper, Solay approached Justin for the first time in days, carrying the Merrills board as a crutch.

Easter was little more than a fortnight away. Assured that the King would find her another husband, she no longer needed to curry Justin's favour. Besides, there was no doubt Justin would reject her.

Was there?

She must be sure of his mind. That was the reason she sought him out. The only reason.

'Easter comes soon,' she said, after losing the third game in a row. She would be glad to be free of Justin, yet huddled over the board, her body warmed with desire and something more she refused to name.

'And this long disguising will be over.'

She pursed her lips against unwelcome disappointment. Over the weeks, she had donned fewer disguises with him. He might not believe she loved him, but had he not noticed something different about her?

She lifted her chin. 'I am not the same person that I was at Twelfth Night. Don't you agree?'

'What I think is not important. It's what you think of yourself.'

'You play word games.' She slammed the leftover pieces down on the board, angry that he had noticed no difference in her and angrier that she cared. 'It is what *you* think and whether *you* can be convinced that I love you that is in question. It is evident that you cannot.'

His dark eyebrows rose and he blinked, for once speechless.

How appalling she had let her tongue run free. She wanted him to reject her, but she should not sound angry about it. 'Forgive me. I should not have spoken thus.'

'Do you think I will leave if you anger me?'

She drank in his obstinate gaze and the stubborn set of his narrow lips, memorising him for later. She might not love him as he wanted, but she felt something for him she hadn't weeks ago.

She wanted to believe in this man, to believe he would

cleave to the law despite the temptation to turn traitor, to believe in choices beyond those made by the stars.

'I think,' she said, rising, 'that you will leave no matter what I do.' Truth, it seemed, tasted of rue as well as honey. 'Because the one thing that has not changed is the one thing I cannot change.'

'Solay.' The word echoed with agony so deep that it stopped her.

'Yes?' she whispered.

Pain etched lines around his mouth and eyes. 'I am sorry. The other night.' Each word seemed pulled from him like a stone. 'I should not have treated you thus.'

She blinked back tears. 'Thank you.'

'The faults are not all yours. They are mine.'

A pretty lie meant to soothe, she thought. Had she taught him something after all?

They walked towards her room together in silence.

'Justin…' she began, then held her breath. He must know that the King's sword was at his back. Glancing around, she saw no one near. She leaned to whisper in his ear, as if giving him a goodnight kiss. 'Be careful. The King watches you. He needs no help from me.'

'But he will get it anyway, won't he?' he whispered back.

Pride straightened her spine and she looked at him. 'No. And the pity is, you do not understand that.'

She closed the door on him, unable to say more. Listening to his fading footsteps, she sighed, relieved this would all be over soon.

Liar.

You didn't tell him you loved him because you were afraid you would have to marry him. Better to find some other man, one who will only require your body and, later, not even that.

Someone who won't care who stares back at you from the mirror each morning.

She skewered the fire with a poker, then picked up Agnes's ivory-backed mirror, peering at the image for reassurance.

Let's be honest, my dear. What do you see when you look at yourself?

And the reflection in the glass seemed blank.

Justin grimaced against the raw wind as the King led his boar-hunting party to Sherwood Forest. Even after Solay's warning, he was surprised when Richard had ordered him to join the party.

The wind stung no more than the memory of Solay's honest outburst. For once, there was no question of how she felt. Well, that's what he had wanted, wasn't it? He could release her, confident that at least he'd taught her something about honesty.

And, he must grudgingly admit, she had taught him something as well. He had wielded the truth as a weapon, trying to keep her away from the things he wanted no one to know.

But her forthright warning had confused him. Had she developed some loyalty to him after all?

His disagreeable mood soured at the sight of a phalanx of unfamiliar knights sporting the badge of the white hart. A King should ride with the trusted barons of his Kingdom, not a collection of random knights.

As the fewterers let the greyhounds loose, Richard galloped ahead to confront the boar alone. Lacking battle credentials, the King was ever eager to prove his courage.

One thrust of the tusk and a boar could split a man in two. Even a King.

Fighting the low-hanging branches, Justin and the rest of the party charged after him, following the barks and squeals.

What would happen to the throne if the childless King were careless enough to get killed by a wild boar?

The thought slapped him like the leaves. If he wondered, Gloucester had, too. He would be all too willing to take his nephew's seat. This was not Parliament's plan for the Council, but was it Gloucester's?

As they broke into the clearing, Richard stood crowing over the dying boar, impaled on the spear. As the horses stamped the soil and the pages' lips turned blue, the animal heaved his last breath on the damp ground, his entrails staining the fading snow.

Justin turned his horse away. A useless kill. They would eat Lent herring tomorrow. Once again the King had wasted coin, even life, for his own amusement. Because he wanted to. Because he could.

Because he was the King.

The party had left the pages to truss the boar. On the way back to the castle, the King, rosy and smiling, brought his horse beside Justin's.

'I understand you are an expert in the definition of treason,' Richard said, finally.

Did every word he said to her reach the King's ear? 'I have studied the law. I know the definitions in all the Statutes.'

'And have you advised the Council on treason?'

He looked sharply at the man. 'The Council needs no advice in this matter. Nothing we do is treasonable.'

'And what about treason not covered in the Statute? What do you advise the Council about that?'

Treason is no jest, he had warned her. But reckless, she had put him in the path of the King's wrath, as surely as the dead boar. 'There is no treason if the law does not name it.'

'Justices on the bench decide that, not words on parchment.'

'But the Justices are sworn to uphold the law.'

The sinister expression turned petulant. 'Why must you fight me on all things?' Richard whined like Justin's six-year-old nephew struggling against bedtime.

'I do not fight you, Your Majesty. There is no conflict between the law and the King.'

'Exactly!' The King's whoop caused his horse to break stride as the castle came into view. 'God anoints the King, so I am the law! Only when all men unite in allegiance to me can there be peace in the realm.'

Suddenly, Justin saw Richard as if for the first time. Here was a man who truly believed he carried the entire realm on his slender shoulders. But the mortar of allegiance must bind to more than a man, else the country would be no more than a collection of warring tribes.

And he knew the King did not understand this, nor did he have the wisdom to learn it. The centre of earthly power while still a boy, he saw a world that had always revolved around his wishes.

'Your Majesty, even a King cannot breach God's law.'

A thin, satisfied smile lingered on Richard's lips. 'You might be surprised what a King can do.'

Justin cleared his throat. 'I have learned not to let Your Majesty surprise me.'

'So what do you think of your bride now, Lamont?' the King said, after a pause. 'Do you not long to have her in your bed? Or have you had her already?'

The vision of her, half-naked on the stone floor, rose before him. He still did not know how he had found the strength to resist her, but Richard's insinuation angered him. 'She will not share my bed unless, and until, we are wed.'

A page helped the King down from his horse. 'Well then, reject her. I shall find her another husband.'

Justin gripped the reins so tightly his horse jerked his head. Wasn't that what he wanted? To be rid of her? 'Not yet, Your Majesty.' Was it jealousy moved his tongue? He resented the King's interference in what had become a more complicated relationship than he had ever planned. 'Until Easter, she is mine.'

And suddenly, the weeks that had stretched endlessly to Easter seemed short, and, instead of being relieved, he glimpsed all the days afterwards, stretching forwards empty without her.

Chapter Eighteen

The riotous morning chorus of birds woke Solay on Easter day before sunrise. Their frantic chirping settled in her blood, whether in anticipation or dread, she was not sure.

Lent was over. Today, after the Easter festivities, she would be released.

Yet until then, they must act betrothed. Justin walked her to the church and sat beside her at the Mass. All the words blurred except those he spoke. Afterwards, at the feast, the long-awaited bite of beef and bacon from their shared trencher tasted no different from yesterday's red herring. Her saffron-yellow decorated egg and Justin's pale green one looked no better than Hibernia's, covered with gold leaf.

Justin's eyes never left her, asking questions his tongue did not.

Just a few more hours and he would release her. Of course he would. She had given up trying to please him.

When the page summoned them, she was surprised to feel Justin's hand take hers, his ring a hard wedge between her fingers.

Truth conquers all.

She gripped his hand, stopping outside the King's chambers, suddenly unsure. 'Tell me. What will you say?'

Something, not quite a smile, tipped his lips. 'What will *you* say?'

Mute, she tried to read the face that had become dear to her, but she caught no hint of what he wanted her to say.

Except that her hand still lay in his.

With a twinge of disappointment, Justin realised she had stopped trying to change his mind. She had not said words of love in weeks, even when he had given her the chance. He didn't know whether she had lost the desire to convince him or simply the hope that she would, but he would play this to the end and force an honest answer.

Yet his palm itched to stroke the dark hair drifting over her breast, to push it over her shoulder and then cradle her head and draw her lips to his.

'Now,' interrupted the page. 'His Majesty awaits.'

She tugged against his hand, but he would not release her as they entered the King's solar.

The King barely glanced at them. 'Lamont, since the Lady Solay has not met your condition, I release you from this betrothal.'

Beside him, she sighed and closed her eyes. Relief or regret?

'Not yet, Your Majesty. The Lady Solay and I are betrothed until and unless I release my condition. You must at least ask her the question.'

Her head had snapped up. He tightened his grip on her hand and she turned to him, amethyst eyes full of something he could not decipher. Pain? Hope? Was she thinking of him or of the Earl of Redmond?

Richard sighed, exasperated. 'So tell us, Lady Solay, do you love him as he demands?'

'I have already told Lord Justin of my feelings.'

What had she told him? That she lusted for him. That he angered her. That she had changed.

But when he asked her one final time, she had not lied and said she loved him.

'What kind of answer is that?' the King said.

A small smile twisted Justin's lips. 'An honest one.'

The King waved his hands to hurry them to the expected conclusion. 'Lent is over, Lamont. Your time is up. Do you believe she loves you? Will you have her to wife? Yes or no?'

She gripped his hand. Behind her eyes, he recognised pain, fear, and something else he couldn't quite capture.

With just a word, he could be free.

'Yes.'

Speechless and numb, Solay loosened her grip on his hand, strangely disappointed, because she had come to know the cadence of Justin's voice.

And she knew that he was lying.

Chapter Nineteen

'Lady Solay, what say you?' The King's eyes shifted between Solay and Justin. 'You must both consent freely for the marriage to be valid.'

Solay stammered, not knowing what to say. For once, she could not decipher Justin's expression.

'Yes' lay between them like a gauntlet.

She looked frantically towards the door, hoping to see Hibernia. Why was he not with them? Had he truly arranged with the King for her to wed another? Perhaps this question was the King's way of letting her escape.

Justin released her hand and she nearly stumbled. Arms crossed, he looked down at her. 'Solay, the time has come to speak of what *you* want.'

What she wanted. As if her desires were important. She suppressed a disgusted shake of her head. What would it feel like to care, as Justin did, only for your own opinion? If she displeased the King, it would not matter that she pleased herself. Unless Solay found a protector, not only she, but her mother and sister, would have nothing.

The King drummed impatient fingers on the arm of his

chair. If she threw away this man, he might not give her another.

Keep both men happy, her mother had said. She couldn't satisfy even one of them.

'It shall be as the King wishes,' she said, bobbing a curtsy towards his bent head.

'No.' Justin grabbed her arms and turned her to face him, ignoring King and protocol. 'It shall be as *you* wish. What say you, Lady Solay? *You* must choose what you want.'

She leaned into his strength, surrounded by the familiar scent of wood and ink. Until now, another husband had been a vague idea, but, faced with the prospect of another man, it seemed impossible that Justin should disappear from her side. She knew the feel of his fingers guiding her elbow, knew the sound of his step on the stairs, understood his favourite opening gambit at Merrills and how to beat it.

Beside him, her traitorous body yearned for the heat they shared and for something more. Lifting her eyes to his dark, demanding gaze, she lost her grip on time and space. Dizzy as when she watched the snowflakes, she clung to him, knowing that if this warmth were ripped away, nothing would ever be the same.

And in that moment, she lost herself.

'Yes. I want to marry you.'

Justin released her and the spinning room righted itself. A smile cracked his face without reaching his eyes.

'You have made your choice, Lady Solay,' the King said. 'Live with the consequences.'

And she wondered whether any of them had chosen what they wanted.

She walked out beside Justin. He did not reach for her hand.

'Why?' she asked, when they were out of the King's hearing. 'Why did you lie? I never said I loved you. You trapped me.'

'Trapped? Oh, no, my Lady Solay. The choice was yours.'
She could not read his face. 'Did you not speak your mind?'

Caught between the King and Justin, she had blurted something. And she was terribly afraid it had been the truth.

'How could this happen?' Agnes moaned, as she and Solay
packed to leave Nottingham. 'It was settled. Now the King is
angry with Hibernia and Hibernia is angry with me.'

The impatient King had decided they would be wed before
they left Nottingham to return to Windsor. Richard was honouring them with his presence and gifting her with a new
gown for the occasion. With the King as witness, their
marriage would never be plagued with the doubts that followed
her mother and Weston. They would be bound through eternity.

Agnes sighed. 'Why didn't you trust me?'

Solay gritted her teeth. There had never been anyone she
could trust before. 'The Duke wasn't there. I wasn't sure.'

Agnes blushed. They both knew where the Duke had been.
The room had reeked of lovemaking when Solay returned.

'It is all Justin's fault,' Agnes said, pouting.

Solay shook her head. 'No, the fault is mine. I made the
choice.' She could blame neither Justin nor the King nor
even the stars.

'So you do love him. If you do, then it will all work out
somehow.' Agnes, addled by her own romance, seemed
willing to believe that love was an excuse for anything.

Yet what was she to call simultaneous comfort and distress
that gripped her in his presence? Her mother had been right.
Unruly want had made her weak. Her body had answered the
question. Now, her heart and her mind had to deal with the
consequences. 'Not the way he wants.'

Agnes gripped Solay's hands. 'If it does not work out, you
could still find a new husband.'

She shook her head. 'Even a King cannot break God's law.'

Agnes waved her hand in the King's gesture of dismissal. 'There are ways. On the wedding night, if he can't…well, then you wouldn't have to…'

Solay laughed at the absurd suggestion, her cheeks hot. Giddiness and terror warred at the thought of bedding him at last. 'I certainly believe he can.'

'Ah, but the witnesses will look for proof.'

It would not be hard to wave a bloodstained sheet. 'He will be my first, Agnes,' she whispered.

One man and one man only. What would that be like?

As Agnes hugged her, Solay smiled. Now that they were to be married, he would not refuse her bed. Even if he hated her, her body might find a way to rule his.

And she might expose his heart, without risking her own.

As the wedding banquet stretched endlessly past sunset, Justin sat next to his bride, wondering how he had got here. He had vowed never to marry, yet the stars seemed to have aligned against him.

Since he and Solay had left the King's chamber, Justin had tried to answer the question she had asked.

Why?

He didn't want to answer. Wasn't sure he could. Hadn't known he would say 'yes' until they stood before the King and he faced losing her to a man whose previous wife had conveniently fallen down the stairs to her death.

So out popped the word. Misplaced chivalry coupled with a final effort to force Solay to choose what *she* wanted.

Still, her choice surprised him. Had she spoken truly? Perhaps he was the one who should be asking 'why'? She must have been desperate to provide her family with the security of a marriage. Or perhaps she had heard the rumours about the Earl's wife.

And only one thing had surprised him more than her choice. His reaction to it.

As he had waited for her to speak, his desire to be rid of her had warred with his fear that he would lose her and he realised he was once again at risk of caring for a woman who cared nothing for him.

One woman had ended up in the Thames because she was to be married to him. At least Solay would have no reason to throw herself into the Thames because she wasn't.

Well, if she were that desperate for a husband, she would have one.

That and nothing else.

As the door closed on the rowdy group that had led them up the stairs, Solay sighed with relief, the taste of red wine and anticipation on her tongue.

Finally, she was alone with her husband.

Solay glanced at him through her lashes. The curve of his jaw, immovable as carved stone, had not changed since they had stood before the church door that morning. Surely, when they were alone behind the bed curtains, he would bend. Surely, now that they were married, he would reach for her and the fire she had felt so often would flame free.

The way to a man's heart is through his stones, her mother always said. Make him feel as if he is the most desirable man on earth.

Solay set aside her fading nosegay of lavender periwinkle and yellow cowslip and wandered the unfamiliar room where Agnes had moved her things. Beneath the aching want and the fear of surrender, she recognised something else in her desire.

A flicker of hope.

They were husband and wife now. She had provided for her family. Could she and Justin truly come together?

Silent, he still stood at the door. Drawn to the window, she looked out at the familiar sky, searching for something to say. 'The stars look beautiful tonight.'

'Then let them keep you company.'

The faint hope she had cradled so carefully crumbled to ash. She turned towards him, the floor unsteady under her feet. 'Where are you going?'

'To find a bed.'

The familiar pain burned inside her. She felt again the cold stone against her bare legs and the hot rage at his rejection. *Until you know who you are,* he had said. Well, she might be a harlot's daughter, but she was his wife now. He could not refuse her.

'Justin, we are well and truly married and your bed is here, with me.' Did he still doubt her past? She gentled her tongue and widened her eyes, for sincerity. 'There has been no other man.' She stretched out her hand, palm up. 'It shall be you and no other.'

She held the pose, her elbow rigid, as anger consumed desire and sweat dampened her back.

His eyes darkened with desire, but he did not reach for her. 'I will not share your bed.'

She pulled back her arm, open palm now a fist. 'It is grounds for ending the marriage if you do not.' Too sharp a tone. She swallowed and tried on a teasing smile, hoping to rile his pride. 'Or cannot.'

No trace of male conceit crossed his face. He showed no fear that his manhood might be questioned. Instead, he mimicked her bantering lilt, twisting his lips into grotesque smile. 'Oh, milady, this is the marriage you so fervently wanted. Do you wish to end it so soon?'

Her palm itched to slap his smug face. She ignored the ache in her chest and tried to think over the angry heartbeats in her ears. What possible reason would he have to refuse her now?

If you knew me, you would want this marriage no more than I. Was he afraid she would discover him a traitor?

She forced her tongue to move. 'You said if I knew you I would not want this marriage. Now that we are married, what is it I must not know?'

'You got the marriage you wanted, Solay. Since you could bring no love to it, you will find no love in it.' He pulled open the door.

'What are you doing?' she whispered, tugging on his sleeve. Drunken laughter still echoed from the floor below, but soon the crowd would want to witness the consummation.

'I will not lie with you, Solay. Not tonight. Not tomorrow. Not for the rest of our blighted lives.'

The drunkards were weaving up the stairway. She pulled Justin's unbending arm. 'All right, but come inside. Sleep on the floor if you must, but don't let them think you did not sleep with me.'

'You made this bed. Lie in it alone.' He pulled his arm away from her and stepped into the corridor.

She looked down the hall, biting her lip. 'What will people think?'

'Whatever they want. You needed money. Our agreement gives you a percentage of my income and rental monies. Give your mother and sister what you will. You need not whore with your husband for it.'

Stunned, she watched him walk off, in full view of the drunkards coming up the stairs.

Gather your wits, Solay. He might not care for the Court's opinion, but you do. If she accused him of neglecting his marital duty, she could end it now. She could be free.

But the King, angry with her, would never reward her with another husband. Without a protector—husband, father or king—she had nothing.

She turned to the crowd and waved. 'He needs to clear his head,' she called out, forcing a laugh. 'If he is to perform his husbandly duties.'

They laughed with her and returned to the hall and their drink. She shut the door. With luck, they would drink to slumber and not mount the stairs again.

She crawled into bed alone, regretting that she had not listened to Agnes and made preparations. She had never imagined he would not take her, once they were wed. If the sheets showed no evidence, it would be her virginity, not his prowess, that would be questioned.

Sliding her hand beneath the pillow, she touched something damp and pulled it out into the light.

A bloody cloth.

She smiled at Agnes's thoughtfulness.

After the castle had quieted, she rubbed the cloth on the middle of the bed sheet. It left a reddish smear. Not much, but enough.

She tossed the cloth into the fire and watched it burn, blaming the smoke for the tears stinging her eyes.

She had got what she asked for, squandered her choice on this man and now she must live with the sorrow. She had never expected love in her marriage. Why did she now regret that her husband did not love her?

Her family would be provided for. Compared with that, her happiness, really, meant nothing. It would be better this way. Better not to hope. Better to live at arm's length.

At least the hate in his eyes would not be her first sight upon waking.

Chapter Twenty

On Solay's first morning as a married woman, the maid removed the bloody sheets with a smile. Late in the morning, when Agnes knocked on the door, Solay assumed a blushing smile and invented a long night of lovemaking for her enraptured audience.

'So you did not need my little gift,' Agnes said.

Solay coughed. 'I…uh…burned it so it would not be found.' Even the truth could be a lie.

But her friend did not notice. 'He's so stern, he frightens me, but it is evident that he desires you. Even the King noticed.'

The King. The thought stopped her tongue.

'Agnes,' she began, trying to look bashful, 'we did not speak of his work. If the King asks—'

Agnes patted her hand. 'Don't worry. The Council's power will be over soon.'

Solay shook her head. 'It's near half a year until November.' And, she had discovered this much, Parliament could easily extend the charter longer if they wished.

Agnes pursed her lips. 'Sooner than that.'

Her stomach turned over. 'What do you mean?'

'I've said too much.'

'Has this marriage come between us, then?'

Agnes laughed. 'Never! The stars brought us together as surely as they brought me my Duke. I'll tell you later, I promise.'

Not comforted, Solay laughed with her. She was hiding things from Agnes, too. But, bedded or not, there were some things a wife deserved to know. How was she to protect Justin if she did not know the truth?

Sly smiles followed her through the halls until she found him at his desk, looking as if he had slept no better than she.

He frowned as she entered. 'So we start our marriage with a lie.'

Which one? she wanted to ask. 'What do you mean?'

'All of Windsor castle is smirking at me and congratulating me on how well I performed my duty last night.'

'Would you have preferred the truth?' Too late to wonder whether she'd made the right choice. 'I could have put it about that you despise my touch.'

A hint of regret shaded his eyes and his cheeks reddened. 'That's not what I said.'

She squashed her quiver of hope. She would beg no more. It was her turn to wound. 'Perhaps I should have told them you were too deeply in your cups to find your way home.'

The anger in his gaze satisfied her. 'That's a lie.'

'Did you wish me to tell them the truth?'

'You did not need to tell them anything.'

'Consummation seals the wedding vows, as you told me many times.'

He frowned. 'Yes, but it was no one's concern but our own.'

''Tis done,' she snapped, anger fuelling her tongue. 'You were not there to be consulted.' She was tired of grovelling for approval that would never come. 'And now that we are bound I must know. What will happen at the end of the year when the Council finishes its work?'

His shoulders relaxed, as if he were glad to be again on impersonal ground. 'If all is in order, the King will resume his rule.'

'And if all is not in order?'

'I will do as Parliament decides.'

'You will not…' She stumbled over the word. *You have given me neither aid nor comfort.*

'Commit treason? You know very little of the man you have married.'

That, she feared, was true. 'And when I asked you directly, you would not tell me.'

'It is time for you to answer a question, wife.' He paced as if questioning an accused criminal. 'Where lies your loyalty? With the King or with me?'

She drank him in with her eyes, this tall, harsh man who was now her husband. She wanted to believe in him, wanted to believe in integrity that bowed to no man, not even a King.

And yet, he feared something.

'Why should I have to choose?' she said, finally.

'The King gathers a private army. Who do you think he intends to fight? The French?'

'Of course.'

'His barons would do that gladly.'

'Who else would he fight?'

'You, of all people, are not that naïve.'

She wasn't, but she couldn't face the prospect. 'You misunderstand the King's intentions. Unless you plan treason, my loyalty needs no dividing.'

As Justin shook his head in disgust, she prayed, fervently, that it would not.

* * *

Justin became familiar with the stars over the next fortnight as the Court travelled back to Windsor. Night after night he lay next to her, staring at the sky, his body burning, and wondered why it had seemed so important to resist her.

In the daylight hours, he would remember.

So he kept her at a distance, even after they reached Windsor, not telling her when he visited London and the Middle Temple again.

For if he lay with her, the last of his resistance would crumble. He would be able to withhold none of himself.

And when she discovered it all, even if he kept his head, his heart would be lost.

Justin sought out Gloucester after the hours of pomp at the Order of the Garter installation ceremony dragged to their conclusion.

The Duke was in a foul mood. 'It sickens me. All this for a lad who's never seen a battlefield,' Gloucester grumbled, as they walked across the Upper Ward to the banquet hall. 'My father created this honour for fighting men. I was not allowed to join until I was four and twenty. Now, he gives the garter to a boy of fourteen and two women.'

Justin was in no frame of mind to listen to Gloucester's complaining. 'I went to London yesterday.'

'Good,' Gloucester muttered, leading him away from prying ears. 'When do we take Hibernia?'

Yellow gillyflowers dotted the Upper Ward and bobbed happily in the spring breeze. It seemed impossible that something so simple and beautiful could still live in the world in which right and wrong no longer existed. 'No judge would issue the subpoena.'

'Why? What was wrong with it?'

'Nothing.' He had checked and rechecked that. There was no legal reason for their reluctance. Judges can be bought for a farthing, Solay had said. She was wrong. Apparently, fear was a strong as a farthing. 'No judge would risk offending the King.'

'Then we'll take him without it,' Gloucester fumed, 'before the King escapes to the countryside again.'

Justin frowned. 'If we violate the law, we are no better than he is.'

'I don't care. We should have clapped him in chains months ago.'

Gloucester's patience, never long, was nearing its end. Unless Justin could make the law work as it should, Gloucester would turn to force and everything he had strived for would be for nothing.

'There's another way. Based on what I discovered in Chester, I believe we can impeach him.'

The man's eyes lit up. Instead of forcing him to answer questions, impeachment could remove him from the Court, or even the country, permanently. 'Are you sure?'

'What he's doing is worse than what de la Pole did and the Commons impeached him.' Impeached him because Justin had laid an inevitable path of legal logic for the Speaker to follow. 'He's gathering a private army for the King.'

Gloucester's sputtering anger drained, leaving his face pale and his lips pursed. The only reason the King would need fighting men beyond those his barons would supply was to turn against them.

He nodded. 'Do it.'

Justin fought a pang of regret. Solay would hate the very thought of putting someone else through what her mother had endured. Besides, if she found out too soon, so would the King.

So he would not tell her.

When had he learned to lie? Had she taught him that?

* * *

A few days later, Solay received a message from home.

She smiled, homesick at the sight of Jane's careful letters. Solay had written home as soon as she returned to Windsor. Would they be pleased at her marriage?

But the message was short and terrible.

Weston's nephew was suing them for the last thing they owned: the dear little house where she had spent the last ten years.

'That house had never even belonged to Weston!' she yelled to the empty room. 'He has no right.'

But time after time, the unfeeling courts had determined what was right, taking property her mother had paid for in never-ending revenge for the fact that a well-loved King could age.

If only the law actually worked, as Justin believed it did, the law might actually help them.

Would Justin?

He still avoided her bed, but he could not avoid his duties as her husband. She had married him to protect her family. Now, she would discover whether her sacrifice had been for naught.

She entered his work room without knocking and spoke without preamble. 'You say you believe in the law.'

His eyes met hers. 'You say it as if you don't think I do.'

'I don't want to exchange meaningless philosophy. I need you to answer squarely. Do you believe everyone has a right to fair treatment?'

'Of course.'

She drew a breath. 'I know someone who is being sued for the last thing she owns.' She did not modulate her tone. 'And the man who is suing her has no right to it. No right!'

He raised his brows and leaned back as her impassioned words bounced off the wall. 'That's for the court to decide.'

She coughed, wishing she had started better. Unruly

emotions were leading her tongue astray. 'This person needs help to fight this lawsuit.'

He leaned back, raising his eyebrows and folding his arms. 'So why are you telling me about this case?'

'She needs a clever lawyer to represent her. Will you help?'

'You've told me nothing about the case. Who is it?'

'I am your wife and I am asking you to do this for me. Do you have to know who it is before you agree?'

'It's a simple question. Who do you want me to represent?'

Would her answer end the conversation? 'My mother.'

Shocked as if she had slapped him, Justin didn't move. 'How can you even ask me to defend that woman?'

'You are judging her without knowing anything.'

Chagrinned, he held his tongue. He had never seen her so direct. 'Tell me.'

'Weston's nephew wants our house. It's the last thing she has—'

'Her husband's nephew?' If what Solay had told him about the man was true, none of his relatives deserved a ha'penny more from Lady Alys of Weston.

She nodded. 'He has filed suit in the civil courts of London that he is Weston's rightful heir, not my mother. That means he's entitled to the house.' Her voice quivered. 'It's all that's left.'

He fought the sympathy her vulnerability raised. Her mother had amassed chattels aplenty she never deserved. 'Is the property rightfully his?'

'You said that was for the law to decide.' At his challenge, her shaky voice turned to steel. 'Or have you judged our case already?'

Her words stung. 'I was asking for the facts.'

She looked at him, head tilted, eyebrows raised. 'You talked as if you already knew them.'

He waved for her to sit.

She did, her voice calmer now. 'The facts are these: he claims my mother never married Weston and that her children were the King's. That would make us...' she hesitated '...that would make her children not eligible to legally inherit Weston's property. In that case, the property should pass to him as the nearest male heir.'

'And were they married?'

He watched her think, wondering what she would say. Her answer could make her legitimate or a bastard. Would she tell the truth? Did she even know it?

'Parliament decreed they were,' she said, finally. 'And with that ruling, Weston was content to take a husband's spoils. Shouldn't that prove the case?'

No wonder she was suspicious of the law. Her family had navigated many of its more unsavoury nuances, just to survive. 'So that would make you the daughter of William of Weston.'

'Legally?' She smiled, sadly. 'I can be the daughter of whatever man the law decrees, but we all know whose womb bore me. That seems all the evidence most men need to decide the case.'

He looked from Solay's challenging gaze to Hibernia's useless subpoena and the questionable outline for the man's impeachment.

If he took on the harlot's case, could he restore Solay's faith in the law?

Could he restore his own?

'I will meet with your mother.' Surely the woman could answer whether or not she had been wed. 'Then I'll decide.'

A flood of happiness washed over her face. 'Alys. Her name is Alys.'

* * *

Justin pulled up his horse before the house at Upminster. Unimpressive by royal standards, devoid of defences except for a placid pond too small to call a moat, it hardly looked worth fighting over. But he had seen men do battle before the judges for even less important property.

He helped Solay from her horse as a young, fair-haired lad jumped down from his perch on an oak-tree limb. The boy ran towards them and threw his arms around Solay as soon as her feet touched the ground.

The boy's head came up to Solay's chin and she hugged back, kissing both cheeks before she faced Justin, her arm still draped around the boy's shoulder. 'Jane, this is Lord Justin.'

He looked again. This, then, was no boy, but the sister.

Now that he looked closely, he could see the girl was on the cusp between girlhood and womanhood, but old enough to be wed. She had the King's fair hair and blue eyes, but while Solay had learned to flaunt her sexuality, Jane avoided hers altogether.

She stepped back and looked him over with a solemn, frank gaze. 'You are her husband now?'

'Yes.' One word. All.

'Is it because the King said you must?'

If Solay hesitated to speak frankly, her sister had no such qualms.

Solay squeezed her sister's shoulder. 'Jane, don't badger him.'

'She deserves an answer.' It was time to face the truth of it squarely. Yet when he answered, he looked not at Jane, but into Solay's questioning eyes. 'I made my own choice.'

In their violet depths, he saw a flicker of hope. Was it possible she cared for him?

Jane turned back to her sister. 'Did you?'

Solay closed her eyes, shielding her thoughts. No, he had never been her choice. Not from the first. But he held his breath, waiting for her answer.

'Perhaps,' she said, 'the stars chose for us one for the other.'

Jane sniffed and collected the horses' reins. 'Well, the stars will not choose for me. I shall choose *not* to marry.'

Solay sighed, watching her take them to the stable, her love for her sister unmistakable in her eyes. 'You see how it is,' she said, simply.

He nodded. Hard as it had been for Solay to find a husband, it would be impossible for Jane.

At the double door, Solay ran her fingers over the pitted wood. 'It does not compare to Windsor, but it is home.'

He fought back the guilt. Certainly, he had given her no new home.

Warily, Justin crossed the threshold, wondering how many of the threadbare tapestries lining the wall had been paid for by the royal purse. No one greeted them. No servants hovered at their beck and call.

Instead of coming to meet them, Lady Alys waited at the end of the Great Hall, sitting as if in a throne room.

Solay led him forward slowly, and as they approached, he decided that whatever riches the woman might have purloined from the crown were long gone. The plate on display was pewter, not silver, and the edge of her skirt, salvaged from the days of glory, was now frayed like a battle banner whipped too long by the wind.

'Mother,' Solay began, 'this is my husband, Lord Justin Lamont.'

She did not rise and he fought the urge to bow, searching the woman's face for a relationship to Solay. Her brows, dark as her daughter's, were plucked into unnatural black slashes. Years of frowns drew lines down from her mouth.

Yet even at twice her daughter's age, he could see a hint of what might have captivated a king.

'I am pleased to meet my daughter's husband at last.' The simple words held an accusation.

'Mother,' Solay began, softly, 'Justin has come about the suit. He must decide whether he can help us.'

The narrow black eyebrows arched. 'Ah, so he has an interest in our land?'

Solay moved to speak and he put a hand on her arm. 'On the contrary, Lady Alys,' he answered. 'From what I understand, you have only this property left, and unless I can win this suit for you, you won't even have that.'

Solay's mother blinked and swallowed, as if she'd had a bite of sour fish.

He could have sworn Solay smothered a smile. 'Justin believes in honest speaking.'

'So I hear,' Lady Alys replied.

'You will never need to wonder at my meaning.'

'Well, we welcome your help, though if I may speak equally plainly, I think you are young for a sergeant-at-law,' she said.

'He is chief legal adviser to the Council, Mother.' Solay's quick defence made him smile. It was the first time she had ever boasted of him.

'It is because of my skill that I earned my degree so young. You need not doubt my ability.'

'I'll know the difference. I used to sit next to the judges to make sure the King's will was done. Then they banned me. Parliament said no woman could ever practise law, but they didn't mean any woman.' Her smile was pure pride. 'They meant me.'

He could not but smile back, despite his remembrance of his father's fury when he heard the Weston woman was interfering with the judges. And he had the strangest sensation that perhaps the King had loved her for her mind.

'The Commons,' she continued, 'is a bunch of witless country dullards who had no right to interfere with the King's wishes.'

He wrapped his temper tightly at her dismissal. 'I see, Lady Alys, that you, too, can speak plainly.' Between her mother and her sister, Solay must have had to smooth over many ruffled feathers as she grew. No wonder she had become circumspect of speech.

'Mother, Justin has not yet decided whether to represent us.' Her eyes held fear that he would not.

'I've never met a lawyer who wouldn't argue whatever side paid him the most. And unless you wish to seize the very land we fight for, we cannot pay you at all.'

'Solay is my wife. I would not expect payment. I only want to see justice done.'

'Justice?' She snorted. 'If you win this case, it will be the first time I have seen it. I have made my way and that of my children with no help from the law.' She reached for Solay's hand and squeezed it and Solay hugged her, awkwardly. 'And still, the King called my daughter his.'

The pride he always assumed came from her royal father seemed instead the gift, or curse, of a mother proud to have risen from humble beginnings to a seat beside the throne.

But he could not let sentiment rule him. 'That does not help us. The suit hinges on Weston being her father. Was he?'

The woman smiled. 'According to Parliament, he was. With that precedent, surely a lawyer with your skills can prove it.'

Her taunt lay like a gauntlet. This woman would have kept the judges examining their logic. The legal argument was clear, but she had not answered his question.

Solay and her mother stood side by side, heads held at the same proud angle, in a shabby hall in the countryside, awaiting his verdict.

Lady Alys, world weary and resigned, seemed prepared for

him to refuse. It would prove that, once again, life had treated her unfairly, that she must battle always alone.

But in Solay's eyes, he saw the hope, the 'please' she could not say and he could not refuse. Whether they lived as man and wife or not, he did not want her to grow old like the bitter woman at her side.

'I will take the case.'

His wife let go a breath and closed her eyes as in prayer. 'Thank you.'

Her mother narrowed her eyes and looked from one to the other. 'All right. Let's begin.'

Chapter Twenty-One

Lady Alys wasted no time showing him the stacks of documents she had kept, itemising the ownership and finances of every holding. Long after sunset, Solay led him up the stairs to the sleeping chambers. Despite his yawns, her swaying hips roused him and, for a moment, he regretted that they would sleep apart.

'My room looks towards the sunrise,' Solay said, pushing open the door. 'I hope you like it.'

He stopped on the threshold, refusing to enter her world. 'I told you we will not—'

'Shh.' She put her finger to her lips and pulled him inside, looking both ways before she shut the door. 'This is not a castle where you can come and go without notice. Mother mustn't know we don't live as man and wife.'

Fixated on the impeachment, on his doubts about Lady Alys, on Solay, he had not grasped what would happen when he went home with her. Truly, she had muddled his head so much that he could no longer recognise the obvious. 'So,' he muttered, a feeble protest, 'again, we start with a lie.'

But the lie was to pretend he did not want her. Rooted to

the spot, his body clamoured for hers. Did he mean to live his life like a monk? He was married to the woman. Why had refused to take her? He was having trouble remembering.

Back against the door, blocking his exit, she lifted her chin, her lower lip trembling in a gentle pout. 'I agreed to your terms. Please honour mine. I do not wish to flaunt our situation before my family.'

He nodded, silent. When he looked at her eyes and saw her honest plea, he could not resist. Just like the first time, something spoke to him, wordless. Irresistible.

She smiled, her entire body relaxing as she let go her grip on the door. 'Thank you.'

While he was working, a manservant had moved his trunk to the left of the room's fireplace. A bowl of dried petals sat on top of it and Solay pinched some between her fingers, releasing the scent of roses. 'All your things are here. I'll sleep on the floor,' she said, 'and leave you the bed.'

He turned his back on the beckoning bed. 'Do you think me devoid of all chivalry? You take the bed.'

'But you are the guest.'

'I'm not a guest. I'm your husband!'

She looked towards the door, as if afraid his shout would carry, then back at him, anger wiping out the pleading in her eyes. 'I was trying to adhere to your wishes, husband. Sleep where you will.'

Since the wedding vows, her patience for pleasing him had evaporated, making her previous simpering over his wishes even more transparent. Worse, he liked this scrappy woman with fire in her eyes who wasn't afraid to tell him what she thought.

He cleared his throat. 'I'll sleep on the floor.'

She pursed her lips, anger gone. 'Forgive me. I must seem ungrateful. For you to help means...' Her voice cracked. She met his eyes, at once humble and proud. 'It means everything.'

'I did not do it for her.'

Cynicism mixed with sadness. 'I understand. My family will be less of a burden if you are not our sole support.'

Had she no faith in him at all? 'I will not let them starve, no matter what happens, but that wasn't why I agreed.'

'Then why?' Eyes wide, head tilted, she reminded him of the little girl who had lost her parrot. The little girl who wanted a birthday, but didn't believe she would ever have one.

He reached for her hair, stroking it, the strands silk against his palm, and then brushed her cheek with his fingers. 'I did it for you.'

She dropped her head against his hands, eyes closed. So quickly, just with a touch, he had made her breath quicken.

He felt the answering throb below his waist.

He stepped towards her, taking her lips as he had wanted to do for weeks. Already boneless, she melted against him, her softness making him harder.

'I wanted,' he whispered, his lips moving against her hair, 'to prove something to you.'

She leaned back to see his face and he loved the hope in her eyes. 'What?'

'That the law can give you justice.'

'I hope you are right,' she said softly, curling against his chest again.

'Perhaps,' he said, not wanting to let her go, 'we could share the bed.'

As close as he had been to taking her, he knew it was madness, but the journey had been long and neither deserved cold stone.

He felt her nod against his heart.

'Just the bed, of course.' He let her go and walked to the far side of the bed, sitting to remove his boots.

Behind him, he heard the rustle of her clothes.

He closed his eyes, but he could see her in his mind. She would unlace her dress, slip it off her shoulders, and her dark hair would cascade down the white skin of her back. The curve of her hip would press gently against her chemise and, if she turned to face him, he would be able to see the pink shadow of her breast through the veil of linen.

Biting off a groan, he decided to keep his clothes on and lay on top of the covers on his left side, facing away from her.

The straw mattress shifted beside him as she slipped under the blanket and he nearly rolled into her. Less than a finger's-breadth away, her scent, rising and falling with her breath, wafted over him.

Back to her, he hugged the edge of the bed. His arms dangled over the side, his legs overshot the end, and he lay, wide-eyed and stiff limbed, staring at the patch of sky and stars he could see through the window. The soft night air of spring stroked his brow.

Beside him, she turned, pounded the pillow, then lay quietly again. He could feel something soft and round nudging him.

He stifled a moan.

'Am I pushing you off?' she whispered.

'No.' He did not trust his voice to say more.

'The bed is small. I'm sorry.'

'Stop being sorry for what is not your fault.'

Her silence vibrated with hurt.

He cleared his throat, angry at himself. 'Perhaps, if we both turned the same way, we could fit more easily.'

Behind him, her breathing stopped. He waited.

'As you wish.'

He rolled over just as she did. Face to face, breath to breath, only the thin blanket between them, he wanted nothing more than to cover her sweet body with his. Her breasts rose and fell, her lips parted, and it took every ounce of his strength to roll away from her.

But he did.

With a small sigh, she nestled against his back and her right arm crept around him, tucking him close. Her hand dangled dangerously close to his stiff member and he grabbed her fingers away from danger and held them against his heart.

'Is this better than before?' Her whisper carried a husky edge.

It was better. It was worse. It was a fire at his back, igniting the desire he so vainly fought. He clenched his jaw against the growl of desire. 'Yes.'

'It's cold,' she said, when he did not speak. 'I'll get another blanket.'

Fresh air cooled his back when she left the bed, and then the blanket covered them both, her quick fingers tucking it too close.

Sweat trickled down his back. He flung off the blanket. 'Let's turn the other way.'

Obligingly, she flipped to her right side and he curved himself against her back.

It was worse.

Now, her full breasts were within reach of his hand, the sweet space between her legs was his to explore, and her neck was open to his lips.

He placed a kiss beneath her ear. He felt her swallow and wiggle back into him. Surely she could feel him, stiff against the sweet roundness of her bottom, still cool beneath the linen shift.

His hand hovered near her breast.

Boldened, she pulled his hand close, cupping hers over it, then snuggled up against his staff.

'Solay.' His voice cracked with a plea and he pulled away, then leaned on his elbow.

She turned on her back, open and tempting, looking up at him, her face hidden in shadows. 'Are you again going to cast me off as a temptress and a tease because I sought to share a bed with my husband?'

Shame clutched at desire's throat. She had done nothing but try to please him, even when she despised him and it was more than he deserved.

I'm sorry danced upon his tongue. 'No,' he said, instead.

'This isn't about the King, is it?'

He shook his head.

They lay side by side, careful not to touch, breathing in unmatched rhythm, staring up at the darkness together.

He swung out of bed and stuffed his feet into his boots, desperate to escape. 'It's not your fault. If you knew...' His words drifted into the dark. He stood, making his feet walk away. 'I will seek shelter in the stable.'

'Whatever it is, Justin, if you decide to tell me, I will not judge you for it.'

Silent, he closed the door behind him. He had planned to close her out of his life. Instead, he craved not just her body, but something more.

Her love.

All his life, he had prided himself on his honesty. Yet he was hiding more from her than his Council work.

He was hiding the story of Blanche.

He had told himself it had not come up. Or that he was waiting for the proper time. But as he entered the stable, inhaling the scent of manure and straw, he faced the truth. He had not told her because he cared what this weak, strong, stubborn, crazy woman thought of him. And despite her babble of forgiveness in the dark, if she knew the truth about Blanche, he would never, never get it.

A bark of laughter escaped his throat and his horse whinnied. How the tables had turned. Over and over, he had judged her for her lies, when all the time, he had been lying to win her love.

* * *

Solay rolled her eyes heavenward, then pummelled her pillow with both fists, sending a puff of chafe dust through the seams. This man, this impossible man, this husband of hers. What was she to do?

I did it for you. An answer she had never hoped to hear. He must feel something for her, but she wanted so much more.

She hurled the pillow against the wall, where it bounced harmlessly to the floor. Sighing, she rose to retrieve it, pausing to look out of the window.

The stable blocked her view of him as surely as the wall around his heart held her back. Yet it seemed this man, afraid of nothing and honest about everything, feared something. She had been so busy trying to protect herself from pain she had been slow to notice his.

She had dreaded the judgement in his eyes, but it seemed clear now that he judged himself just as harshly as he judged others. How painful it would be, to find yourself lacking every day of your life.

Who had taught him that?

His father. A judger. She had suffered from an absent father. Perhaps his had been too ever present.

She raised her eyes to the stars, spilled like a thousand wildflowers across the sky, searching for patterns. She had a husband, but, it seemed, she would never become a wife. Despite her every effort, Heaven's plans for her had not changed. She had done her duty for her family, but she was still alone.

This, then, was to be her life. Unable to please her husband, perhaps she could at least please herself.

It was time to discover what that meant.

Chapter Twenty-Two

The next morning, Justin splashed off the smell of the stable with cold water from the stream. He entered the kitchen, surprised to find Solay there, flour dusting her arms like snow. The room was basking in the heat of the oven.

He knew little of domestic duties, but he had never seen a lady up to her elbows in bread dough. Yet she kneaded the loaf as if she had done it many times. 'Is the kitchen maid ill?'

She smiled. 'We have only the two servants. Mother and I do most of the household tasks. Jane helps in the garden and the stables.'

He had barely noticed last night, but thinking back, he had seen only an older couple helping with supper and carrying his trunk up the stairs. Despite Solay's desperation to marry, he had never fully realised how far the King's mistress had fallen. 'No wonder you want to stay at Court.'

She shook her head. 'I'd rather be here. The whole Court seems like a disguising.' She dipped and twirled around the room, scrunching her face into that of a simpering courtier. 'What does the King think of this? Will the King approve of that? When does the King want to eat? What if I'm hungry when the King isn't?' She broke her pose and shook her head. 'We can't even go to bed or waken or break fast if the King does not wish it.'

Surprised, he laughed at her imitation of the flatterers at Court. 'I thought it was your sole ambition to make a life there.'

'That's what Mother wanted.'

Rooted in past glories, the harlot had foisted her dreams on to her daughter. 'She coerced you into going?'

Solay turned the full force of her violet eyes on him. The look said *the King called me his daughter*. 'I wanted to go.'

Her pride mixed in some alchemical way with her vulnerability. Together, they gave her strength he was just beginning to understand. 'And you got what you wanted.'

'I got what I needed.'

A husband. You. She might as well have said the words aloud. He winced at the honesty he had demanded. Neither had illusions about this marriage. Why did he crave something more?

'And what do you want now?' He held his breath, wanting it to be something he could give.

Silence stretched before she answered. 'What do *you* want, Justin?'

He opened his mouth to scold her for asking what he thought before she would speak. Then he realised he was evading her question. He had berated her for not speaking her mind while he had concealed his own.

He cleared his throat. 'I would like to be a Justice of the Peace.'

'Like your father?'

He nodded. 'I want to bring the fairness of the law to ordinary people.' It sounded foolish, said aloud. Why had he shared dreams she would disdain?

'So you do not want a life at Court either.'

'I never did.'

She reached into the oven and pulled out two finished loaves. 'I understand. You have never liked the King.' No criticism tinged her voice.

The scent of warm bread filled him with peace and Westminster seemed far away. 'It's not just the King.' Always he had asked for her honesty. It was time to share his own. 'Sometimes I fear the Council has become more concerned with their own power than with the common good.'

'So as a Justice, you could ignore all that?'

'The King cares little about what happens with most people in the countryside.' He smiled. 'And they return the favour. Many don't care who the King is, let alone worry about his household expenses, unless he asks for more taxes. Nor do they care about the war unless they have to serve.'

She paused in her kneading. 'Even now, King and Court dominate Mother's thoughts.'

'So that is what I want, Solay. And you?'

'I want my family to be taken care of, for Jane to be happy.'

No surprise. It was why she had wanted a husband. 'But what do you want for yourself?'

Her eyes met his without barriers. 'I misrepresented my knowledge of the stars. I want it to be real.' She broke off her gaze and pummelled the dough with her fists. 'I want to learn their secrets.'

He had hoped, foolishly, she might have said something about wanting a life with him. 'No one will teach you.'

She leaned on her arms and glared at him. 'You ask what I want and the first thing you do is disapprove. Why should I share anything with you?'

He recognised her princess voice, the one that said *I can*. Wasn't that what he had tried to teach her? No wonder she did not dream of a life with him. She had just accepted his crazy desire to follow in his father's footsteps. Then he sat here dewy-eyed over baking bread, unwilling to do the hard work of supporting her dreams. 'You're right. I'm proud of you for deciding what you want.'

He wanted to hold her, but not just for the physical fire. To cherish her, somehow.

She smiled, as if she had seen it in his eyes, and then looked away. 'And when I discover what the stars have in store for me, then I shall want that,' she said, in the teasing tone that hid her feelings, 'so as not to be disappointed.'

Relieved to be sparring with her once more, he breathed again. 'So you will seek justice in the Heavens and I on earth.'

She touched his arm, her fingers leaving white smudges on his sleeve. 'Justin, if there truly were justice in the world, I would trust you to find it.'

He grabbed her hand, feeling like laughing with joy, and kissed her palm, the flour clinging to his lips.

Perhaps here, away from the Court, they could find peace.

Solay's mother had hoarded her legal documents as tightly as her jewels. Over the next few weeks, Justin read every one.

He set up a table in the upstairs solar, alternating between reading them and working on the impeachment document when his mind grew tired of the details of property ownership. He could have asked for a clerk's help, but he could trust no one else with either task. He let Jane sort the documents and keep them in order, a job she seemed to enjoy.

He was learning a few things from Lady Alys's business acumen. It was common knowledge that the King's mistress had accumulated wealth far beyond her right and her station. He had never known how cleverly she had done it.

Forced to leave her old life, Lady Alys had left many things behind, but not even one of her documents of ownership. There were papers supporting control of at least fifty proper-

ties in twenty-five counties, an accumulation of land an Earl
might have envied. Had she been a man, she would have sat
in the House of Lords.

Some of the properties were gifts of the King, yes, but the
income from many more came under her control in other
ways, all perfectly legal. In fact, she might have given those
judges good advice.

Yet in all this mass, there were no loving letters between
husband and wife. No exchange on affairs of mutual holdings.
Perhaps a jealous King wanted no reminders of his rival, but there
should have been at least a scrap that would bolster his argument.

'How goes your work?' Lady Alys's voice at his back
startled him.

He put down a document and rose. 'You have a wealth of
information.'

'The documents for this property clearly show my right to it.'

'Until Parliament acknowledged Weston as your husband.
Then it all went to him.'

'Which should make my daughters' inheritance clear.'

'You speak of normal circumstances. Your daughters are
universally acknowledged to be the King's. If they are to
inherit, I must find a way to prove they are legitimate offspring
of William Weston.' Any children born during the marriage
would legally be the husband's unless he disavowed them.
'Can you even prove you were married to him when they were
born? You have all these documents. Is there nothing con-
nected to the marriage?'

'Lost, I'm afraid.'

Or destroyed. The woman cared for her wealth more than
her husband. 'There must have been witnesses to the
ceremony.' The witness of the community was sufficient to
prove marriage.

'None living.' She turned her back on him, pacing to the

window, the frayed edge of her gown, dragging the floor. 'Why do I need witnesses? Parliament decreed we were married. That should be enough.'

'Perhaps it would be if Lady Alys of Weston were not involved.'

The mother looked over her shoulder at him with a sad smile. 'Ah, so justice is not blind?'

Reluctantly, he shook his head. 'Perhaps it never was.' His pompous arguments about the law sounded foolish now. He had scoffed at Solay's cynical views, but she was wiser than he. It seemed impossible for Lady Alys to be treated fairly by the law.

She swept past him to leave, pausing at the door. 'This property is all I have left to protect my daughters' future. I hope,' she said, a furrowed line between her brows, 'that Solay did not make a mistake in asking you to take the case.'

'So do I,' he answered.

Despite Justin's prediction, Solay found a local physician who agreed to teach her something of how the stars affected healing.

She would return from a day's study, flushed and happy from her walk, chatting of all she had learned, more irresistible than ever.

Now, as he ached for her day after day, the glimmer of a life together beckoned like the first star of the night. And his pallet, once a haven, had become a lonely cavern.

Still sleeping apart, they had fallen into a habit of taking a walk after supper, away from the prying eyes of her mother, often returning after the rest of the house was abed.

'Today, we spoke of the five aspects of the planets,' she explained, munching the last bite of a meat pie, watching the sky turn red and the stars emerge.

'What does that mean?'

'That's how they relate to each other in the sky.' She licked her fingers, then ticked off the list. 'Let me see if I can remember. Conjunction means they appear in the same space. In opposition means just what it says, as if at opposite ends of a string. Square is like this.' She held up thumb and first finger to form a corner. 'Then there are two others, trine and sextile.'

'How do you remember all that?' The terms made his head spin.

'It can be no more complicated than the machinations of the law,' she said, smiling. 'Here, let me draw it out.'

She grabbed a stick and traced a circle in the dirt. As he watched her elaborate, intersecting lines, he had to admit there seemed a certain logic to the system.

'But what good is it to know what the stars say if you cannot change their decree?'

She looked up from her drawing, her eyes steady. 'So you know what cannot be changed. For example, it is the planet Venus, cruel fate, who decrees whom we love. You cannot demand love of someone as if it were a pound of flour in the market.'

'Venus?' He raised his eyebrows and forced a smile. Demanding her love in order to consummate their marriage. Had he ever been so foolish? Yet Venus seemed as logical as anything about love, which seemed to strike at will and whimsy. Which seemed to be striking him.

She raised her chin. 'When I am skilled enough, I will read my chart, and yours, if you will let me. Then we will see what fate has planned for us.'

'You will not. The King forbade it.' He should never have let her pursue this. If she displeased the King, he could have her tried as a witch or worse. And Justin would not be able to save her. He would fail her just as he had failed Blanche.

A dimple he had never noticed flashed in her cheek with a lopsided smile. 'I thought you cared naught for the King's opinion?'

'I care about you.'

She searched his eyes, as if for once unsure whether he spoke the truth. He leaned towards her, his lips brushing hers. Her touch sent a shiver down his spine and back to his arms, which of their own accord, circled her.

His lips would not leave hers. Hungrily, he kissed her, cursing Venus, or God, or Fate, or his own treacherous body for giving him the one woman he could not refuse.

She gave herself totally. No teasing, no luring, no trying to entrap him. Just soul-deep surrender. As if she had truly forgiven him everything, even those things she did not know.

He broke the kiss.

Unable to let go of her, he held her close, chin on top of her head. Both breathed as if they had run a long distance. Her heart battered his chest, trying to break through. Her body always called to his, much as he'd fought it, but now, a sense of peace lay alongside the wanting, luring him to the dream that he might some day deserve love, too.

His mind struggled to regain control. His breathing steadied. He did not let her go.

'Solay…' He looked up at the sky, unable to meet her eyes, but knowing what he must say. 'Solay, I'm going to London.'

She stiffened. 'When?'

'Next week.'

'Why?'

'I need to file a response to Weston's suit.' And meet with Gloucester on the impeachment, but he let that pass.

'Will you come back?' she whispered, though there was no one to hear.

It would be easier to stay away, to disappear into his

work and avoid the temptation of her body day by day and the gnawing pain of hiding his secrets. But there was a peace in this life, in this odd existence, that he was reluctant to leave. 'I'll return within a fortnight. But I want you to know something.'

'What?' She stiffened her elbows, as if expecting a blow.

'I cannot guarantee the outcome of this suit,' he began, 'but you have my oath. I am going to do the best I can.'

Under his chin, nestled against his throat, she nodded.

He let her go, then, and met her eyes, wanting to see that she believed him, berating himself for raising hopes he did not know whether he could fulfil. His vaunted earthly justice seemed more uncertain than ever.

'I know you will.'

'Now I need your oath, Solay.'

She did not answer 'of course', as the old Solay would have. 'My oath on what?'

'You must promise me to hide your studies when we return to Court.'

She smiled. 'Now the Great Truth-Teller wants me to keep secrets.'

What had happened to the woman who sought only to please? 'To protect you from the King's anger, yes. Promise me.'

She shook her head. 'You wanted me to speak my truth, Justin. It's too late now to change your mind.'

And the pain that poured through him as he faced what it would mean to lose her was just as terrible as he had always feared.

Justin's absence left a gaping hole in her world.

She missed their games of Nine Man Merrills that stretched longer as the daylight lengthened. She missed watching the sun set and the stars come out. Afterwards, he would walk her to her room, his hand at her back, and leave her at her door with a kiss, nothing more. But everything.

Except for wanting to be his wife in every sense, she could have lived this way always.

Now, without him, though her skin welcomed the warm spring sunshine, the air that filled her lungs was not as sweet. This, then, was what it meant to miss a lover.

'Are you sure he won't deliberately lose the case?' Her mother's harsh question interrupted her thoughts.

Solay threaded her needle expertly, darning a rip in Jane's last whole tunic. 'Yes.'

Her mother shook her head. 'You trust him too much.'

'Perhaps, but if he lost, it would only make us a greater burden on him. Besides, he believes everyone deserves justice.'

Her mother gave a brusque laugh. 'How can you know what he believes? He does not share your bed, daughter.'

Solay's needle slipped, jabbing her thumb. She sucked the drop of blood away. She should dissemble, reassure, gloss over the problem, lest her mother think something was wrong with her marriage.

But something *was* wrong.

She put down the needle. 'No, Mother, he does not.'

'Not for want of desire,' her mother said. 'Any fool can see what lies between you.'

Solay blushed, staring down at the half-mended tear. She had thought the desire would fade, but it had not. Sometimes she could almost see the want wrap itself around them like some undulating serpent in the Garden of Eden. 'You warned me.' What kind of strength did her mother have, to resist such a force of nature?

'So have you bedded him?'

She shook her head.

'Why not?'

There was a moment of silence. She picked up her needle and shrugged her shoulders. 'He demands my love before he'll bed me.' She smiled, trying to make light of it.

'And what do you demand?'

'How can I demand anything? I am lucky to be married at all.'

Her mother sat straighter. 'The King called you his daughter. Justin is the lucky one.'

'He doesn't see it that way.'

The black eyebrows arched. 'Are you certain? He is not here for love of me.'

I care about you. It was more than she had thought she might ever have, but a long way from *I love you.* 'We are bound. He feels his obligation.'

But she did not want him bound by oath. She wanted him bound by love, just as he had wanted her. And she laughed at herself for the foolish way the fates had turned.

'I have seen the way you watch him,' her mother said, looking up from her knitting. 'You have fallen in love with him.'

Solay's cheeks went cold. Deny, she should deny it. But she was tired of lies. 'Do you think he knows?'

Her mother laughed. 'Of course not. Men are hopeless that way.'

'It's strange, isn't it? That was his condition and I fulfilled it, but now I dare not tell him.'

'Why?'

For all the reasons her mother had warned her against loving in the first place. *Because he is too important. Because he holds my life in his hands. Because if he does not approve of me, I have no life.* 'He wouldn't believe me.'

Her mother cocked an eyebrow. 'I can understand your want of his body, but I cannot understand why you want more.'

'He's...' She shook her head, laughing at herself. 'He's stubborn and pigheaded and judgemental, but he has honour and integrity.' She went on her knees before her mother, gathering the blue-veined hands in hers. 'He really believes, Mother. He believes truth and justice are possible here on earth. He believes so much that he makes me believe in them, too. And if he ever says "I love you," I'll believe that, too.'

'Have I taught you nothing? You must trust no one.'

'But I'm married to him.' Sweet relief even to say it. No man could put them asunder. Justin had promised that.

'Married, yes, but unless you share his bed you cannot know him and have no way of influencing him. You must end this separation and lie with him or you will be totally at his mercy.'

She looked at her mother's frightened face, pity staining her love. In the worry she saw there, she recognised the life her mother had led, one in which not even the sharing of bodies was sacred. Always something was held back. The body was never traded without a price. A prostitute not paid in coin, but in loyalty and influence.

And she did not want that life. Not in the court, not in the bed. Justin had taught her that much. She did not know how far she could follow his path, but she could no longer follow the old one.

'When I lie with him, it will be because I love him and for no other reason.'

Fear darkened her mother's eyes and she squeezed Solay's hands until her nails left marks. 'Listen to me. You were the King's subject before you were born. You will be the King's subject no matter who your husband is, no matter whether your husband lives or dies. Always, always, your first loyalty must be to the King. Before your husband, before your family, even before God.'

'No, Mother. My first loyalty must be to myself.'

Her mother drew back her hands and clasped them in her lap, as if she would never touch Solay again. 'Then it seems I have no daughter.'

Solay pushed herself up from her knees. 'You have a daughter, Mother, or else Justin and I would not be here. But you no longer have a pawn.'

And she thought her mother stifled the hint of a smile.

Chapter Twenty-Three

'Solay, can I talk to you?' Jane, a gangly fifteen, shifted awkwardly from foot to foot at the threshold.

Solay looked up from puzzling over her birth chart. Each planet, each house was an uncertain victory she must earn without asking the physician directly. He thought she was interested only in herbs and healing. 'Of course.'

Jane's pale hair was gathered behind her, out of the way, and as she entered the room, Solay recognised the curve of breast and hip beneath the tunic and tights. How could the girl have grown so much without her noticing?

Jane began without preamble. 'What will happen to us? Without the house?'

Her words stole Solay's tongue.

Jane had been only five when they fled to the country, too young to remember much about her father, the Court, and its trappings. Her mother had planned for Solay to return to Court. Jane was to stay at home, tending to her needs as she aged. Solay had been schooled in airs and graces while Jane grew as she liked, half-wild, playing outdoors and with animals and books her primary companions.

Now, their indulgence seemed thoughtless and cruel. Dear God, if they lost the suit, how could this naïve, half girl live without the protection of this house?

She took a breath. Jane had always embraced the truth, even when she did not like it. 'We shall be at Justin's mercy.'

'Will he find us another house?'

Jane's question shredded the final bit of the gauzy dream she had clung to. Her fragile truce with Justin had created a timeless bubble that closed out King and Court. Now, reality loomed. What would happen to her mother and sister if the suit were lost? Even the King could not find a husband for a woman who knew only horses and books.

'Yes. Yes, I'm sure he will.' She had just extolled his virtues to her mother. Justin was a man who would do his duty. She knew him that well.

'He likes me a little, doesn't he? He said I was helpful with the documents he needs.'

Solay's heart ached. Beneath her boyish bravado, Jane had grasped for the first time the lesson Solay and her mother had always known: her life depended on pleasing others. 'Of course he does.'

'When I asked about the law, he explained some of it to me and didn't seem to mind. Maybe I could be useful to him. Like a clerk.'

'Don't worry, Jane. Everything will be all right.' But as she hugged her sister, she decided she could avoid the issue no longer. She would ask Justin when he returned, and pray she liked his answer.

After Jane left, Solay pulled out a new sheet of paper. Could she find a hint in the stars of what was in store for her sister?

She drew the square of the Water Carrier, Aquarius, for Jane's birth date, then sighed. She had had little luck in developing her own reading. In the centre of her chart, Cancer the Crab crouched unsteadily, waiting for the proper planets to surround him.

She was not at all certain that what she had filled in was correct. In the Fourth House of family, she had expected a grand planet, a sign of royalty and power, Mars, or even Jupiter. Instead, according to the tables, the House sat empty.

It must mean she had much yet to learn.

Justin's trunk arrived home two days before midsummer, so all the next day, Solay listened for his horse, not sure until the moment she heard it that he would really return. Jane, eager to please, flew out the door, ready to lead the beast to the stable.

Solay was right behind her. As he dismounted and handed the reins to Jane, Solay slipped her arms around his waist and held him close, loving the feel of his arms tightening around her.

'I missed you,' she whispered into his chest, and thought she felt a nod above her head.

She pulled away, afraid she had revealed too much, but his eyes held a softness and his lips a smile. The sun caressed her face, but, gazing at Justin, she felt the dizziness of the snowfall. He bent his head. Her lips opened to him.

'Justin! What is the news from London?' Her mother's voice commanded attention.

Their mouths, so near a kiss, dissolved into smiles.

Solay sighed. 'She will want every detail.'

'I know.' He waved to Lady Alys at the upstairs window, then turned back to Solay and took her lips, hard, fast and with promise. 'I missed you, too,' he whispered.

Both Lady Alys and Jane had endless questions about the state of the suit. Solay was not alone with him again until the late-day sky turned pink. She relished each warm hour of summer, so they sat outside to catch the last of the daylight.

He took a sip of mead and stretched his legs as the pink clouds caught fire, then turned golden orange.

'Justin, did you hear news of Agnes?'

He frowned. 'It is said she now shares a room with Hibernia, as well as a bed.'

We are to be together, Agnes said. This must have been her meaning. His wife in the castle; his mistress at Court. It was happiness enough. Unless…

'Justin, the subpoena—what happened to it?'

He took a sip of mead, not meeting her eyes. 'Nothing. It is no more.'

She could not help but smile. If Agnes could find happiness, perhaps she could, as well. She twirled the stem of golden flowers she had picked. 'Shall I tell you what I have learned while you've been away?'

'Please.'

She thrust the stem close to his nose. 'This is Saint John's Wort. It can be boiled in wine and drunk for inward wounds or made into an ointment for those on the skin.' He listened patiently while she listed all the plant's uses. 'It's a herb of Leo, which is ruled by the sun, the gold of the flowers.'

'Piss-a-beds are yellow,' he said, grinning. 'Are they flowers of Leo, too?'

She wagged her finger at him, certain of her knowledge. 'Don't mock me. 'Tis just as logical as the law.'

He laughed, cleansing all fear, and looked up at the darkening sky. 'It's good to be back. I could barely see the sky at day's end in London.'

'It did not look the same when you were gone.' She hugged the silent moment of peace, working up the courage to ask him. 'Justin, what happens next?'

'What do you mean?'

'If we lose the house.'

Lines furrowed his brow. 'Do you doubt my ability?'

'No, but I do not have your faith in justice. I cannot leave my family's fate in the hands of the law.' She strangled the flower's stem, gripping it until her knuckles turned white. 'We are not powerful. My mother has enemies still, even you—' She bit her tongue.

He covered her hands with his. 'Solay, I knew my obligations when we wed.'

She nodded, looking down at his hand covering hers. Her family had become his burden, just as she had planned.

Unable to meet his eyes, she looked up at the sky. The first, faint star pierced the darkness. *I wish for his love, not just his duty.*

He put his arm around her and followed her gaze. 'You love the summer, but there is less time to see the stars.'

She leaned into his comfort with a sigh. There would be no more talk of the future. 'True, but I don't have to shiver as I watch them.' She lifted her arm. 'Look. There is Hercules.'

He squinted at the sky. 'Where?'

So she drew the constellation of Hercules with her finger until he finally saw the upside-down kneeling warrior with his lifted club.

'Come,' he said, finally. 'I have something for you.'

She followed him to the room where he opened the trunk, lifted out a large, flat volume, and laid it in her lap. It was as big as a small table and he had to help her hold it. 'I found this in London and thought of your birthday.'

She pulled back the leather covering it to reveal a bound volume. She opened it with reverent fingers, her eyes wide as she realised what she held. 'It's a Kalendarium.'

He leaned forward, turning pages, pointing out each treasure. 'Here are the tables of the position of the sun in the zodiac on every day of the entire year. And here is a list of all the eclipses.' He pronounced the unfamiliar words carefully. 'It tells the proper time for bloodletting, so the physician will be impressed with your knowledge.' He turned the pages carefully. 'And here are all the charts.'

She touched the pages with reverent fingers. 'It's magnificent.' The copyist had filled the pages with clear, neat script. Such a volume would surely cost as much as a small cottage.

'I thought,' he said, his voice rough, 'that if you were going to anger the King, your readings should at least be accurate.'

The symbols blurred before her eyes.

He reached over to catch a tear. 'Don't cry. You'll spot the pages.'

She blinked, trying not to weep. 'Thank you.'

He rose and moved around her room. There was nowhere, not even the bed, that he could make his. 'Solay…'

She held her breath, not wanting to interrupt. Never had Justin been a man to have trouble speaking his mind.

'I want to stay with you tonight.'

'Of course.' She reached for the laces on her gown, vaguely disappointed. She wanted to be his wife, yet this seemed so cold now.

He took her hands in his. 'No. Just—stay.'

Her chest lightened with relief. 'I would like that.'

Together, they put the precious volume aside. She rose, feeling a stranger in her own room. He removed his boots and lay on his back on top of the bed. She unlaced her shoes and lay beside him, staring at the ceiling, afraid to touch him.

He would see her rumpled hair when she woke, might kiss her before she had freshened her mouth. Would he still want her after that?

Wordless, he slipped his arm under her shoulders, pulling her head to pillow on his shoulder.

And she slept until sunrise.

* * *

Justin woke to find himself sprawled across a bed empty of her.

He threw an arm over his eyes to block the sun, wondering what she would say to him this morning. He had held her until she fell asleep. Nothing more had happened.

Nothing physical.

Something more than their bodies had bonded, but it was fresh and fragile and he was not yet certain whether to trust it.

The smell of baking bread made his stomach growl and he swung his legs out of bed, glad to be back with her.

He had missed her more than he expected. Through the busy days at Westminster, the work on the impeachment document and conferences at the Inns at Court, he would yearn for the peace of sunset. But at day's end, the sky turned red, then blue and the very stars reminded him of her.

He had been right about one thing. Truth drew you closer. Lies built walls.

Parliament wouldn't meet until the autumn, but he and Gloucester had met surreptitiously with two key members of the Commons to outline their plan of impeachment.

And he had found himself using the very methods he despised. Deceit. Stretching the Statutes. He had become the very thing he'd vowed to fight, manipulating the law for what he thought was a good end.

What happens next? she had asked. He was beginning to ask the same. After Hibernia, would Gloucester seek to depose the King himself?

He could tell her none of this so he told her the subpoena had gone away. A truth, but a lie, for it had been replaced by something even more dangerous: a plan to impeach Hibernia.

So he added another crime to the list of those he could not

confess. All his distrust had only come back in kind. Now, she did not even trust him to protect her family.

He splashed some water on his face and reached for a towel. The time had come. Once he shared her bed, once he was fully her husband, his body would know what his mind could not: whether he could be certain of her.

Chapter Twenty-Four

Solay spent the day poring over her precious present, admiring page after page of tables, neatly written in dark brown ink. There were even two letters illuminated in gold. She saw and heard little else all day, neither the sun's movement through the sky or Justin's step at the door of their bedchamber.

'Take off your apron,' he whispered in her ear, hands on her shoulders. 'There'll be no more work today.'

Heat spread from her cheeks to her centre. Did he mean to take her in the middle of the day?

The memory of a stone corridor in Nottingham made her damp between the legs.

She turned, trying to look stern, but a little smile kept tugging at her lips. ''Tis full light.'

'Exactly. And I have plans to celebrate your day.'

'My day?'

'Tomorrow is your birthday, is it not?'

This was the first birthday she could ever claim. She had always loved Midsummer's Eve, when the sun ruled the sky for longer than any other day, and now, now she knew why. 'It is, but you have already given me a gift beyond measure.'

'Well, the whole village begins celebrating tonight. You must join them.'

The laugh that escaped was pure joy. 'It's St John's Day they celebrate, not mine.'

He arched a brow. 'Well, either way, we're going to join the festivities.'

It's my day, it's my day. She sang the words silently, as she pulled on her good indigo-dyed gown. It was really St John the Baptist's Day, but she would pretend the celebration was for her. Tonight, she and her husband might share a bed. And more.

They asked the others to join them, but Solay's mother insisted she was too old and Jane too young, so Justin and Solay escaped alone.

'I hear the young people stay up the whole night,' her mother said as they left.

Justin's smile suggested what they might be doing. He took her hand as they left for the village and the tingle she felt spoke of promises for later.

Their dower house was attached to a castle that had passed to yet another absentee lord since Lady Alys lost her rights to it. The steward, mindful of summer's endless days of cutting hay and shearing sheep, had ended the midsummer work day far short of sunset, set up wooden trestles with cakes and ale, and joined the serfs in a brew.

Justin tugged her hand and pulled her over to the table full of small loaves of St John's bread. He picked up one and broke off a piece for her. 'Here's a bite of birthday bread.'

She took it, her lips brushing his fingers. More than the sun warmed her cheeks. On the other side of the green, the physician and his wife smiled and waved. They must think him a foolish love-smitten husband.

As they wandered the green, her every move echoed his, as if the air were water, rippling between them.

At the edge of the green, a shallow stream, too wide to jump across, ran merrily towards the Thames. Courting couples sent little wooden barks with candle stubs and precious wishes out into the stream, cheering when the boat touched the other side safely, meaning a wish would be granted, and moaning if the little boat sank.

'There's a good candle wasted,' she muttered, looking at them with longing as one of the little craft sank and doused a candle and a wish.

'The night is short. Do you want to make a wish?' he asked.

She nodded. She would cherish the gift of this day for ever.

Two village boys had carved extra bits of wood and gathered candle stubs, glad to trade them for Justin's coin. Solay knelt in the grass, dabbling her fingers in the stream, as Justin melted candle wax on the wood and stuck the stub in it.

'Shall I write your wish on the boat?'

She shook her head and reached for it. 'I know what I wish for.'

Holding the rickety boat steady with both hands, she knelt on the grassy bank, reluctant to let it go. As long as she held it, wish and candle intact, she had hope.

Justin sat beside her, close, as he had been all day. 'What do you wish for?'

She met his eyes, knowing he must recognise the want in hers for the first night of their life together. She saw want and something more in his gaze. Could she believe it?

Shaking her head, she looked down at the little bark. 'It must be secret or 'twill not be granted.'

She closed her eyes and let the boat go.

He held his breath with her as it rocked from side to side, splashing water on to the candle wax before it righted itself. Then, in the middle of the stream, another woman's wish drifted towards it, riding the downstream current.

'Go around!' he cried, waving to the other bark as if he could change its course.

In vain. It rammed Solay's and both careened wildly. She gasped. He grabbed her hand and she thought he held a breath. Did he care so much then, if her wish came true?

Would he feel the same if he knew what it was?

They bobbed back and forth on the water, then the other bark capsized as the young woman who sent it groaned, then laughed as her beau stole a kiss.

The little prow of Solay's boat touched the opposite bank and she gave a little cry of joy.

Justin hugged her. 'So,' he whispered, tickling her ear, 'now will you tell me your wish?'

What would he say if he knew she wanted them to be husband and wife? Safe in his embrace, surrounded by his scent, she parted her lips to tell him.

Then she stopped.

Every time she had tried to lie with him, he had refused her. Refused her so violently that everything that had come before was tainted. Instead of telling him, she wanted to cling to anticipation, still hoping, like the little bark, that it might touch the bank.

Later. Later she might tell him.

She sat back on her heels on the soft grass. 'I wished,' she said, smiling softly, 'to know *your* birthday.'

She thought disappointment touched his eyes. 'That's all?'

'And do not lecture me about being forbidden to study. The King is not here today.'

He laughed then. She was beginning to love the sound. In giving her a celebration, he had given himself one as well.

She held her breath as he studied her, trying to decide whether to trust her.

'All right. You shall have your wish. I don't know why I

didn't tell you long ago.' He leaned close to her ear and whispered, 'I was born a fortnight before Christmas.'

The vibration of her laughter tickled her heart. 'I was right! You were born under the sign of the Archer,' she said, unable to resist a prideful smile.

'But you were not sure, or you would not have wanted to know so badly.'

For the first time, it was a comfort that he understood her so well.

They joined hands and turned back to the green, where the boys held impromptu races while the men brought fallen branches from the orchard to pile on the bonfire.

A tall lad set a torch to the pile, sending sparks crackling towards a cerulean sky. The younger boys grabbed brands from the fire, then raced up and down the green like shooting stars. A few, the brave ones, leaped over the fire's flames.

She glanced sideways at him. Ale in his right hand, he watched the jumping boys. 'I used to do that,' he said, nodding at them. 'There's an art to it, to guessing when the flame will dip and timing your jump.'

His smile reminded her of the boy who had thrown snowballs in Windsor's Upper Ward and she longed to give him boys of his own to play with. 'Did you ever get burned?'

He shook his head. 'No, but when I singed my good tunic I got a lecture from my mother.' His left hand toyed with her fingers, lifting each in turn. 'I bet I can still clear it,' he said. A wicked smile tugged at the corner of his mouth.

'No!' She clung to his hand, but she couldn't keep him from rising. 'What if you fall into the flames?'

He simply laughed and downed the dregs of his ale. 'Watch me.'

She covered her face with her hands, peeking through her fingers, trying to remember how much ale he had drunk. At least he didn't stagger as he crossed the green. A dark figure against a sky of stained-glass blue, he looked back and waved, as if to be sure she was watching.

She waved back, gritting her teeth.

'They're all boys at heart, milady.' The physician's ample-bosomed wife had come up beside her to watch.

'What if he's hurt?' Barley seeds and eggs would be useless against a severe burn.

'Don't worry,' the woman said. 'Now be sure you're watching him or he'll do it again to make sure you saw him.'

She took a deep breath. 'If he's doing it to impress me, I'd rather he do something else,' she grumbled.

Justin was the next in line to jump when she saw the night's first star. *I wish for him to be safe.*

He took a running start and leapt.

Just as he jumped, the blaze soared skyward and he passed directly through the flame. A tongue of fire licked his tunic and it ignited before he crashed to the ground.

Solay ran, her heart in her throat, knowing only that he must not die.

He rolled away from the fire, smothering the flames as he went. She reached him before any of the men, falling to her knees, pounding the flames with her bare hands, vowing in incoherent thoughts that if he lived, she would no longer wait to bed him.

Thumping his back, she pounded the last smouldering spark on a ruined tunic.

'Ouch! Stop it! I'm unhurt.' He sat up and waved away the men who had run over to help.

She cupped his soot-streaked cheek. 'Don't you ever, ever do that again. Now let me look at it.'

Miraculously, Justin's back was red, but not blistered. The physician joined them, applied a cold cloth, and reminded Solay to apply ivy and comfrey when they returned home.

Justin stood, arching his back, and stretched out his hand to help her up.

She wanted to throw herself into his arms and cry in relief, but his grin was too cocky to be rewarded, so she let him help her up with what she hoped was royal disdain. 'I am beginning to understand your mother.'

He hugged her shoulder. 'I told you I knew how to do it.'

She shook her head. 'Enough foolishness. We're going home so I can get you out of that tunic and keep the cold compress on.'

He smiled and put his arm around her shoulder, pulling her to him. 'No need. It'll itch for a few days, but I've had worse.'

She put her arm around his waist, careful to avoid his singed back, and snuggled against him, shaking her head.

The sun's final blush left the horizon. The older folks drifted off to bed. What was left of the night belonged to the young. The village lads, the ones more interested in kissing than bonfires, slipped into the shadowed orchard to be alone with the girls.

As they walked up the path to the house, a moan drifted behind them on the clear night air.

'Midsummer's Eve is a night for lovers,' he said, the whisper raw in his throat.

His breath rose and fell, whether from the exertion of the jump or from want of her, she didn't know, but if she was to have her Midsummer's Night wish, she would have it now.

Here, there was no castle, no Court, no King. Only the two of them and the stars.

She wrapped her arms around him, raised her face and kissed him.

The wind caressed her throat like another hand of loving. All her fears lifted. She lay back in the grass and he undressed her, not gently, for his fingers shook with urgency. She writhed with anticipation, with some spark that moved her relentlessly towards him.

And the touch of the warm night air on the tip of her breast felt like his breath.

His fingers stilled.

Her muscles held their breath. Surely he would not reject her now?

She opened her eyes. 'Do you find me…pleasing?'

'You know I do. No more games, Solay.'

'But even so, you didn't, you wouldn't…' She stumbled, afraid to say the words. 'I thought…'

'That I didn't want you?' He stroked the hair away from her forehead. 'How could you not know?'

And if she didn't, he showed her with a kiss. He drank her lips and searched her mouth with his tongue, loving her inside and out. Then his kisses trailed down her neck with little nibbles that made her laugh with joy.

'You are mine, Solay,' he whispered. 'By this act, we shall be truly wed.'

He pushed her skirt away, and she unlaced his shirt and tangled her fingers in his hair, seeking the hidden heat of his chest.

She wanted to see him, to relish the sight, but now was not a time to look and savour. That would come later, after they were sated and the moon had risen.

With awkward fingers, lips and tongue, she explored his chest, his neck, the crook of his arm. His skin salt was on her tongue. He twisted now, hungry as she, shucking off his chausses until only the fragile barrier of skin came between them.

She reached for him, the heat of his staff branding her palm before he pulled away. Leaning on his arms, he loomed over her, dark against the cobalt sky.

Surely he would not resist her now.

'I want you,' she said. 'Please. I'm crazed by it.'

He shook his head, his breathing ragged. 'I want you to be ready.'

'I am ready.' She rolled her eyes to the heavens and grabbed his arms. 'I'm telling you the truth.'

He shook his head, slowly. 'Not the way you will be. Lie back.'

She did.

He leaned over her, holding her arms down with each of his. Her body swelled, aware of his eyes on her, just as they had been that night so many months ago.

This, this was so much more.

She opened her mouth, hungry for him to fill it, but instead of kissing her again, he took her breast. The soft scrape of his teeth sent lightning between her legs. They opened of their own accord, melting with anticipation.

Without lifting his head, he slipped his fingers inside her, teasing, preparing, until it seemed the entire world had collected at that one point. She thrust towards him, wanting to take him in everywhere, through her skin.

He was right. She had not been ready before. When he slipped inside, the opening that had seemed too small to hold him matched him perfectly.

Her breath and her body were one. There was inside and no outside, no difference between his skin and hers. No up or down. No earth or sky. Just this swirling oneness, dizzying as the fall of snowflakes.

'Look at me,' he commanded.

Her eyes fluttered open. Moonlight showed her a glimpse of his eyes and when she saw the fierce possession, she gripped him even more tightly. His eyes, relentless, wouldn't release hers. As he stroked her, she spiralled upwards, holding him so tightly that it seemed they would be joined for ever.

Eyes locked with his, just before his loving stole her speech, the words burst free.

'I...love...you.'

Then she cried out, and so did he, and then they lay together, needing no words.

And over his shoulder, she could see the stars, scattered across the heavens in a constellation she had never seen before.

Chapter Twenty-Five

The next morning, Solay opened her eyes as sunlight kissed the sky, creating the world anew.

Behind her, Justin held her tightly against him, his hand cupping her breast. His even breathing against her neck told her he slept. Relieved, she lay still, needing time to think about what she would say.

He rolled over on his back, wincing as the grass touched the burn, but he didn't wake.

She followed the rise and fall of his chest, wanting to thread her fingers through his hair again. Now that she had known him, he suddenly looked fragile as well as strong. If the heart that had pulsed against hers stopped, surely hers would follow it into death.

I love you.

She had meant every one of those three words. Now, they lay like rubies scattered on the path for him to gather.

Would he?

What if she asked *Justin, do you believe me?*

What would she do if he said 'no'?

Yet she wanted to ask another, even more frightening question.

Do you love me?

Such a foolish wish. But when he looked at her, the way he had loved her last night, oh, now she knew what Agnes had meant. Such loving opens the soul.

Now, her soul lay naked.

Waiting for him to wake, she sat up to watch the sun slip over the edge of the horizon. Bright and yellow and hot enough to sear her eyes, it burned a hole in the orange sky.

And it illuminated dark corners, shining light where she had never thought to look.

That was another, larger question.

Why was it so important to him that she love him?

I love you.

Justin lay on his back, arm flung over his eyes, savouring the words drifting through his memory, heady as the scent of roses.

If she had said it at any other time, he would have explained, excused, resisted. He could have told himself she didn't mean it.

He would have been safe.

But even Solay could not dissemble at that most elemental moment. Could she?

He pushed aside the doubt, wanting a moment of peace. He yawned and stretched out his arm, uneasy that she was no longer within reach. Sitting up, he rubbed the burn on his lower back and looked for her.

Wrapped loosely in the unlaced dress, she sat hugging her knees to her chest and gazing out at a golden-orange sky.

He moved behind her, pushed aside her dark curls and kissed the curve of her neck. She arched in answer, and he reached for her breasts, ready to love her again.

She stiffened and pulled away. 'Tell me about the other woman,' she said. 'The one you were betrothed to.'

The peace lay shattered.

'Why do you want to know?' When she knew the answer, her *I love you* would vanish. He had known loving her would lead to this, yet he took her still.

She put her hand over his, gently, but would not let him turn away. 'You are the one who has preached the power of truth.' Her violet eyes met his, full of acceptance, but demanding honesty. 'I told you I would not judge.'

He sighed, resigned. He should have told her months ago. 'You must know something already.'

'I know you were to be wed and the girl died.'

She did not know the worst. 'What more must you know?'

'I want to know what happened.'

He looked down at an ant crawling on the grass, trying to steady his thoughts before he was forced to speak. Why must a woman carve a man open, pick out his innards and expose all things private? 'There's not much to tell.'

'So about this, then, you cannot be fully honest.'

Shamed into speech, he spat the words as quickly as he could. 'Her name was Blanche. She came to me wide-eyed and tempting and I…' He shrugged.

'You and she…?'

'Yes.' He closed his eyes against the vision of their mating, a tepid thing in the end, over as soon as he finished what she came for.

No. A woman could not lie in the moment of joining.

'How old were you?'

He opened his eyes and filled them with Solay. She had promised forgiveness, but that was before she knew. 'Youth does not excuse me. I was already at the Inns at Court.'

Did he see a wisp of disappointment in her eyes?

'So you agreed to marry.'

He nodded, trying to remember whether honour or hope

had driven him the hardest. For those few weeks, he pretended he was loved without reserve, without judgement. A lie. All of it.

He had not been loved at all.

'The banns were read. Our families rejoiced.'

Each hard-won confession fell into silence. Each time, he hoped he had revealed enough to satisfy her.

But she probed again. 'Then what?'

'It became evident that she was with child.'

Solay looked down, as if thinking of the seed he'd planted last night. She was silent a long time. 'You would not be the first couple to anticipate the final vows,' she said, finally. 'But I did not know you had a child.'

'I don't. A week before the wedding, she confessed the babe was not mine and she told me she loved the father.'

Blanche's words, long buried, burst to life. *I could never love you. You love the law more than you will ever love a woman.*

'Then why didn't she marry him?'

'Because he was already married.'

He thought he heard her gasp, but he fixed his eyes on the ground and stabbed at the dirt with a short stick, knowing she would ask for the rest.

'And what did you say?' she said, finally. 'After she told you the truth?'

'I told her she had made this marriage and now we both must lie in it.'

'A marriage neither of you wanted.'

The stick between his fingers snapped. 'I knew you wouldn't understand. By the law, we were already wed.'

'So you chose to live a lie to abide by the letter of the law?'

He frowned, wishing for the old, accommodating Solay. 'There was no other way.' *It's what must be done, son.*

'Did you look for one?'

He flinched and hurled the broken stick at a tree. 'She was wrong! She trapped us. The banns are binding. There was no escape.'

Silence stretched up to the calm blue of the summer sky. He breathed again. Perhaps this would satisfy her.

Perhaps she wouldn't ask what happened next.

But Solay would not be fooled. 'She found one, didn't she?'

Her question seized his throat like murderous hands. This, this was what it was like for other people, those terrified by the truth.

She let him sit without answering for a long time, but she never looked away. And she never said *you don't have to tell me.*

'Yes,' he said, when neither the grass nor the wind nor Solay's eyes offered an escape. 'She went down to the river, loaded her pockets with stones, and took herself and her unborn babe to the bottom of the Thames.'

And because Blanche had not told her parents the truth, neither could he. Blanche's mother had shrieked and torn her hair. *She's condemned to the Seventh Circle of Hell for ever.*

Solay tugged his fingers from their fist and laced their hands together. 'I'm sorry. I'm so sorry.'

He pulled his hands away, grabbed another twig and snapped it. 'She shouldn't have lied.' He no longer knew whether he argued with Solay or with his past. 'If she'd just been honest from the beginning—'

'Yet when she was honest and wanted to leave the marriage, you refused her.'

'It was not me! It was the law.'

'So this time, you made sure you had a way out.'

He searched her eyes and knew she had seen through him, through everything. *I have a condition.* He heard the echo of his voice, desperate to control the feelings for her that had swamped him, even then. 'I would not risk that again. And I could not force someone else into a marriage with someone they didn't love.'

'Do you love her still?'

He rummaged amid the painful images, searching for the answer. 'I'm not sure I loved her at all.'

'Yet you had not taken another bride.'

He shook his head. 'You may blame Blanche for that.'

'*You* do not blame Blanche. You blame yourself.'

Pain ripped through his chest, sharp as an arrow. He could see her still. He always would. Her blue eyes, first seductive and then, on that last day, so full of pain. He could have set her free with one word. She and the babe would have lived.

He must admit the truth to Solay, then lose her. 'I killed her. That's the truth I haven't told you.'

'No,' she whispered. 'That's the lie you've told yourself.'

Shocked, he searched her face. No judgement touched her eyes. No blame. Only compassion and tenderness and understanding.

He resisted her comfort. 'You can't know. You weren't there.' He had worked so hard, hoping that some day, he could bring enough justice into the world to atone for his sin. 'My judgement was her death sentence. I can never forgive myself for that.'

'Until you do, she holds you at the bottom of the river with her.'

And the love in Solay's eyes as she held out her arms looked like absolution.

Chapter Twenty-Six

Solay and her mother sat quietly in the solar later that week when she decided to brave the subject of William Weston.

Justin had faced his past. Perhaps she could do the same.

Her mother was reading documents in preparation for the case. Odd, that the mysterious William Weston consumed their lives as fully as the King once had.

She hardly remembered the man her mother had married. He had swirled into their lives when she was eleven and was gone within two years, most of that spent persuading Parliament that he was Lady Alys's legal husband. Three years ago, when he died, they did not even see him laid to rest.

Yet he had married her mother. And the few times she had seen him, though he had barely spoken to her, he had watched her like a dog stalking a deer.

She took another stitch, then put down Justin's tunic. 'What was William Weston like?'

Her mother looked up from the parchment. 'Why do you ask?'

Solay smoothed the singed threads' edges and shrugged, as if the answer were of little consequence. 'How can I not be curious? Our lives and our lawsuit revolve around him. Did you know him well before your marriage?'

Her mother's gaze did not falter. 'He was at Court. One knows people at Court.'

'Did I ever see him there?'

'You were very young. He was much in Ireland. The King sent him to subdue the rebellion.'

'What was he like?'

'A man. Just a man. Certainly not a king.'

'What did he look like?'

'What does it matter?'

'I want to know.'

'It was a long time ago.'

'He was your husband. Don't you remember?'

Her mother sighed. 'He was much older than I.'

'So was the King.'

'As I remember, he was tall, strong and had very dark hair.'

'What colour were his eyes, Mother?'

'Blue, like the King's, but deeper.'

'When did you marry him?'

'I don't remember.'

Solay put down her mending and stared. 'You don't remember? How can you not remember your marriage?'

Yet there was much her mother had not remembered. Her birthday. Jane's.

'What difference does it make?'

'It makes a great deal of difference in this lawsuit.' All her life, she had known some things were not to be spoken of. She had never questioned. But not now. No longer. 'Justin trusted me and I trusted you, yet you have no proof that you ever wed the man and now you say you can't even remember?'

Red spots flared in her lined cheeks. 'You are cruel and you know nothing.'

'I know you are not telling the whole truth.' She crushed Justin's tunic in her fists and stood. 'If Justin loses the case, the fault will not be his alone.'

Lips pursed, her mother let her leave the room without a word.

She dropped the mending in their chamber and went to his workroom. He should know, at least, what her mother had said.

At the door she paused, relishing the sight of the straight, strong back her fingers had stroked this morning before they rose. For a moment, nothing else mattered. If only the two of them could close the door on the world for ever.

She sighed and he turned and smiled to see her. The pile at his left elbow had dwindled. 'I'm almost done.' His fist tapped the stack in frustration. 'There's nothing here.'

'Mother has done her best to hide the truth. She claims not even to remember the day they were wed.'

'There's no record of it.' He waved the stack, the last few documents. 'Another deed, another bill of sale—'

A folded document with a broken red wax seal slipped out.

She sank on to the bench beside him and stared at the cracked imprint of a lion rampant. The Weston seal.

She picked it up, her hand shaking. Undated, it carried only a few lines, written in an informal hand with no signature.

News of the birth of your daughter has reached me. I hope all went as you wanted. This amethyst brooch is hers. When she is grown, tell her the truth.

And an icy certainty chilled her spine.

'What is it?'

'A note from Weston. Accompanying a birth present to me of an amethyst brooch.'

An amethyst brooch like the one the King had sent back to her mother. It was yours, once, Solay. A gift from your father.

And all this time, she thought her mother had meant the King.

"It seems," she said, forcing her lips to move, "that I am no more royal than you are."

He grabbed the letter, skimming the lines, vague enough that if the King had read them, he might have been fooled. 'There could be another explanation. Perhaps Weston was currying favour with the King.'

She gripped her elbows, trying to cover the emptiness. She had pranced proudly at Court, but her very presence was the biggest lie of all.

'"The King called you his daughter." That's what Mother always said. Not that I *was* his daughter.'

His jaw settled into grim determination. 'Come. It is time for your mother to tell the truth.'

He rose, but she stopped him. 'No. Stay here. I must do this alone.'

Bits of her life floated across her memory as she walked to her mother's solar. No wonder Weston had spent all they had. He must have counted it small payment for having his child stolen.

She stood in the doorway, the note trembling in her hands. 'Why didn't you tell me, Mother?'

Her mother looked up. Her eyes flickered to the letter, but she did not reach for it. 'Tell you what?'

'That I am not the daughter of a King.'

Colour drained from her mother's face and she seemed to shrink inward, ageing before Solay's eyes. 'You were not to know,' she whispered, looking towards the door for someone listening. 'No one was to know.'

It was true, then. Alys had smuggled another man's child into the bed of the King. Discovery would surely have meant death.

All her life, Solay had clung to her royal blood, the only thing that made her special. Now, even that was a lie. Her entire existence was an elaborate disguising.

A hollow ache opened in her chest, but she didn't know whether the pain was for herself or her mother. 'Why?' She refused to whisper. She was done with secrets. 'Why did you call me the King's?'

'He could have no children.'

'How could that be? The man fathered ten children.'

Her mother shook her head, staring at the floor. 'That was in the days before. Later, he could no longer…' She couldn't say the words.

All of a sudden, too much made sense. A precise birthday would allow too many calculations. 'Jane, too?'

Her mother nodded. 'Her fair hair was a lucky accident.'

'And were you married to Weston when we were born?'

'It was part of the bargain. I helped his career with the King.'

Solay sighed. 'Tell me one true thing, Mother. One thing that was done out of honest feelings. Something you did for something other than personal gain.'

'I loved him.'

Love. Her mother had never used the word before. 'Who?'

'The King.'

'Loved him so much you made love with another man?' The idea was absurd. 'You never even called him by his name.'

She straightened her back and lifted her chin, once again the most powerful woman in the realm. 'He was the King, not some ordinary man.' She looked up at the ceiling, seeing things far away. 'He still needed to be as powerful in bed as in battle. It was the one thing I could give him.'

It was necessary for me to portray a desirable woman. 'The King would not call that love.'

Her gaze returned from the past. 'No, *you* would not call it love.'

And as she looked at her mother's face, she realised how much love that took.

But in the end, the deception was all for naught. 'It is over, then. Now, everyone will know who fathered me.'

Her mother grabbed her arm, her nails sharp on Solay's skin. 'No!'

She lifted her mother's fingers away and rubbed the four crescents on her forearm. 'How can it matter now? The King is long dead.'

'I did not do it only for him. It was the only thing I could give you. I will not let you destroy it.'

'Even if it means losing the house?'

Her mother lifted her head, the moment of desperation shed. 'What is one house to the daughter of a King?'

Nothing, it seemed. A house could be bought anew.

Solay left the room, moving in a body she no longer recognised. In her left hand, she clutched Weston's words with fingers that no longer seemed to belong to her. She touched her cheek, wondering whether she wore the same skin as when the sun rose, then stared at her right hand, veins blue with the blood of a man she'd considered a stranger.

Standing in Justin's doorway, she let the air fill her chest, each breath an effort.

'It's true, then,' he said.

She nodded, searching his eyes, praying she would find forgiveness. 'They were married. I am his daughter. So is Jane.'

'And you never suspected?'

She laughed, sadly, remembering her puzzlement at the emptiness of her Fourth House. 'No, but the stars knew.'

He squared the stack of documents as if the matter were closed. 'So you and Jane are Weston's only legitimate offspring. When we prove you are Weston's daughter, the property will be yours.'

'We are not going to tell them.' The certainty came across her, strong as her mother's lifetime of pride.

'Do you think ignoring the truth will change it? Why can't you just be who you are?'

Crushed in her damp palm, Weston's note stuck to her skin. 'Be who I am?' She heard a scream. Was it hers? 'Who am I? Suddenly proven I'm not the King's daughter. That leaves me only what I've been called all along: the daughter of a whore.'

He who so loved to speak the truth was struck dumb when she uttered it. And the small sense of triumph she felt at his pain died. If he loved her, he would understand.

But he'd never said he loved her.

'You've been like all the others.' She spoke with an unearthly sense of detachment as her marriage lay smashed before her. She was a different woman now. Not the King's daughter he thought he'd married. 'You look at me, but you see her.'

'That's not true.' His jaw clamped around the words, releasing no others.

'You've demanded I prove my love again and again. What if I ask you to prove you love me?'

She waited. For interminable minutes she waited while he stood there, unable to move from the cage he'd built.

'Even a whore's daughter deserves love, Justin.' The whisper almost choked her. 'And she needs it so much more than the daughter of a King.'

His silence was her answer. She locked her hope away with her illusions. The reality of her life was before her. And knowing all her mother had sacrificed, she knew what she must do.

She walked to the table and picked up the candle he had lit, touched it to the note from Weston, and flung it into the hearth. No one else would ever know. Even Jane. 'There's your blessed legal proof. Fleeting as a flame.'

He knelt to reach for it, but grabbed only ash. Black smoke drifted up the chimney and the note disintegrated into powder, like passion, not something that could last.

He looked up at her. 'I wanted to save this house for you. Is perpetuating a lie more important?'

'Not for me. For her.'

With a sigh, he rose and engulfed her in his arms. 'If it's that important to you, I will do as you want.'

Burrowed against his tunic, she consoled herself with the solid feel of his arms and the reassuring thump of his heart. If she could not have his love, then this, this must be enough.

She lifted her head, drinking in the softness of his brown eyes gazing at her. 'An Act of Parliament says they were wed. If Parliament can control a King, it should allow us to keep a house.'

'What will you say,' he said, 'when they ask you?'

'I will tell the truth.' She smiled, sadly. 'The King called me his daughter.'

Chapter Twenty-Seven

Justin watched Solay leave to prepare the evening meal, wishing he had a right to speak his truth.

What if I ask you to prove you love me?

Her question stuck in his belly like a sword thrust. Buffeted by his demands, the King's threats and her family's needs, sustained by pride or anger or by knowing who she was, she had demanded his love.

And it was too late. Much, much too late. While he had required her to convince him of her love, he'd fallen for her.

He stared at the empty doorway and laughed with a sad abandon, for she had neatly turned the tables. Now, if he told her he loved her, she would never, never believe him.

All his posturing, all his accusations, all his arguments were vain attempts at denial. He had implied she was not worthy of love, but all the time he was the unworthy one. She had forgiven him, but he could not forgive himself.

Words alone would not be enough to claim her. He would have to earn the right, to show her, with deeds, not words. He must give her what she wanted most in the world.

This house.

He stacked the documents and blew out the candle. He had dallied here because he loved to be with her, but tomorrow, he would return to London to better prepare for the case. What he had must be enough to convince a judge.

And then, what he did must be enough to convince Solay.

Solay shivered as October's raw wind swept the few remaining leaves from the trees in the courtyard of the Middle Temple, relieved that her statement to the judge was over.

Justin walked up to her. As she stood next to him, for the first time in months her skin felt warm and whole.

'What do you think? How were my answers?' she asked. The opposition's lawyer had been a mean-spirited man, accusing her of lying at every turn. 'Have we a chance?'

'I'll do everything in my power.'

'But…?'

'But it will depend on the whims and the prejudices of the court.'

She shook her head. 'At one time I wanted to hear you admit that the law was flawed. Now, I wish you'd tell me that justice will be done, no matter what.'

He put his arm around her, pulling her close. 'Justice will be done. No matter what.'

And just to hear him say it made her smile.

'Now,' he said, 'Here's something happier to think on. Agnes is back at Windsor. I thought you would like to see her.'

She nearly skipped. 'Oh! That would be wonderful.'

'If we start early tomorrow, we can be there before day's end.'

'Thank you.' She squeezed his arm in gratitude. She had barely seen him in the weeks since he left the house. He was, if anything, more gaunt than ever. 'You have not been eating enough.'

'I live in chambers and eat in the common hall. The cook cannot compare with you.'

'Have I finally taught you the art of flattery? My cooking is not so good.'

'I said nothing about the food.' He grinned. 'Only that the cook could not compare with you.'

Her laughter pealed and his smile broadened. 'So tell me,' she said, moulding her body against his side as they walked, 'what has kept you too busy to eat?'

'Parliament meets next month. There is much to prepare.'

'More subpoenas?'

'No. An impeachment.'

Her every muscle went rigid.

She forced herself to softness again, afraid he would notice her reaction. 'Oh?'

'I'm sorry. I knew it would bring unpleasant memories.'

She shrugged. The Court seemed years away. What did the intricacies of power matter now? She had her husband and he had promised to take care of her family. 'Who has earned the wrath of the Lords and Commoners?'

He stopped and looked at her, his eyes searching her face. A restless wind fluttered through his hair like fingers, but the narrow set of his lips did not part.

He's wondering whether he can trust me. After all this, he still wonders.

She reached up to lace her fingers with the wind in his unruly hair. 'It's all right. I only asked because I knew it was important to you.'

A shadow of the old suspicions lingered in his eyes. 'I must be sure you will not tell the King.'

Her hand slipped on to his cheek and he pressed against her palm. The King, still on gyration, had forgotten all about her. She knew where her loyalties lay. Everything she needed now, Justin held. 'I am your wife, not the King's.'

He took a breath, and released a sigh. 'Hibernia. It is Hibernia.'

She swallowed a gasp, then forced her lips to smile. 'Hibernia,' she whispered, wanting to know nothing more. 'No, I will not tell the King.'

But how could she keep this secret from Agnes?

The question still haunted her as she hugged Agnes the next day. Her friend's round face had narrowed somewhat, but she glowed with an inner light.

'You look happy,' Solay said, settling into a chair before the fire.

'I am. The King has made Hibernia justice of the Northern Counties.' She put a solicitous arm around Solay's shoulder. 'And you? How goes marriage to Lord Justin?'

Solay tried to smile. 'I am content.' The happiness of a mistress was beginning to look more appealing than the state of her marriage.

'You do not love him, I know.'

Solay shrugged, not correcting her. If she opened her mouth to confide, the truth would escape.

'Oh, Solay, I'm so sorry. All the happiness you saw for me is coming to pass. There is something wonderful I must tell you.' Firelight reflected in Agnes's soft blue eyes, as if it burned inside her. She closed the door. 'But you must keep the secret.'

Solay's heart was heavy with secrets. Surely it would crack with one more. 'Agnes, I'm not sure—'

Agnes sat and gripped Solay's fingers. 'We are to be married.' Each word was a smile.

Solay shook her head, sure she misheard. Justin's set jaw

flashed into her mind. *One man and one man only.* 'But he is already married.'

'He has put his wife aside.'

Solay touched Agnes's forehead with the back of her hand. Surely a fever had taken her senses. 'Agnes, that is not possible.'

'Ah, but it is! The King's own lawyers wrote the papers and sent them to the Pope months ago, along with a special appeal from the King.'

'By all the saints,' she whispered. The King now placed himself above even God's law. 'And his Holiness agreed?'

'He did not object. Their marriage is dissolved.'

'On what grounds?' Solay whispered weakly, surprised to hear Justin's words in her mouth.

'Grounds? I know not, neither do I care. But it is all thanks to you.'

'Me?'

'The Duke told me last winter that he had petitioned the Pope and he asked me to marry him, but I hesitated. Then, when you told me what was in the stars, I knew God had destined us to be together!'

Solay's stomach turned over. She clutched Agnes's shoulders, forcing her to meet her eyes. 'You mustn't do this.' How naïve she had been to think that her reading would cause no harm. 'There was more I didn't tell you. The stars predicted disaster!'

Agnes's smile never faltered. 'You are my friend. You would have warned me of danger.'

You would have warned me. Her fingers turned to ice and she could not look away from those trusting blue eyes. Before she left this room, she would betray someone.

Agnes, seeing her shocked face, patted her knee. 'Don't worry, Solay. The worst is nearly over for all of us, including the King.'

Grateful for a change of subject, she let her hands fall to her lap. Let Agnes talk. It would give her time to think. 'You mean Parliament will not renew the Council's charter?' She prayed so. Perhaps then there would be no impeachment.

Agnes shook her head. 'It's more than that. The Council will be destroyed. The King has arranged it with the judges.'

An uneasy feeling rippled through her. As little faith as she had had in the law, it sounded strange to hear such a thing spoken aloud. 'What do you mean?'

'The King called a secret meeting of senior judges and they rendered their legal opinion. They said Parliament cannot impeach anyone without the King's approval.'

She tasted remembered bitterness. 'They did not believe so when my mother was brought before them.'

She should have found it amusing. She should have been able to share it with Justin and laugh. *See, even the King seeks the counsel of the judges.*

But Agnes was not smiling. 'The judges said the Council members are all traitors.'

'Traitors?' Her blood ran cold. 'How can that be? The Council was created by Parliament. They've violated none of the tenets of the Statute of Treason.'

'They said it is the word of the King that is the law, not the statutes.'

Suddenly, everything Justin had said became clear. If the King put himself above the law, then neither the laws of Heaven nor of Earth were sacred.

'So you see,' Agnes said, smiling, 'it means the King doesn't have to do anything they say.'

For all her years at court, Agnes remained naïve about the ways of power, unless it affected her personally. It meant much more than that. Once condemned as traitors, they would all be hanged. Drawn. Quartered. Dead.

All perfectly legal.

Not Justin. Oh, please, not Justin. 'When? When will this happen?

'By the time the Council's charter expires all will be ready.'

'But Parliament!' Amazing what straws she clutched, expecting Parliament to save instead of condemn her world this time. 'When Parliament meets, they will confirm the law.'

'The King has thought of that. He told the sheriffs that anyone elected to Parliament this fall must be "neutral in the present disputes".'

Solay did not doubt that the sheriffs would manipulate the elections.

What will you do, she had asked Justin, if the King has not reformed? Always his answer had been what was right and legal. Now, his respect for the law left him vulnerable to those who cared only for power.

Solay rose. Justin must flee. She must keep him safe.

Agnes put a hand on her arm. 'You must not tell your husband.'

Husband. She had used the word so lightly once. 'I cannot let him die.'

'Then you do love him, yes?'

'I will not let him sit in ignorance and be destroyed. Agnes, if I mean anything to you, please, please help me.'

Agnes pouted. 'He's a stubborn, ill-dressed dullard. How can you love such a man?'

Solay's smile warred with her tears. 'And Hibernia is a peacock who laughs too loud. How can you love such a man?'

Agnes dabbed at her eyes with her sleeve. 'Big oafs.'

'Would that they let us rule the world instead,' Solay said.

Agnes laughed. 'What a world that would be! Full of nothing but music and needlework and love.' She sighed. 'All right. How can I help?'

Solay stood, knowing what she must do. 'I need to see the King. Now. And no one but you and Hibernia must know.'

She must be careful and swift. She knew only one thing she could trade for Justin's life.

Agnes guided Solay, bundled in her cloak, via the private corridors and directly to the King's personal solar, where he and Hibernia were relaxing before the fire.

Startled and angry, he rose and growled at Agnes, 'What is this intrusion?'

'The Lady Solay begs a word.' Agnes backed away to stand with Hibernia.

'What is it, Lady Solay?' the King asked.

'Forgive me, Your Majesty.' She dipped in a deeper curtsy than usual. 'But I have information that is vital you know.'

'So? What is it?'

'First I would ask a favour.'

'No bargains, milady. I have already given you more than you deserve. Tell me the information. Then I will decide if I will grant any favours.'

She took a breath, trying to steady the panic in her belly. 'I believe Lord Lamont is planning to impeach the Duke.'

The King laughed and sipped his leftover wine. 'Ah, Lady Solay, marriage has finally made you a better informant. But you only confirm what I already knew.'

'What? How?' Shocked, she forgot to watch her tongue. Had she betrayed Justin for naught?

'I had spies in the Middle Temple who keep me informed. But at least you have belatedly proven your loyalty. I had reason to wonder, since you married a traitor.'

There was the confirmation. If she did not succeed, Justin would die. 'It is for his sake that I have come.' She took a deep breath. 'He plans to move against Hibernia on the morrow. If the Duke is to escape, he must go tonight.'

'I should never have let him back into Windsor.' He slammed the goblet on the table and turned to his friend. 'Call the guards. Take Lord Justin to the dungeon.'

Agnes gasped.

Before he could move, Solay knelt, her knees no longer strong enough to hold her. 'Please, Your Majesty. I will keep him occupied tonight. By tomorrow, the Duke and Agnes will be far away. Then if you will let Justin escape Windsor unharmed tomorrow, I will keep him with me where he will trouble you no more.'

'Why should I?'

'Parliament meets next month. You have many challenges ahead. Wouldn't you like to know what the stars have to say? Give me some time to prepare, then I will come to you whenever you choose.'

His eyes shifted and she recognised the fear that drove the power. 'Go to Chester,' he said to Hibernia. 'Both of you.'

Hibernia took a final swig of wine. 'I'll gather your badged men and return within a month. We will crush the Council before Parliament even sits.'

Solay gasped. 'An army? Will you not put them on trial?' Surely that was why he had gone to the trouble of speaking to the judges. She had expected Justin to have his day in court. She had expected justice.

'They've broken the law,' the King said. 'They do not deserve its protection. Traitors deserve to be hunted down like wild boar. By the time their charter expires, we will wipe them off the face of the earth.'

She rose, fearless because, if Justin were dead, she would not want to live. 'If you do not spare him, I shall not read.'

He eyed her in silence. 'Even a King cannot control the battlefield.'

'Leave that to me.' Justin had always disdained illegal force. Surely he wouldn't join the Appellants army? 'Just let him escape tomorrow.'

The King's eyes turned gentle and he nodded. 'So, Lady Solay, it seems you do love him after all.'

'Should he ever discover our bargain, Your Majesty, I do not believe he will see it that way.'

'Your Majesty?' A shaky whisper. Agnes.

'What?'

She had stood in the shadows behind the Duke, but now she stepped forward. She sank to her knees, her head down as if ducking her head at the King's temper. 'Forgive me, Your Majesty, but if the Duke and I are to leave tomorrow, might we be wed tonight with your blessing?'

Solay's heart squeezed. The King and the Duke exchanged glances.

The King's said *what you ask is impossible*.

The Duke's said *please*.

The King sighed and reached out to lift Agnes to her feet. 'I will call the priest.' He looked over his shoulder. 'Would you stay as a witness, Lady Solay?'

She wanted to protest that the banns had not been read. That she was not even sure that a divorced man could remarry. She wanted to say that if she stayed away too long, Justin would wonder where she was.

And she looked at all the hope and happiness in Agnes's eyes and could not refuse.

For now she understood what a woman would do for love.

Chapter Twenty-Eight

Justin put another log on the fire, knowing the autumn chill would make her cold.

He waited for her, his body only slightly less patient than his mind. She had been with Agnes since after the evening meal. What did women find to talk about for so long?

He had planned this evening for weeks. He had even reread the romances, to see what the heroes did.

But his body and hers—well, she had been right about that all the time. Their bodies did not lie.

He had planned the fire, the wine and cheese, the gown, and most of all, the loving, to get to the quiet time. After she had exploded at his touch, in the peace after the lovemaking, he could hold her and whisper *I love you.* Then they would laugh and whisper of the future. Of where they would live. How many children she would give him.

The door opened and she was there.

'Husband.'

His wife. After all. His wife.

'You were gone a long time.'

Fear flickered in the depths of her purple eyes, but it must have been a trick of the firelight.

'Agnes and I had much to say.'

Relieved she did not talk of it, he took the cloak from her shoulders and flung it across the bed, then poured Burgundian wine into the goblet, resenting the need to look away from her. 'I wanted to spend the evening with you.'

'Oh, yes,' she answered in a fierce whisper. She sipped the wine, and looked at him over the rim of the cup until he was lost in her eyes.

He took the goblet from her hands, then ran his fingers through her hair, delighting in her shudder. Her eyelids drooped with pleasure. Then, she caught his hand and kissed his palm, tickling it with her tongue.

He crushed her against him and took her lips. Already he was hard, his careful seduction wiped from his head. She answered his tongue with hers, sharing the same urgency that had nearly driven them to mate in the corridor at Nottingham.

Reluctantly, he pulled away. Tonight must be more than that. Tonight, he would worship her with his body. Then, surely then, she would know.

She reached for him and he captured her hands and brought them to his lips, tickling the little valleys between her knuckles with his tongue. 'Tonight, I will pleasure you.'

She laughed, huskily, and pulled him towards the bed. 'Can we not both be pleasured?'

'In time. You shall be first.'

He turned her around, like a limp doll, and slid the surcoat off her shoulders.

'Wait. Here.' He reached for what he had hidden in his trunk. 'Open this.'

'What is it?' she asked, but he let her discover for herself, delighting in her gasp as she pulled the robe of purple silk from the box. 'It's beautiful,' she said.

And he knew his search of London for one that would match her eyes was worth it.

'Put it on,' he said, hungry to see her wear it.

Shy now, she pulled the bed curtains, giving herself privacy to change. He ripped off his clothes, burning with heat that came not just from the fire.

When she stepped into view again, his body rose to meet her.

The robe fitted her like a lavender shadow, caressing the curve of her hip, sculpting the shape of her breast, and veiling the darkness between her legs.

'I feel like a princess,' she said, running her palms over her hips and thighs. 'Thank you.'

He managed to choke out two words. 'Sit down.'

She settled in the middle of the bed, her back to him, the blue-black strands of her hair tumbling over her shoulders, fine spun as the silk. He pulled her against his chest, loving the feel of her hair on his skin.

He reached for her breasts, each a perfect fit in his palm, and teased the tips with a squeeze.

A low moan rumbled in her throat. 'Take me now.'

He laughed. 'Always so impatient. Not until you are ready.'

She twisted to face him and put her arms around his neck, whispering against his lips. 'I am ready.'

'I'm a better judge of that.' He parted the silk and slipped a finger into her. Sheathed inside, he felt her grip his finger. She was wet, but not as wet as he would make her.

'Lay back.'

She obeyed, but only by kissing him and pulling him down with her. He had a mad moment of wanting to make love on the cursed cloak, as if that would mark her as his instead of the King's.

Instead, he rolled over, pulling her with him, and kicked the red velvet on to the floor.

She did not turn her head to look.

He pushed her boneless legs apart and knelt between them. The robe, open in front, exposed the untouched pale skin of her inner thighs. In the shadows, the dark nest was even blacker than he remembered.

She pulled his hand to her lips and put the finger inside her mouth that had been inside her, her tongue a sweet echo of the pressure inside.

Heat washed over him, from the fire, from her, from within him, and he nearly exploded right then, but he gritted his teeth. Tonight was to be hers. He must show how much he loved her.

He pulled his hand back and let his fingertips roam from her shoulder to inner elbow. She arched against him, writhing, reaching, nearly ready, as she claimed, then his fingers caressed her inner thighs and brushed between her legs.

She stretched wider, an involuntary invitation.

'How do you know what to do? How do you know how to make me so wild?'

He smiled. 'I just listen to your body. Now lie back.'

And he bent his head to kiss her.

When she felt his tongue, she nearly leapt off the bed.

Tongue, breath, a thousand fingers roamed around and inside her. With each touch, each kiss, she spiralled higher, until she felt as if she really were dissolving, as if all barriers would be gone and they would merge into one being.

She stiffened at the thought. If they did, if they were finally and for ever that close, surely he would know everything she had done before she said a word.

All night long, he caressed her, yet each time she reached the brink, all she had done rose like a wall in her mind.

So throughout that long, luscious night of lovemaking, not once did she reach her release.

* * *

He woke, dull with failure, the mid-morning sun bright in his eyes.

Their bodies had always been their one sure connection. Now, even that had failed him.

It all began as he had planned. She had screamed, she had moaned, she had gasped for breath. But not once did she cross into the Elysian abandon where he wanted to take her.

Now, she clung to him, her head on his chest, the dark silk of her hair spilling over his loins, her breathing too erratic for sleep.

'I did not please you.'

She lifted her head, meeting his eyes. 'Yes, you did.'

'Not enough.'

'The fault was mine, not yours.'

He shrugged her away and swung his legs off the bed. 'I thought we were done with lying.'

She lifted her chin. 'I could have pretended, but I did not want to…lie.'

He walked over to the basin, splashing water on his face, cold as the realisation of what she had said. He wiped his face with a drying cloth, wishing he could wipe away the vision of her face in ecstasy in the half-light of Midsummer's Eve. 'So your body has lied all along.'

Eyes wide, she scrambled from the bed and wrapped her arms around him. 'No. You must believe me.'

He pressed her cheek against his chest and held her close, not wanting to face her eyes, no longer sure he could tell her truth from her lies. But even betrayed, he wanted her again. But he wanted not only her body. He wanted whatever it was she could not give.

He let her go and turned away, pulling on clothes, desperate to leave the room and his failure. 'I'll get you a sop.'

* * *

Tears choked her throat and spilled over as soon as the door closed.

So this, then, was the price of lies. To destroy the one true thing they had shared.

Now, out there, he would discover the truth and suspect her part in it. And when he came through that door again, he would bring with him the lonely future she did not want to face.

Chapter Twenty-Nine

When she heard the door creak, she closed her eyes. So soon their peace was ended. Now, she must persuade him to leave Windsor quickly, or everything she had done would be for naught. And how could she sway him now that the bond of flesh had broken?

When she opened her eyes, he loomed larger with each silent step he took towards the bed. Strength and power, hard as carved stone, nothing remained of her lover except a lock of uncombed hair, still rumpled from sleep.

'You knew.' Instead of the hot anger she had expected, his voice shimmered icy certainty. 'You knew and you said nothing.'

'Knew what?' She must find out what he had discovered before she could release the rest.

'Stop it, Solay. Hibernia and Agnes have disappeared. There's even wild talk that they are married, though that's impossible. You saw her last night. She must have told you.'

'Yes.' She forced her voice to stay soft, low. 'It's true. They married in the King's private chapel and left before dawn.'

He gripped the bedpost and glared at her. 'And you pleased them and the King with the blessing of the stars, no doubt.'

'I told her there was hope she might be happy.' So many, many months ago.

'The man is already married!' He clung to the post as if the world was careening beneath him. 'He cannot take another wife!'

She must stay calm, speak softly, explain things step by step so he would understand what he must do, else he would be in the dungeon by sunset. 'Hibernia is no longer married to the Duchess.'

'That's not possible.'

'But it is. The Pope allowed Hibernia to put his wife aside.'

'On what grounds? They are related by neither blood nor marriage.'

She wanted to share the story with him. *See, Justin? When Agnes told me, I asked the same thing.* But the time for shared smiles had past. 'He did it because the King asked him.'

Momentarily stunned, Justin stared at her. 'But the King is on earth to enforce God's laws through man's. He cannot violate them.'

Blind. Still he was blind. 'If Pope and King agree, your precious, immutable law, God's or man's, has no more power than their desires.'

He paced the room, pounding his fist into his palm, as if looking for someone to hit. 'Mismanagement of the Privy Purse, exalting Hibernia to the rank of a King's son, refusing to fight France—these were all reprehensible. But to allow the man to put aside his wife, the King's own cousin, for his Bohemian mistress is an outrage.'

She let him argue with the walls, knowing she must tell him much, much worse.

'The Council will not tolerate this,' he concluded, flatly.

'The Council will have no say.' She slid off the bed and

circled her arms about his waist, wanting to hold him when he heard the worst. 'The King has declared the Council traitors.'

He staggered as if the word was a sword blow. She could not hold him. 'What?'

A question, from a man who never questioned. It bent her heart. 'The King asked a panel of judges for their legal opinion on the Council's actions. They told him that to obstruct the wishes of the King was traitorous.'

'No.' His stunned face was that of a child whose favourite toy lay broken before him. 'That's not right. That's not the law. No judge would say that.'

Always, always, he saw only the world he believed in, a world in which good and bad, white and black, battled uncompromising enemies, never sullied with messy grey.

'Just because you defy power for right you expect everyone to do the same. There are many, even judges, who do not want to spit in the King's eye.' She touched his arm. 'Most just want to be left alone to live the life we dreamed of. A life in the country, where we speak of the King only if he rides through on his way somewhere else.'

He shook his head. 'The Council has done nothing to violate the Statute of Treason. We can prove that at the trial.'

She took his face between her hands, forcing him to look at her eyes. 'You think justice is blind, but it is you who cannot see. There will be no trial. Hibernia has gone north to gather an army that will hunt you down and kill you, all of you.'

He blinked, then realisation touched his eyes. 'If the King will not honour the law, there is nothing left but brute force.'

She sighed, his pain tight in her chest. Finally he understood. She had been right all along. And she had not wanted to be right. 'Now, gather your things. We must leave quickly. We'll be safe in Upminster.'

'If the King does not respect the law, no one is safe. Gloucester was right. We will have to take up arms against him.'

'No!' Now she was the one in shock. 'You hate war.'

'I would rather die in battle than in a traitor's noose.'

She had hoped she would not need to tell him all. 'You
won't be hanged. If we leave now, he will let you live.'

'What do you mean? How do you know?'

'He promised.'

'Who promised?'

She lifted her chin. 'The King.'

His eyes met hers and she knew everything was about to
change in some final, terrible way.

At his silence, she broke the gaze, lifting her cloak and
shaking it, as if all were settled. 'But we must escape this
morning while everyone is distracted by Hibernia's disappear-
ance. If we go home and stay out of the fight, the King will
let us alone.'

'I don't know whether to be disgusted by your treachery
or stunned that you think I would believe the promise of a
King who's never kept one.'

Anger burned her cheeks. 'Would you have preferred I let
him take you?'

'I can see why you are a survivor. Nothing else, no one else
matters but what you want.'

'You matter!' She drank in the stubborn set of his jaw, the
pain in his brown eyes, the cleft in his chin, all the little things
she loved. 'Why else would I bargain for your life?'

'And what is worth so much to the King that he would give
up the joy of my death?'

She swallowed and touched her fingertips to her lips. How
could she not have seen that he would ask? 'I told him I would
read his stars for the coming year.'

'Valuable, to be sure, but that's not all, is it?' Light

dawned in his eyes. 'You told him about the impeachment. Everything I told you, my wife, my helpmeet, went straight to the King's ears.'

'It wasn't like that—'

'I loved you and you betrayed me!'

His shout bounced off the walls and she tried to clutch the echo of the word before it slipped away. Loved. Once, but no longer.

'I did what I had to do to save you,' she whispered.

'I even thought it might be true, what you said.'

'It *is* true.' *What you said.* He could not even say the words *I love you.* Could not even understand that she loved him so much that she would save his life, even if it meant losing his love.

'Don't expect me to believe you.' There was grim determination in his eyes, in the set of his jaw. 'If you really loved me, you would have honoured my principles.'

'Instead of keeping you alive?' She turned on him with the vengeance of a warrior. 'You don't want love. Love isn't enough. You want love on your own terms. It isn't enough that I save your life. I must save it by your rules, rules you just admitted don't apply to the world we live in.'

She shook with the effort to push it into his stubborn brain. 'Don't you understand? I don't want you to die.'

He snorted. 'Yes, it would be useful for you to keep me alive. That way, if the King loses and the Lords win, you can come crawling back to me. Don't expect me to welcome you. Or maybe I will. Maybe I'll welcome you by saying "let's have a roll in the hay". That shouldn't be too hard for a harlot's daughter.'

Of its own accord, her hand flung itself at his face, the slap stinging her fingers, leaving a red imprint on his cheek.

'You don't deserve the love I've wasted on you.' She gasped for breath, but he had stolen the air. 'I sold my soul for your life. You owe me the courtesy of saving it, at least today. We are leaving for Westminster. When we get there, you can warn your beloved Council and raise an army and start a war or do whatever you please. I'm going home.'

He shook his head, sadly. 'If Hibernia can dump an inconvenient wife, you can certainly be freed of an inconvenient husband. You've finally convinced me, my dear. If I return alive, I will find a judge who's not too particular to set us both free.'

The thought of losing him ripped her heart away, but he had never, truly, been hers. If he hated her now, it was not because of the past or because of her mother. It was because of what she had done.

She wanted to put her arms around his waist and hear his heart beat for the last time, but the few feet that separated them were as wide as the Channel. 'All this time, you've demanded love, but you know nothing about it. Love has its own laws, Justin, and they care nothing for your legalities.'

He turned away without a word, as harsh and cold as he had been the day she first saw him.

She closed her eyes, unable to watch him go, and waited for the sound of the door closing. It was long in coming.

'Goodbye, Solay.'

She didn't answer. There was nothing to say.

Chapter Thirty

For the next two months, as the Lords Appellant gathered their men to stop Hibernia's army, Justin had no thoughts, only feelings.

Rage, at her, at the world, at the King, even at Gloucester, burned through his veins and drove his preparations for battle.

Her betrayal cut more deeply than any sword's blow. Convinced of her love, he had succumbed to the temptation to believe her. Now, because of her deceit, they were marching to fight Hibernia on the field instead of in court.

And if he sometimes remembered that he owed his own life to her devil's bargain, he ignored it.

But in the dark hours of the night, when the winter stars watched over the sleeping soldiers and even the exhaustion of his body would not let him rest, he could not turn away the memory of the forgiveness he had found in her flesh.

Then, the vision would dissolve into their last, angry words.

Over and over, he saw the scene until the clash of swords and the bump of shields could not blot out the truth. *You don't want love. You want love on your own terms. Love has its own laws, Justin, and they care nothing for your legalities.*

The answer screamed at him from the darkness. The failure was not hers alone. When she made her own decision, uncowed by his opinions, he had cut her down without mercy. He should have cut out his tongue instead.

All the time he had insisted she prove her love when he had done nothing to earn it.

So he marched towards a final confrontation, hoping a blade would find him because he didn't want to live, now, without her.

And all that kept him alive was knowing there was one more thing he must do for her.

At the sound of an approaching horse, muffled by the December snow, Solay put down her bite of mincemeat pie.

Huddled in the upstairs solar around the only fire in the house, she and her mother exchanged a wordless glance over Jane's head. Who would come to their door on Christmas Day? The country was at war and marauding armies threatened civilians as well as soldiers.

Yet when she opened the shutter, she hoped, as she always did, that she would see Justin.

Under a shadowless afternoon sun, a peaceful white blanket hugged the cold ground. Justin would have liked the snow, she thought, wondering where he marched, whether he was cold. Praying he was safe.

She shook off the feeling. She should be planning to cajole another man into marriage. Or less. After Justin cast her off, even to find a man who would take her as a mistress would be no easy task now.

'Is it him?' her mother asked, her voice soft with compassion. They had become close over the months, bound by the foolish things they had done for love.

She shook her head. 'It's a squire, alone.' She peered more

closely, catching her breath when she saw the badge of the white hart. 'He's come from the King.'

Her mother stood as he pounded on the front door. 'Jane, light a fire downstairs. Solay, bring him to the Great Hall. We must greet the King's messenger with honour. What will he think that we have no wild boar to serve him on Christmas Day?'

Downstairs, Solay opened the door to a shivering boy, with chapped lips and a runny nose, who looked barely older than Jane. Had the King no seasoned men left?

Her mother waited in the Great Hall, seated before a hearth that yawned empty where a Yule Log should be burning. Jane touched a brand to some of their precious kindling. The boy eyed the flames with longing.

'The King commands the Lady Solay to come to him,' he said, when his teeth stopped chattering.

'Where is the King?' she asked, dreading Windsor at Yuletide.

'London.'

His answer told her little. Had Hibernia's men beaten the Council's army? Then where was Justin?

'I trust his Majesty is in good health,' her mother said, in her most regal tone.

The boy's reddened cheeks paled. 'His army was defeated a fortnight ago.'

Her mother swallowed a gasp.

Solay sagged, relief pouring through her veins. Justin was on the winning side.

Agnes was not. 'Where is the Duke of Hibernia?'

The boy inched closer to the fire. 'No one knows.'

She gripped her hands and bowed in silent prayer for Agnes and for forgiveness. Without Solay's cheery assurances, her friend would never have married Hibernia. Now, no doubt she was cursing Solay for false predictions of a happy future.

Never again would she shade her words. Her study of the stars had become a sacred calling. She would not dishonour it with a lie.

Her mother, ashen-faced, sat unmoving, her hands gripping the arms of the chair. 'Does the King still reign?'

The boy leaned forward, whispering as if spies lurked in the chimney. 'The King and his councillors have locked themselves in the Tower. The Lords Appellant approach the city. No one knows what will happen when they arrive.'

So the Lords had triumphed and Richard wanted to know whether this was his hour of death. She had spent the autumn and early winter with Justin's gift and the King's chart. She knew what she would tell him.

'Jane, I will need the horse at dawn.'

'Must you go?' A note of fear rang in Jane's voice. 'You'll miss Saint Stephen's Day. We had planned—'

Her mother put a hand on Jane's shoulder. 'Hush, child. It is an honour that the King summons her.'

And more. It had been the price of Justin's life. She prayed he still had it.

Tiny snowflakes skipped around the Tower's courtyard as the squire took Solay's horse.

It was Yuletide and she had come to the King again.

She clutched a folded chart beneath her cloak, and followed a guard upstairs and through corridors until he paused before a closed door.

'Wait in here,' the guard said, knocking. 'I'll tell them you've arrived.'

A voice answered beyond the door, 'Come.'

Heat from a brisk fire washed over her as she opened the door. A broad-shouldered man looked out of the window at the snow falling into the Thames.

She caught her breath. 'Justin?'

When he turned, she searched this stranger's features for the husband she had known. Cheekbones carved sharp lines in his gaunt face and new muscles curved his shoulders and arms. He had wielded a sword, then, despite his hate of force.

He took a step towards her.

She matched it.

He did not take another. 'Solay.'

A question echoed in her name and she longed to answer it. She wanted to run into his arms, to pretend they were still on a midsummer hill, watching the sun rise over a beautiful new world.

She straightened her shoulders. Their summer closeness had been swept bare as the trees, the halcyon days of love a midsummer fancy. That hill was miles and months away and she had traded his love for his life. There would be no forgiveness.

'The King sent for me,' she said.

'I know. I wanted to see you first.'

His last words had cracked the stone of her heart in the engraving. *If the Lords win, I'll just say 'let's have a roll in the hay'.* She could not bear it if he said that. 'You won a great victory over the Duke.'

'Solay, I found Agnes.'

She took that step and then another. 'Is she all right? Where is she?'

'She's safe. I took her to the convent at Readingdon.'

She pursed her lips against sudden tears. How fleeting Agnes's joy had been. 'Thank you.'

He held out a handkerchief and she took it, unsure whether she cried for Agnes or at Justin's unexpected kindness.

'Sit,' he said. 'Please.'

He motioned her to a bench by the fire and pulled up its

companion. She untied her cloak and placed the King's chart on the table.

He leaned forward, elbows on his knees, his fingers near enough to touch. 'We haven't much time and I have much to say.'

She closed her eyes against the memory of his hand caressing her hip, but she could not shut out the familiar hum that linked them. It sang in her blood and turned her centre to molten metal.

She leaned away, struggling to remember her mother's lesson. *Don't trust the wanting.* But in the last year, all the certainties she had clung to—the power of the King, her birthright, her ability to please, her attempts to influence the future—all had melted like snow. Only the wanting remained, binding them as strongly as it had that first moment, as if nothing had come between.

'What is it you would tell me?'

'I have drawn up papers that give you the income from three of my London houses in perpetuity.'

She thought she had accepted her fate, but hearing his cold calculation turned her tongue to lead. *I will find a judge who's not too particular and set you free.* They would be no different from all the other former lovers at court, averting their eyes with a nervous cough when forced to pass in the carolling ring.

He had not waited for an answer. 'It's the only way I could—'

She held up her hand to ward off his words. 'Thank you. You are generous.' There would be enough for food and firewood and feed for the horse and a new gown for Jane come spring time. Now, she only wanted to return to home, where the sight and the scent of him would torture her heart no more. 'We will be quite comfortable.'

'No.' Despite being on the winning side, his eyes were hollow with irreparable loss.

Dread crept up her spine. 'There is something more?'

'The courts grind like millstones, no matter who sits on the throne. I lost the suit. You have lost the house.'

She reeled, breathless, at this final blow. 'I should have told the truth, despite what Mother wanted, I should have—'

He gripped her knee and shook it. 'The fault is not yours. You were right. I can't guarantee justice on earth. I'm sorry.'

His eyes spoke as strongly as his lips. And as she looked at the dear face she would not see again, the last little wall that had kept her heart safe crumbled.

'Then it was not to be,' she whispered. 'I know you did everything you could.'

How foolish she had been, chiding him for his conditions. All the while, she had held back one little portion of her love until he had earned it. And now that he no longer belonged to her and she had nothing to gain from him, she had never loved him more.

The guard knocked and opened the door without waiting. 'They are ready for her.'

'Tell them we are coming,' Justin said, and the guard withdrew.

She tried to rise, but he grabbled both her hands in his. 'You must know before you go. You are walking into a den of lions. The Lords no longer argue over law or even justice. They talk of a new King.'

She shivered. A new King would not be crowned while the old King breathed. 'What has that to do with me?'

'They think the stars will tell them Richard's reign is over.'

She swallowed the fear fluttering in her throat. She had been too long away from Court. Focused on the heavens, she had forgotten to think of earthly snares. 'Who would they see on the throne?'

Gloucester was the son of the old King, but he was not the

only one who could make a claim. And the others would relish the title of Kingmaker.

'Richard only lives because Gloucester cannot get them to agree to make him King. Slant your words with care.' He squeezed her hands between his. 'Gloucester will be there. He wants you to predict Richard's death.'

'And if I do not?'

'He will accuse you of practising black arts.'

She did not need to ask the penalty for that. 'So he sent you to warn me that Richard's life is not the only one hanging in the balance.'

His finger touched her cheek, bringing her gaze back to his. The urgency in his eyes had nothing to do with lust. 'I will protect you. I swear.'

She rose and his hand dropped away. 'I know you will try.' But they both knew it was an empty promise.

When she turned, he dropped her cloak over her shoulders and whispered in her ear, 'What will you tell him?'

She had no husband, no home, no surety left in her life except the learning that had given her a glimpse into Heaven. Strange, what stayed, what didn't. 'The truth.'

There was nothing else left.

Stunned, Justin watched her walk out of the door without waiting for him. Belatedly, he remembered she knew the Tower as well as he and caught up with her halfway down the corridor, grabbing her arm to stop her.

'That will save you if the truth is what they want to hear. Is it?' he whispered fiercely, uncertain who might overhear.

'You will find out when the King does.'

Her tongue had become tart over the last year. 'You are good at games. Spout some nonsense they can interpret as they please. They won't know the difference.'

She never broke her stride. 'I will not seek to please Gloucester because he now holds the power.'

'When did you become a warrior for truth? You've bent it much further for much less reason.'

'You don't even care what the truth *is*.'

'Tell me later. After this is over.'

'So the great defender of truth wants me to lie?'

'If it will save your life, yes.' He would break any oath, defy any rigid soulless code that wouldn't let her live.

'Then how can you be angry at what I did to save yours?'

The ground shifted beneath his feet. 'You never craved the King's power, did you?'

'Only his power to give me what my mother and sister needed.'

Loyal to flesh and blood and friends, she had sacrificed everything else for those she loved. For him.

He cupped her face in his hand. 'You are stubborn, foolish and incredibly brave,' he said.

A flush touched her cheek, but she turned away without a nod or a smile.

And as the guard opened the door, Justin had no idea what she was going to say.

Shaking, Solay swept into the room. Finally, too late, Justin had understood. But she would not violate her vow. Not to please him, or Gloucester, or even the King. She had worked too hard to find the truth.

When she paused, face to face with Richard, she stumbled to a curtsy. But no command came, neither to rise nor to kneel. She looked up through her lashes, keeping her head low.

The proud King she had known was gone.

Richard was slumped in a rough chair, his wife within touching distance. Faithful Hibernia no longer stood beside him. Instead, Gloucester and the other four Council members circled the room, ready to pick his bones.

She glanced up at Justin, who raised his eyebrows and shrugged. She had been prepared for Gloucester alone. It seemed the other Council members would not trust his report.

A cask of wine had been tapped, and red drops of Burgundy spotted the floor. The smell of fear hung in the air beside that of the leftover wine.

She rose, and Richard did not prevent her. Sunken above thin cheeks, his blue eyes had become those of a trapped and angry animal. 'It seems a crowd has gathered to hear my fate, Lady Solay.'

'I shall tell it the same, Your Majesty, whether to a crowd or to you alone.'

He did not move, but the Queen waved a hand for her to proceed.

She spared a glance for her scowling audience. Besides Gloucester and the grizzled Earls of Arundel and Warwick, she was surprised to see Henry Bolingbroke and the young Earl of Nottingham, both Richard's age. How things had changed since those snowy days in his castle.

She cleared a place at the table, moving aside two half-empty wine goblets.

'Wait,' Gloucester said, before she could sit. 'I must have your oath that you will interpret the stars truthfully.'

Justin spoke before she could. 'Gloucester—'

'I asked Lady Solay.'

She smiled at Justin and shook her head. This, she must do alone. 'To come among you, I have risked death.' She would speak the truth for herself, not for him. 'I would not risk it on a lie.'

And she did not really care whether anyone except Justin believed her.

'Then swear on the grave of your father, the King.'

Justin's hand tightened on her shoulder. She reached up, covered his fingers with hers, then touched the amethyst brooch pinned near her heart.

'I swear on the grave of our late and beloved King Edward.' She looked at Gloucester. 'Your father.' Then at Richard. 'Your grandfather.' And finally at Justin. 'And the man who called me daughter.'

Gloucester's mouth twitched, as if he were not satisfied, but could not think why. 'Proceed.'

She settled at the table. Justin poured a goblet of wine and set it at her right hand, then stood behind her, his hands on her shoulders.

She started to shrug him off. Their marriage was over. She must go on alone. But the feeling of him, warm at her back, comforted her.

She let him stay.

As she unfolded her chart, Gloucester and the others moved closer, peering over her shoulders as if they could decipher the neatly labelled squares and triangles.

She cleared her throat and concentrated on the chart, letting everything else fall away. 'In the twelfth year of his Majesty's reign, there continue to be powerful planets in the Twelfth House, the house of enemies.'

Richard slumped in his chair with a tired laugh and looked around the room. 'You need not look to the stars to know that. Just look around the room.'

'We are not enemies of the King,' Gloucester said, glowering at his nephew.

The Queen snapped at them, protecting Richard like a cub. 'Do you claim you are his friends?'

'We are friends of the realm,' Gloucester answered.

'Then perhaps,' Solay continued, 'you belong in the

Eleventh House, the house of courtiers, councillors, and friends both false and true.' She raised the goblet with a shaking hand and touched it to her lips. Still, her mouth tasted of dust. 'Here, the planets show disruption, change and even endings.'

'Endings?' Richard asked. 'Of the Council or of my councillors?'

It was so quiet, she could hear Gloucester swallow his wine.

'The stars do not have men's names attached,' she said, relieved for once that she did not know the truth.

She continued through the houses calmly, speaking of wealth and possessions, of brothers and fathers, of sickness and health, of love and marriage.

No one spoke again until Gloucester sputtered an interruption. 'What you say is meaningless. It tells us nothing.'

'Not so,' she answered, evenly. 'Look at the Tenth House. It is the house of Kingship. There have been shadows in this house during the last year, but now, Saturn leaves this house and Jupiter enters.'

'What does that mean?' Gloucester said.

Richard sat straight and smiled at Gloucester in the old way. 'Beneficence to the King and punishment to my enemies.' His kingly voice had returned.

'You were born of royalty and born to rule, Your Majesty,' she said. 'I know the signs.'

The signs so lacking in my own chart.

Anne's quiet voice floated softly into the hush. 'You have not spoken of the Eighth House.'

Bolingbroke, eager. 'What is that one?'

Richard answered for her. 'The House of Death.'

Silence blanketed the room.

'Well, Lady Solay, answer him. What is in the Eighth House?' Gloucester asked.

'Nothing.'

'Nothing?' Richard's voice cracked.

'The heavens have given us no guidance.'

His glance skittered to his foes, then he leaned forward. 'I did what you asked,' he whispered, though they all could hear. 'Can you tell me no more?'

She heard the plea in his voice. He wanted to know whether he was to live or die. Yet no matter what the stars said, what she said now would determine his destiny.

'The stars do not guarantee the future, Your Majesty,' she said, loud enough for all the lords to hear. 'They only tell us what circumstances will test us. We create our own lives by meeting our fate bravely. You were born a King, Your Majesty. As long as you honour the laws of the realm and the advice of your barons, I'm sure the stars will shine favourably on you so that when you die, whenever that may be, you will still be our rightful King.'

She held her breath.

Richard pursed his lips, as if reluctant to capitulate, then sighed. 'The King embodies the law and so must fully express it. I always welcome the instruction of my dear uncle and the other lords in these matters.'

Gloucester glared over her shoulder at Justin. 'It seems your wife parrots your opinion, Lamont. You must have told her what to say.'

Justin's hand tightened on her shoulder.

She felt the war within him and covered his hand with hers. 'He told me what I would face in this room. Only I could decide how to meet it.'

'It is I who agree with my wife, Gloucester,' Justin said. 'Richard is the King Heaven has given us. The law of earth can do no less.'

Behind Gloucester, the others murmured assent. His shoulders slumped. There would be no more talk of a new King.

She stood, letting Justin's hand fall away, and met each man's eyes. Gloucester's angry ones, so like the old King's. The minor Lords Appellant, by turns wary, relieved and irate. Then she looked into the Queen's grateful brown eyes with a woman's understanding. Richard's gaze now showed kingly pride instead of craven fear.

She turned to Justin.

His eyes were full of warning and fear and affection and a strange sort of pride.

Gathering her chart, she walked out beside him, their bodies joined by that invisible cord that had bound them from the first.

My wife. I agree with my wife.

Hope rose in her heart.

She glanced over at him, looking for the little quirk of his eyebrow, for the twitch at the edge of his mouth that came just before a smile. She watched brown hair curve around his ear and the blunt fingers that had brought her to ecstasy. She watched all these things for what might be the last time, and heard him say nothing.

'I spoiled Gloucester's plans,' she said, finally. 'What does that mean for you?'

'I shall leave his service. We will both be glad of it.'

'Will you be safe?'

He smiled. 'Are any of us safe?'

'What will you do?'

'What I was trained to do. Practise the law.'

They returned to the little room, where the fire had burned to embers and her cloak was welcome in the early winter darkness.

He had called her brave, but to be brave before the King had risked only her life. To be brave now, with him, would risk her heart.

But she would do it anyway.

She reached for his hand, wanting that touch one more time.

Unable to look into his eyes, she played with his fingers, watching them as if they were magic, unable to tell him goodbye.

But he spoke instead.

'Stay with me, Solay,' he said, stroking the back of each of her fingers, one by one. 'Perhaps justice can only come from the Heavens, but I think we can find love on earth, now.'

She held her breath. If he took back his words, she would have this one memory: the crackle of the fire, the taste of leftover wine, the scent of cedar and ink, his clenched jaw and that whisper of hope in his dark eyes.

'Have I convinced you that I love you?' she asked.

'I have become convinced that I love you.'

'If I say I love you, will you believe me?' She wanted him to say yes. More than she'd ever wanted anything in her life.

'Should I?'

She lifted her head and caught the twitch at the corner of his mouth. 'Yes, you should. And be honoured to have earned the love of the daughter of Lord William Weston and Lady Alys Piers.'

He wrapped her in his arms. 'We are already bound by the laws of heaven and earth.'

'And more than that,' she said, needing the silly white cloth again as she looked up at him. 'We are bound by the laws of the heart.'

He swept her into his arms then, and it was hours before the kiss was complete.

Epilogue

Solay opened her eyes to the midsummer sunrise and a kiss from her husband. She laughed against his lips as the baby inside her kicked with satisfaction.

'Good morning, my love,' he said. 'Your day has come again.'

Despite all convention, Justin persisted in celebrating St John's Day as if it belonged to her instead of the saint, and he was planning to spoil their child the same way.

'Isn't it nice that my day happens to be the longest one of the year?' Later, they would all join Justin's brother and his family for their first midsummer celebration. 'All the more for me to enjoy.'

He bounded out of bed. 'Wait. Stay right there. I'll be right back.'

She rolled over, content, as he slipped out of the room.

They had come back to the country from London for the midsummer celebration, leaving the bustle of the city and Justin's law practice for the dower house on his brother's property. It was small, no grander than the house in Upminster, but her mother had been happy here.

And Jane? She wished she knew how to make her sister

happy. Justin had a marriage offer in hand from a wealthy London merchant, but when they broke the news, Jane ran from the room crying and had barely spoken since.

Solay curved her arms around her growing stomach, hugging her soon-to-be-born babe, wondering what the stars in the sign of the Virgin had in mind for this one. They had been right about the King. The next session of Parliament had been stormy. Safely away from Court, she and Justin had watched, horrified, as Richard's chief advisers had been tried, convicted and killed.

But the King kept his life. And the throne.

Hibernia and Agnes had escaped across the Channel to the Low Countries. She missed her friend, but she was glad they had finally found a place to love in peace.

Justin opened the door. 'I've a birthday gift for you.'

She sat up in bed as he pulled something from behind his back.

Inside a small cage, a bright-eyed, shocking green popinjay blinked and cocked his head. Open mouthed, she stared at the alert eyes.

'Awk!' the bird squawked.

'Teach this one to talk and you'll always have a companion who mimics you.'

Her eyes lit up and her laughter pealed out like bells.

There would be more, later. An appointment for Justin as Justice of the Peace in a village near the Thames, where their house would have windows facing east so she could always see the sunrise.

But for now, this, this would be enough.

Author's Afterword

This story was inspired by real people and events, though I have taken many fictional liberties.

The notorious mistress of Edward III, Alice Perrers, who I called Alys Piers, was reviled by the chroniclers as greedy, avaricious and power-hungry. She sat on the bench with the judges, was impeached by Parliament, and was accused of stripping the rings from the dead King's hand. Alice's trial, the convenient appearance of her husband, Lord William Windsor, and the later lawsuit with his nephew over Great Gaynes in Upminster happened much as I described.

Alys had two daughters: Joan and Jane. (I ignored her son for the sake of the story.) Little is known of the girls, not even their exact years of birth. Their parentage is also the subject of speculation. And some reports call them both Joan.

We do know that Joan the Elder married a lawyer, Robert Skerne, and they lived in Kingston-on-Thames. A monumental brass with their images is still there, marking their tombs after a seemingly long and prosperous life.

Everything else about Joan in this book comes from my imagination—her return to Court, interest in astrology—and any role in Richard's reign is strictly conjecture.

For the historical figures in the book, I have tried to adhere to actual events during 1386-7. King Richard was ordered by Parliament to submit to a Council of Lords Appellant, headed by his uncle, the Duke of Gloucester. To escape their control, he did go on a 'gyration' across the country. And he did submit ten questions to a panel of judges, who then declared the Council traitors. History also suggests he had some interest in astrology.

The character I called the Duke of Hibernia is actually the Duke of Ireland. He divorced his wife with the Pope's blessing and ran away with one of the Queen's ladies, Agnes Lancerone. As I've tried to show, the King's favouritism for Ireland, and his flouting of the laws of marriage, triggered the Lords' decision to go to war with the King's men, who were soundly defeated. Ireland fled the country and died abroad. I chose to believe that Agnes went with him.

No one knows exactly what happened between the Lords and the King during his imprisonment in the Tower, but there is speculation that he was removed from the throne for a time.

History has not looked kindly on Alice Perrers or the Duke of Ireland. I have tried to show them as human beings, with both flaws and strengths.

Richard survived this 'constitutional crisis' and emerged stronger than ever. Eventually, he took revenge on those who had thwarted him. In the end, he was deposed and killed and the new king was Henry Bolingbroke, who had been one of the Lords Appellant in the Tower.

* * * * *

Melita had been expecting a chaste quick kiss of the generic variety. But this kiss with Sully was the kind that sparked a dying flame to life. The kind of kiss you can't plan for. The kind of kiss memories are built on.

The memory of her murdered lover, Nemo, came to her then and she made a starved little noise in the back of her throat. She raised her arms and threaded her fingers through Sully's hair, pulled him closer. Felt his body settle, then melt into her.

In that instant her hunger for him grew, and his for her. She pressed herself to him with more urgency, and he responded in kind.

Melita came out of her kiss-induced memory of Nemo with a start. "Wait a minute." She pushed Sully away from her. "You bastard!"

She spit two nasty words at him in Greek, then wiped his kiss from her lips.

"I thought you deserved some solid proof that I'm still in one piece." He started for the door. "The clock's ticking, honey. Come on, let's get out of here."

"That's it? You sucker me into kissing you, and that's all you have to say?"

"I'm sorry. How's that?"

He didn't sound sorry in the least. "You're—"

"Getting out of this godforsaken prison cell. Stop whining and let's go."

"Not if I was being shot at sunrise. Go. You deserve whatever you get if you walk out that door."

He turned back. "Freedom is what I'm going to get."

"A second of freedom before the guards in the hall shoot you." She jammed her hands on her hips. "And to think I was worried about you."

"If you're staying behind, it's no skin off my ass."

"Wait! What about our deal?"

"You just said you're not coming. Make up your mind."

"Have you forgotten we need a boat?"

"How could I? You keep harping on it."

"I'm not going without a boat. And those guards out there aren't going to just let you walk out of here. You need me and we need a plan."

"I already have a plan. I'm getting out of here. That's the plan."

"I should have realized that you never intended to take me with you from the very beginning. You're a liar and a coward."

Of everything she had read, there was nothing in Sully Paxton's file that hinted he was a coward, but it was the one word that seemed to register in that one-track mind of his. The look he nailed her with a second later was pure venom.

He came at her so quickly she didn't have time to get out of his way. "You know I'm not a coward."

"Prove it. Give me until dawn. I need one more night to put everything in place before we leave the island."

"You're asking me to stay in this cell one more night...and trust you?"

"Yes."

He snorted. "Yesterday you knew they were planning to harm me, but instead of doing something about it you went to bed and never gave me a second thought. Suppose tonight you do the same. By tomorrow I might damn well be in my grave."

"Okay, I screwed up. I won't do it again." Melita sucked in a ragged breath. "I can't leave this minute. Dawn, Sully. Wait until dawn." When he looked as if he was about to say no, she pleaded, "Please wait for me."

"You're asking a lot. The door's open now. I would be a fool to hang around here and trust that you'll be back."

"What you can trust is that I want off this island as badly as you do, and you're my only hope."

"I must be crazy."

"Is that a yes?"

"Dammit!" He turned his back on her. Swore twice more.

"You won't be sorry."

He turned around. "I already am. How about we seal this new deal?"

He was staring at her lips. Suddenly Melita knew what he expected. "We already sealed it."

"One more. You enjoyed it. Admit it."

"I enjoyed it because I was kissing someone else."

He laughed. "That's a good one."

"It's true. It might have been your lips, but it wasn't you I was kissing."

"If that's your excuse for wanting to kiss me, then—"

"I was kissing Nemo."

"What's a nemo?"

Melita gave Sully a look that clearly told him that he was trespassing on sacred ground. She was about to enforce it with a warning when a voice in the hall jerked them both to attention.

She bolted away from the wall. "Get back in bed. Hurry. I'll be here before dawn."

She didn't reach the door before he snagged her arm, pulled her up against him and planted a kiss on her lips that took her completely by surprise.

When he released her, he said, "If you're confused about who just kissed you, the name's Sully. I'll be here waiting at dawn. Don't be late."

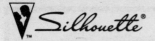

Romantic
SUSPENSE

**Sparked by Danger,
Fueled by Passion.**

Onyxx agent Sully Paxton's only chance of
survival lies in the hands of his enemy's daughter
Melita Krizova. He doesn't know he's a pawn in the
beautiful island girl's own plan for escape. Can
they survive their ruses and their fiery attraction?

*Look for the next installment in the
Spy Games miniseries,*

Sleeping with Danger

by Wendy Rosnau

Available November 2007 wherever you buy books.

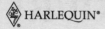

Charlie fell in love with Rose Kaufman
before he even met her, through stories her
husband, Joe, used to tell. When Joe is killed
in the trenches, Charlie helps Rose through
her grief and they make a new life together.
But for Charlie, a question remains—can
love be as true the second time around?
Only one woman can answer that….

Look for

The Soldier and
the Rose

by
Linda Barrett

REQUEST YOUR FREE BOOKS!

 Harlequin® Historical
Historical Romantic Adventure!

2 FREE NOVELS PLUS 2 **FREE GIFTS!**

YES! Please send me 2 FREE Harlequin® Historical novels and my 2 FREE gifts. After receiving them, if I don't wish to receive any more books, I can return the shipping statement marked "cancel." If I don't cancel, I will receive 6 brand-new novels every month and be billed just $4.69 per book in the U.S., or $5.24 per book in Canada, plus 25¢ shipping and handling per book and applicable taxes, if any*. That's a savings of close to 15% off the cover price! I understand that accepting the 2 free books and gifts places me under no obligation to buy anything. I can always return a shipment and cancel at any time. Even if I never buy another book from Harlequin, the two free books and gifts are mine to keep forever.

246 HDN EEWW   349 HDN EEW9

Name _____ (PLEASE PRINT) _____

Address _____ Apt. # _____

City _____ State/Prov. _____ Zip/Postal Code _____

Signature (if under 18, a parent or guardian must sign)

Mail to the **Harlequin Reader Service®:**
IN U.S.A.: P.O. Box 1867, Buffalo, NY 14240-1867
IN CANADA: P.O. Box 609, Fort Erie, Ontario L2A 5X3

Not valid to current Harlequin Historical subscribers.

Want to try two free books from another line?
Call 1-800-873-8635 or visit www.morefreebooks.com.

* Terms and prices subject to change without notice. NY residents add applicable sales tax. Canadian residents will be charged applicable provincial taxes and GST. This offer is limited to one order per household. All orders subject to approval. Credit or debit balances in a customer's account(s) may be offset by any other outstanding balance owed by or to the customer. Please allow 4 to 6 weeks for delivery.

Your Privacy: Harlequin is committed to protecting your privacy. Our Privacy Policy is available online at www.eHarlequin.com or upon request from the Reader Service. From time to time we make our lists of customers available to reputable firms who may have a product or service of interest to you. If you would prefer we not share your name and address, please check here. ☐

HH07

HARLEQUIN® *Romance*®

New York Times bestselling author

DIANA PALMER

Handsome, eligible ranch owner Stuart York knew Ivy Conley was too young for him, so he closed his heart to her and sent her away—despite the fireworks between them. Now, years later, Ivy is determined not to be treated like a little girl anymore…but for some reason, Stuart is always fighting her battles for her. And safe in Stuart's arms makes Ivy feel like a woman…his woman.

Winter Roses

Available November.

HARLEQUIN®

Mediterranean
NIGHTS™

Not everything is above board
on Alexandra's Dream!

Enjoy plenty of secrets, drama and sensuality
in the latest from Mediterranean Nights.

Coming in November 2007...

BELOW DECK

by

Dorien Kelly

Determined to protect her young son,
widow Mei Lin Wang keeps him hidden
aboard *Alexandra's Dream* under cover of
her job. But life gets extremely complicated
when the ship's security officer, Gideon Dayan,
is piqued by the mystery surrounding this
beautiful, haunted woman....

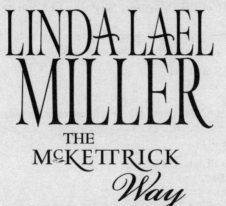

Silhouette

SPECIAL EDITION™

brings you a heartwarming
new McKettrick's story from
NEW YORK TIMES BESTSELLING AUTHOR

LINDA LAEL MILLER

THE McKETTRICK
Way

Meg McKettrick is surprised to be reunited
with her high school flame, Brad O'Ballivan,
who has returned home to his family's
neighboring ranch. After seeing Meg again,
Brad realizes he still loves her. But the pride
of both manage to interfere with love...until
an unexpected matchmaker gets involved.

—— McKettrick Women ——

Available December wherever you buy books.

COMING NEXT MONTH FROM

HARLEQUIN®
HISTORICAL

- **CHRISTMAS WEDDING BELLES**
  by **Nicola Cornick, Margaret McPhee and Miranda Jarrett**
  (Regency)
  Enjoy all the fun of the Regency festive season as three Society
  brides tame their dashingly handsome rakes!

- **BODINE'S BOUNTY**
  by **Charlene Sands**
  (Western)
  He's a hard-bitten bounty hunter with no time for love. But when
  Bodine meets the woman he's sworn to guard, she might just
  change his life....

- **WICKED PLEASURES**
  by **Helen Dickson**
  (Victorian)
  Betrothed against her will, Adeline had been resigned to a loveless
  marriage. Can Christmas work its magic and lead to pleasures
  Adeline thought impossible?

- **BEDDED BY HER LORD**
  by **Denise Lynn**
  (Medieval)
  Guy of Hartford has returned from the dead—to claim his wife!
  Now Elizabeth must welcome an almost-stranger back into her
  life...and her bed!